'A gloriously self-aware satirical romp through the terrors of relationships, family life and survival. Philip Roth meets Cold Feet'

Helen Lederer (*Absolutely Fabulous, Losing It*)

'Spencer Brown is endlessly inventive and delightfully, dependably silly, like a joy-seeking missile'

Richard Ayoade (*The IT crowd, Submarine*)

'Hilarious and heart-warming'

Andi Osho (*Live at the Apollo, Curfew*)

'Very funny. Peep Show combined with Outnumbered. But you know. In a book'

Josh Howie (*Josh Howie's Losing It, BBC Radio 4*)

'Is there a term for chick lit for men? If so, this is it. Tom Cooper is an aspirational figure for the men of today'

Omid Djalili (*The Infidel, Live at the Apollo*)

the REBUILDING OF TOM COOPER

SPENCER BROWN

Marotte

www.marottebooks.com

First published in 2019
by Marotte Books Ltd
51 York Avenue, London SW14 7LQ

www.marottebooks.com
Text © Spencer Brown 2019

A CIP catalogue record of this book is available from the British Library.

ISBN 978-1-9161526-1-8

Typeset by Elaine Sharples
Printed and bound by PULSIO PRINT

Cover design by Liam Relph

For Sarah

Wednesday Morning

'Where's Mummy?'

It's the first thing that Arthur says when he wanders into my room.

I don't know how to answer. The worst part of me wants to lead with 'getting stuffed by a stranger', but the better part prevails. Besides, I don't want to end up inadvertently starting the sex conversation. Or giving him a completely fallacious idea about the techniques involved in taxidermy.

'Um… Mummy's out.'

'When's she coming back?'

'I'm not sure.'

'…Where's Mummy?' Carrie's decided to join us, stretching the sleep out as she yawns.

'She's out,' Arthur interjects.

'When's she back?'

'He doesn't know,' says Arthur. Carrie looks at me questioningly.

'Who's taking me to nursery?'

'Looks like it'll be me today.'

'But Tuesday's not your day.'

She's right. Tuesday's not my day. Unfortunately, it's Wednesday. She really has no idea what day it is.

'I'm doing it this week.'

'OK.' They both shrug and go out of the room.

Is this how it happens? How you tell your children their mother's left? *She's out, I don't know when she'll be back.* Every day that passes they become more and more suspicious, until around

1

the time of puberty when they finally realise she's gone. But by then it's no big deal anyway.

I need to have a talk. I take them through for breakfast and start to assemble their regular cereal combos – Weetabix and Coco Pops for Arthur, Weetabix and Cheerios for Carrie. I should sweeten the deal.

'You can just have Coco Pops and Cheerios today if you want.'

'But it's not the weekend,' says Arthur.

'It's not the weekend,' echoes Carrie. *Shut up, you have literally no idea whether it's the weekend or not.*

'That's all right,' I shrug. Carrie seizes the opportunity and nods like a crazy person. But Arthur's suspicious.

'Has something bad happened?'

'What do you mean?'

'Last time you let me have just Coco Pops in the week, Grandad had died… the other time was Christmas,' says Arthur.

'Don't worry, no one's died.'

'Is it Christmas?' Carrie asks. Jesus, this puts the whole days of the week thing in the shade.

'It's not Christmas. Look – you both need to sit down.' They move to the table, and even Carrie is starting to sense that something's wrong. I start speaking to the accompaniment of slurping and spoons against china.

'OK. Now, what I'm going to tell you might make you feel a bit sad and a bit confused. It might even make you feel a bit angry.' Sad, confused and angry: these are emotions they can understand. I'm dealing with this well.

Slurp.

'Your mummy and I both love you very much.' Slurp. Slurp. 'But Mummy has decided that maybe she doesn't love Daddy any more. So Mummy and Daddy won't be living together from now on.'

'Mummy's stopped loving you?' Carrie turns this over in her head. I nod. She thinks for a while. Then a look of panic takes over. 'Will Mummy stop loving *us*?'

'No. Don't be silly.' She's about to cry. Fucking Sally. 'Mummies and daddies always love their children. It's just sometimes they stop loving each other.' Carrie takes this in, trying to process.

'So... who does Mummy love now?'

'She doesn't love anyone,' I tell her, 'she just—'

'Austin. I think Mummy loves Austin,' Carrie interrupts. *Austin? Who's Austin?* I have literally no idea who Austin is.

'Who's Austin, Carrie? Daddy doesn't know Austin.'

'He's a man me and Mummy meet sometimes in London.'

'London? What? When!?' I'm trying to stay cool. This is not how this was meant to go. 'When did this happen, love?'

'When I'm at nursery.'

'You can't go when you're at nursery.'

'No, silly. I don't go to nursery those days.'

'You don't...' I'm at a loss for words. I mean, for God's sake. It's a Montessori. It's one thing to be fucking someone behind your husband's back – but taking your kid out of pre-paid childcare...

'We did it yesterday.' I have to clarify – yesterday for Carrie just means some time in the past.

'Yesterday? Tuesday?'

'No, today is Tuesday, silly. We can't do it today yesterday.'

Montessori was Sally's fucking idea. I would have been perfectly happy with a normal nursery. That was free. But no, we're paying for Montessori and our daughter still doesn't know what fucking day it is.

But this is not over. Arthur has yet to make a contribution.

'I think she loves Peter.' Another name I don't know. Why do I feel I've lost control of the conversation? Carrie doesn't miss a beat.

3

'No, Peter is silly. No one would love Peter.' She knows Peter too? How do they both know Peter!?!

'When did you meet Peter?' I ask.

'We see him all the time,' says Arthur. 'He's nice. He comes over when you work late.' *Shoot me. Shoot me now.*

'It might be Luke.' says Carrie. No more names; please no more names.

'It won't be Luke. Luke is just Mum's friend.'

'Maybe Gary then?' Gary. For God's sake.

But at least I know Gary. And I know he's a nob. He's Arthur's friend Henry's dad. And completely unthreatening. Far worse looking than me and he has a really annoying voice that's constantly breaking like he's a teenager about to go through the big change. Sally and me used to take the piss out of it all the time. Phew. A moment of calm amidst the storm. I come in all Zen.

'Well, I don't know about the other three, but I'm pretty sure it's not Gary.'

'Hmm...' muses Carrie. 'Well, Mummy was kissing Gary when he came to pick Henry up on the play date, but maybe she doesn't love him.' *Thanks for clarifying that, darling daughter.* I don't believe this. Is she shagging bloody everybody?!? Arthur agrees with his younger sibling.

'I think you're right. She likes *kissing* Gary, but she doesn't love him. I said he was annoying and she agreed.'

They have opinions on this. They have actual opinions. Jesus – why didn't these fuckers sit *me* down for a conversation?

I can't take any more. This has to stop.

'Well,' I say, trying to sound authoritative. 'I think we're just going to have to not know for a while. Maybe we'll find out soon, but sometimes it's better not to draw conclusions before you have all the evidence.'

4

Carrie opens her mouth to talk. 'But—'

I cut her off. 'Let's not introduce any more names into the mix.' Carrie looks a little crestfallen, but I've got to take care of myself as well.

'Why don't you both go to your bedrooms and get dressed?'

'I can't do it,' says Carrie.

'Just go and find your clothes. I'll be through in a sec. Daddy needs a few minutes to himself.'

They leave. I'm pretty sure I hear Carrie mention the name Michael on the way out.

And then I'm alone with my thoughts.

Three guys. Maybe four. For God's sake. Although, you have to admit doing that behind my back with a full time job was logistically impressive.

I sit there for a few seconds in silence. Or as near to silence as it gets with two kids and a flat with one too few rooms to accommodate a family. Well, most of a family.

I feel numb. Empty.

I go to get myself a bowl of cereal. I get the Weetabix from the cupboard, but change my mind.

I think I deserve just Coco Pops today.

Work

Word gets round work pretty quick about Sally. I stupidly mention it to Carly at the photocopier, and soon everyone knows. Lucy's the first to come and talk to me.

'Sorry to hear about Sally. That must really hurt. Do you want to talk about it?'

I pause. They say when men talk about their problems, they're looking for solutions, whereas women just want to share how they feel. That's bullshit. I'm not sure there *is* a solution to this. But I do want to tell her how I feel. How much it hurts that I've been abandoned, rejected. I don't want to be one of these idiot men who just bottles it all in. Copes with pain by cracking bad jokes.

'No thanks. I'm all right.'

Well, at least I didn't crack a joke.

'Well, if you change your mind...' I nod, gratefully. I've only spoken to this woman once before, and she's supporting me. It's so weird. It's not long before Annie comes over too.

'Heard about your wife. I remember her from the Christmas party. I have to say I'm not a hundred percent surprised.'

'No, we liked each other then.' Annie doesn't do a good job of covering her scepticism.

'Well, if you need to talk about it...'

'Thanks.'

This is nice. Maybe not all women are awful. Most of them seem pretty damn lovely. Which makes it all the worse that I managed to choose a bad one.

It's 11:00 am before the first male approach. Andy, my immediate boss, comes over.

'Hey, Tom. Look – that report that's due. Take another week if you need it.'

'Thanks Andy. I appreciate that.' *Take another week?* Why, yes. Yes, I will.

But it's not just him; Anthony overhears, clearly inspired by the male-on-male action, and wants to join the party.

'Don't worry about the spreadsheets either. I can get them done myself.'

'Thanks Anthony.' Oh my God. This is awesome. No report, no spreadsheets. The next few days are really starting to open up for me.

Then John turns round in his swivel chair. Now let me be clear

– I hate John. John hates me. John is my arch-nemesis. I hate his little weaselly face, his stupid elongated beard; I hate everything about him. We don't talk. We haven't for about two years, since the first day he started working here when we went out for a beer and realised we hated each other. But even he wants to be part of this.

'Look – that pint you owe me; don't worry about that either.' *Wow*. I mean, I was never going to get him a pint back anyway, but now it's official. This is more like it. Maybe the male way *is* better. Practical solutions. They're not letting me express myself, not letting me discuss my feelings, but I just got a free pint and what amounts to a week off work. Men get a bad rap, but this has done a damn good job of cheering me up.

Carol comes over. She's the office manager, the only person here over fifty-five. She looks like you want a granny to look – none of these weird asymmetric haircuts and multi-coloured dye jobs my mum swears by. But I appreciate the fact that she's bothering to talk to me. Probably for some more 'emotional stuff', but still…

'I heard about Sally; it must be very tough.'

'Thanks, Carol. I appreciate that.'

'Well, I just want to say – it's going to be a difficult few months. I know from when my husband left that it can be very lonely. So, if you ever need some company…'

What a nice woman. She really is a nice woman.

'Well, I've got my kids to take my mind off things,' I smile. Carol is not smiling; she is looking me straight in the eye.

'Yes, but there're certain forms of company your children can't provide you with.'

I pause for a second. Is she saying what I think she's saying? I think she's saying what I think she's saying.

'All I'm saying is, if you ever need some kind of… relief. You can give me a call.'

Yeah, definitely what I think she's saying.

7

'Um. Thanks, Carol. That's very nice of you.' I'm not going to take her up on it, but I should at least express a little gratitude for the offer.

She smiles, nods a 'you're welcome', and heads off back to her desk. Then she turns back.

'I'm very good with my hands,' she says before leaving.

Wow. I think I just got offered a hand-job by Granny Carol. I guess you could call that 'practical'. Just goes to show you should never accept stereotypes. I wonder if she'd expect me to return the favour? Don't get me wrong, I'm not going to take her up on it, but I appreciate the gesture.

It's funny being a man. If some 60-year-old guy approached a recently separated woman and said he was 'available for physical relief' it would be despicable. Repulsive. He'd be fired. And rightly so. But the same thing happens to a man, and you're like 'well, good to know I've got a back-up in the bag.' What a nice woman. She really is a nice woman.

And then it strikes me. I'm single.

For the first time since I was twenty-nine years old, I'm single. I've been so busy thinking about the kids, and Sally, and what's happened, that it hadn't even struck me there's a future. And I'm in it. Alone. With no-one.

And I'm old.

Well, thirty-nine, but that's old. I've got baggage. I've got kids, a broken marriage. That's off-putting. What if I never find anyone? Am I going to die alone? I've got – what – forty years ahead of me? ALONE? I'm **ALONE**. My future is a mass of emptiness punctuated by Carol's occasional hand-jobs. OH GOD. I've started accepting them now. What is wrong with me? What the hell is wrong with me?

I run out of the office through the fire exit and into the emergency stairwell beyond. Standing on the concrete steps, surrounded by bare walls, I can hear my breathing echo through the right-angled space around me. I sit down, feeling the cold of the step through the seat of my trousers. And I start to cry. It's only taken fifteen hours, and I'm crying like a 39-year-old baby.

That's when I see her standing there – some woman from another office. I haven't seen her around before. And now she's caught me in the act.

'Bad day?'

This is embarrassing. I try to get myself together.

'Laptop's on the blink again. Lost a memo I was writing.'

She's clearly seen me crying, but is nice enough to pretend she hasn't. She's kind of cool looking but not too try-hard. Probably from the dotcom company downstairs. She's dressed in a loose-fitting shirt and cardie, but doesn't seem like she's in costume as a 'creative person'. She's wearing heavy-framed specs that look like they do in eyewear adverts, rather than the face-distorting bottle bottoms I rock when I'm not in lenses. It's kind of annoying. But she smiles at me sympathetically. It's amazing the difference a smile can make.

'Must have been a long memo.'

'I'd nearly completed a whole paragraph.'

She laughs. 'Well, as someone who's lost a few memos herself, you just have to move on. There's plenty more memos waiting to be written.'

I'm not quite sure how to continue the conversation. I'm pretty sure this is all a metaphor, but there is a small chance we are just talking about memos. I go with the metaphor.

'I've only just lost that one,' I explain. 'I don't think I'll be starting any new memos for a while.'

If this *is* just about memos, I just sounded like the weirdest office worker ever. I'll know in a second when she moves onto minutiae of formatting.

'Well, they'll be there when you're ready for them.' She offers a conciliatory smile and heads off up the stairs. 'Oh, and remember to double space after a full stop.'

She disappears. Now I'm really confused.

But I feel a bit calmer. I sneak back inside and tidy myself up in the loos. I'm a wreck, but that's to be expected. Besides, a cool-looking stranger just told me there'll be more memos out there when I'm ready for them. Maybe she knows something.

When I'm ready… Right now, it doesn't feel I'll ever be.

Friday

It's 7:30 and the babysitter, Lacey, turns up. I'd forgotten we'd booked her.

'Oh – I'm sorry – I forgot you were coming. Is it all right if we leave it for tonight?'

She looks at me resentfully. 'I turned down going to a party so I could do this. So no, it's not all right.'

'Oh, OK.' I toy with the idea of paying her and telling her to leave, but I can't face just chucking money down the drain. 'I guess I should probably just… leave my flat then.'

'Guess you should.'

We stand there for a few moments looking at each other. And there I was thinking I might have regained some agency over my life… I grab my coat and head out.

Standing in the cold about three metres away from my front door, I try to work out what the hell I'm going to do. Maybe I could go and see a movie. I used to see movies on my own when I was younger. There's nothing wrong with it. Something arty. Yeah, that'd be good. Seeing a film in French is basically like learning a language – I'm improving myself. True, there is a slightly greater chance of seeing boobs, but that's by the by. This is adult education. A movie for sophisticated adults. An adult movie. Hmm. I'm doing it – there's no reason a single life shouldn't be a rich life.

Ten minutes later and I'm in the pub. Everyone around me is having fun, while I'm there nursing a pint, pretending like I'm waiting for someone.

Maybe it's good to have some time on my own. Time to digest what happened. To think about why she left. I can't help but feel it's all my fault. Maybe she didn't find me interesting any more. She always seemed to switch off when I'd try to tell her something, her eyes drifting towards the ceiling.

But it's not like we were that different. Sure, she'd choose cream rather than custard with a crumble, but it was only ever the small things… And I've been pretty stable. It's fucking hard when you have kids, but I've kept it together.

Maybe she didn't want that. Maybe she wanted the drama. A life of fights and arguments and Mediterranean-style passion. That's how it used to be before we got married. I thought she just felt secure so didn't feel the need anymore. Maybe she was just bored.

Three pints in and my mind's even less clear. I've started a list of things I did wrong. From pants on the floor, to missed bin days, to pushing Carrie off a swing (*if you want to go that high, hold on tight, you bloody idiot*). I'm constantly checking my phone to see what time it is: I can't go back till ten – that'll be three hours, Lacey doesn't do less than three hours. Still one and a half to go…

It strikes me I could go and see Mark and Karen. Mark and Karen are my best friends from university, plus they only live round the corner. If one of them is in, they might be up for a chat. I haven't told them about Sally yet. If they're out, well…

11

maybe they've got a slightly less unpleasant babysitter than me. I could talk to *her* while I wait to go back. It's weird staying in with your own babysitter, but someone else's… that doesn't seem like freakish behaviour at all.

A few minutes later, I'm standing outside their door. I see the silhouette of someone approaching through the glass panels. It's Mark.

'Hey!' I say.

'Hey. What are you doing here? I didn't know you were coming round.'

'Sally left me.'

His face drops. All irritation towards my unscheduled appearance is gone. He seems genuinely surprised. Well, at least I know *he's* not fucking her.

'Oh God, Tom. I'm so sorry.'

He ushers me into their hallway. 'When did this happen?'

'Three nights ago. She just walked out – said "I'm leaving you" and went.'

'Did she tell you why?'

'No. But according to Arthur and Carrie she's sleeping with about four other guys.'

'Four?!? Oh my God,' says Mark. 'Although, you've got to admit it's logistically impressive.'

'That's what I said.'

'Is everything all right?' Karen pokes her head out of the kitchen door.

'Sally's left Tom.'

'Oh, fuck. I'm so sorry, Tom. We're just having dinner – do you want to come through for a bit?'

'Sure, thanks.' Karen leads us through into the kitchen.

'She's sleeping with four guys,' Mark fills her in.

'Four?!'

12

'Maybe,' I tell her. 'That's just second-hand from the kids. Although if Arthur's right – one of them is Gary. I mean – who'd want to fuck Gary? It'd be like banging a Muppet going through puberty.'

Karen stops in her tracks a few steps into the kitchen.

I follow her through. And the situation becomes clear.

They're mid-dinner party. And everyone has heard every word I've said.

'Oh, God. I'm sorry – I didn't realise you had people round. I'll get going. You don't look like you have space for me anyway.' I start to turn round.

'We were just leaving.'

A woman stands up. I think I recognize her. What's her name? My mind starts working in slow motion. Harriet? Shona? Samantha? Yeah. *Samantha*... Samantha: Gary's wife.

There's a man sitting next to her. From his diminutive stature and the fact that he has his head in his hands, I'm pretty sure it's Gary.

'No offence to you, Sam. Some people have a thing for Muppets.' She doesn't look impressed. 'I always kind of fancied Miss Piggy.'

Slightly Later

The one plus point of the whole Gary situation is they've now got a couple of spare puddings. Mark is a great cook, but Karen usually does the desserts and she is PHENOMENAL. Tonight it's homemade crema catalana which is like a crème caramel but with orange and more independence.

The other guests are really sympathetic. Well, once they've confirmed none of their names came up.

13

'You need to get straight back on the market. Find some hot woman and shag it out of your system,' Mark advises.

'It's only been a couple of days,' I say.

'All the more motivation. Take the opportunity. *I mean, what if she comes back?*' Karen gives him a look of horror, but Mark is mid-flow: 'You'll be kicking yourself if you miss the opportunity for a legal shag.'

'Is that what you'd do?' Karen interrupts.

Mark smiles. 'You'd never leave me, darling.'

'I'm thinking of it now.'

One of their friends, Rachel, joins in. 'I've got a mate who's getting divorced – I could set you up if you wanted.'

This is ridiculous. It's been three days. Of course I don't want to be set up. What is wrong with these people? Just give me some time to get my head together. But Mark's on a roll.

'Is she pretty?' he asks.

'She's a very nice person; she's very pretty.'

'She's not pretty,' (her husband, Jeremy.) 'Women always say other women are pretty when they're not.'

'That's not true.'

'Oh – is that right?' continues Jeremy. How are *they* not divorced? 'Let me ask you a question. Your friend, Rosslyn; is she pretty?'

'Of course she's pretty.'

He turns to me, victorious. 'Back end of a bus.'

'That is so sexist,' Rachel says, 'you'd never say that about a man.'

'Because I wouldn't say a man was attractive. If someone asked me, I'd say, "I don't know".'

'In case you accidentally fucked him?' says Louise, another of Karen's friends. She's annoyingly right-on, but Jeremy does need to be taken down. He seems to have mistaken this situation for a gathering of men.

14

'OK, then,' says Rachel, turning to me. 'Tom. Is he attractive?'

No. Please don't involve me in this – Jeremy's not even my friend.

Jeremy looks me up and down, defiant. 'Let's see. OK – here's my answer: I don't know.'

'But if you had to say one way or the other. Is he handsome or not?' pushes Rachel.

'Can we not do this?' I protest. 'I've just had my wife leave me – and "back end of a bus" is the only answer that won't make him sound like a misogynist.'

Jeremy takes affront to this. 'So you're on their side now?'

'Um…' I'm arguing with bloody Jeremy. This is not what I came here for. I need to de-escalate the situation, but Jeremy is having none of it.

'OK,' Jeremy retorts. 'No. He's not handsome. He's not "back end of a bus" level, but he's not handsome.'

This is why you have friends, so they can boost your confidence before you go out into the world.

'Well, I'm glad we got that sorted out,' I say, 'thanks for the info.'

'It's not info,' says Rachel, 'because actually – you *are* quite handsome.'

'Oh,' I say. 'Thanks.' Back in the game.

'He's not the worst,' says Karen smiling. 'Just a shame he's got such a terrible personality.'

I smile back. It's nice to have friends. Even if you have crashed their dinner party and split up one of the couples they invited. It's good to have some people who actually care about you.

'You should get back out there, but only when you feel ready,' says Karen. 'There are a lot of women who'd be lucky to have you.'

'And let me know if you want me to fix you up,' says Rachel.

'I know someone too, if you want?' Louise joins in. 'Although, she is a bit "right-on".' Jesus – if you think she's right-on she probably no-platforms vegan Gender Studies lecturers for being too right-wing.

'See: plenty of women you've never met are out there waiting for a bit of the old Tom magic,' Mark joins in. 'Plus, there's a good chance Gary's wife will be back on the market from tomorrow if you're interested.'

Saturday

The kids are starting to freak out.

It's understandable. Their mum's just gone. Disappeared. The world's shittiest magic trick. She hasn't even called since Tuesday. It doesn't make any sense. Then again, Louise from last night was telling me when she was eight her mum just suddenly up and left. She still saw her occasionally but she said it was like she'd become a stranger. One minute she was Mum. And then she wasn't.

But Sally's not like that. She's a great mum. I don't know why she'd do this. Fair enough; she doesn't want to be talking to me, but she should at least be talking to the kids. When it comes down to it, that's what I'm really annoyed about.

At noon, my mobile starts vibrating. It's Sally trying to FaceTime. That's got to be a good sign – people don't FaceTime unless they want a proper conversation. I hand-brush my hair quickly in front of the mirror and pick up.

'Sally… hi.'

'Can you pass me over to the kids?'

I pause for a second. 'Can we maybe talk for a bit first?'

'I don't think that's a good idea. I just want to talk to the kids.'

Hmm. Turns out Sally not calling the kids wasn't what I was annoyed about.

16

I sit there on the other sofa – watching the back of an iPhone while my kids chat to their mother. I can hear her voice, but all I can see is a sideways apple with a little bite taken out of it. It looks a bit like a weird cartoon Japanese kitten from this angle. This is what our family looks like now. Two separate groups with a phone between us. Like being stuck behind someone filming at a school play.

And then it hits me. It's not just our relationship that's over. It's our family.

The realisation totally blindsides me – like we're in the middle of a game of *Mallet's Mallet* and someone secretly substituted a sledgehammer. *Word association game – mustn't pause, mustn't hesitate… the one with the most bruises loses. 'Love' … 'distance'… 'separation'… 'divorce'… 'custody'…'Tom?' '… er…'* Bang… and he's unconscious on the floor.

Life as I knew it is over.

And I have no idea what's going to happen next.

September/a Bit of October (Kind of Lose Track…)

The next month or so is a blur. I sink into a deep depression. I'm not sure if anyone around me can tell. I just keep going through the motions of my life, like one of those memory foam mattress that keeps its shape even though no one's lying on it anymore.

But inside I'm dead. An empty space playing a loop of self-recrimination. Trying to work out what I did to make her leave. What made her so unhappy she was willing to destroy our family.

I'm lumped with all the childcare as Sally needs to 'sort out her living situation'. Maybe it's good. Time to think isn't what I need right now. Sally takes the kids for the day most weekends. Every changeover is like a Cold War prisoner exchange. Even in person she doesn't want to talk to me, refusing to make eye contact, to acknowledge my presence. Maybe she feels guilty, bad for what she's done. I can't but help feel it's more likely she just hates me.

And I thought we didn't agree on anything anymore.

Monday

Four weeks later, and it's half term. I decide to take a few days off to go to my parents'. I don't think I can cope with the holidays on my own, and I need to start thinking about getting my life back together. About returning to the world.

Of course, I tried to get my parents to come down to me, but as Mum explained:

'Dad's got a car show, there's a tennis committee meeting, I've prepaid for three Zumba classes, and let's not forget my hair appointment. If I start cancelling Tiff on a regular basis, I'll lose my Friday morning slot, and then where would I be at the weekend?' Ostracized from the local community because of your offensively natural-looking hair, that's where.

Anyway, what it comes down to is this: if I want some free childcare and a chance to get my head together, I have to travel. So I'm heading up the M40 to the sunny climes of commuter belt Birmingham, to spend a few days in the village I grew up in.

We arrive at 'Glebelands' a.k.a. Versailles at about two. My parents have recently installed a fountain on their driveway. It wasn't a good choice. Whereas fountains are perfectly fine in front of a chateau, in the context of a 1970s suburban house, even Louis XIV may have found them a little 'ostentatious'. The driveway around it is still being built. They've managed to take away the previous owners' beautiful front garden and replace it with enough concrete to lay the foundation for a shopping mall. Forget the rainforests, we could have a significant drop in global warming if we stopped the remodelling habits of provincial septuagenarians. Coupled with a thermostat that doesn't see the irony in Spinal Tap's 'turned up to eleven', they could be the biggest threat to the environment since the Trump administration.

'Tom! Park on the road – you can't go on the driveway,' Dad calls, running out of the house in slippers like he's stopping a national emergency. I park up and the kids go in with him, leaving me to carry the bags and talk to my parents' racist builder. He's heard I'm from London.

'Used to live in London, you know,' he announces as I try to walk past.

'Oh, right.'

'Born and bred there. But I moved up here. Best decision I ever made. Love London but it's not the same anymore, is it? It's different. You know what I mean.'

I want to pretend I don't. He's said no words that say what he means. Unfortunately, I'm pretty sure exactly what he means.

'Not quite sure what you mean.'

'You know. *London*. It's not for Londoners anymore, is it?' Yep, I was right. OK, parry. Go for the joke.

'Well, I'm as responsible for that as anyone. I'm from here.'

'That's not what I mean,' he says, his face instantly deadpan. *I know it's not what you mean, idiot. Have you not noticed from my reactions I probably don't want to join the alt-right?*

'What I mean is—'

'Uuuuuuhhhh.' I do a massive stretch, and make this weird noise. Any blind person in the near vicinity would think I'd just come. Is this how I stop someone from saying what they actually mean? What kind of hide-your-head-in-the-sand kind of anti-racist manoeuvre was that? I've just ostriched my way out of a confrontation.

'Anyway, I'd better go in. Can't let Mum look after the kids on her own.' *Yeah, right. That's the only reason I'm here.* 'Besides, she's probably toasted me a bun.'

'Don't want it getting cold,' replies the builder. *No, that's probably how they eat them in Istanbul.*

I pick up my bags and head inside. I'm ashamed of myself. But what's the point of arguing? He's not going to change. He's just a broken record that has foolishly been given the right to vote.

I chuck the bags into the double-glazed porch, only to find they've locked the front door. How fucking secure do these people need to be? I knock and wait.

Through the window of the porch, I look at the builder. He doesn't know any better. He was just born before me. Didn't have any education. Didn't read any books... It makes me wonder. Could I have been like that? If I hadn't done all right at school, hadn't gone to university, would I be spouting the same ignorant opinions I'd picked up from a tabloid? It scares me to think about it. About how fragile it is – not being a dick.

I stand there, trapped in my own thoughts in a purgatory made of PVC. It's the same with everything. Maybe we never make any real choices – we're just a product of our particular cocktail of genes bounced around life by circumstances beyond our control. We could end up a racist, an annoying co-worker, or just someone who marries the wrong woman. Maybe it's no one's fault – maybe these things just... happen.

I feel a lightness come over me for the first time since Sally left. Life might be bad. But maybe I didn't do anything wrong. Maybe it's not my fault. My dad comes and lets me in, and for the first time in years going into my parents' house feels a bit like walking into heaven.

Although judging by the heat of it, it's more likely to be the other one.

Later

We sit having a late lunch in the Saharan heat of my parents' conservatory.

'Can't we eat in the dining room?' I ask.

'You know we don't eat in the dining room,' says my mum.

'Why would you? That would be like cooking in the kitchen, or living in the living room.'

'There's no need to be sarcastic. And we don't live in the living room anyway – we mainly use the snug, so who looks silly now?'

Arthur and Carrie aren't eating their food. I blame myself. I'm always serving up multi-coloured meals, and now they're sitting there in front of plates of beige. Chicken fingers, chips and… what I think are baked beans with the sauce rinsed off. She knows Carrie doesn't like tomatoes so she's clearly gone for a pre-emptive strike. Either that or she now treats lunch with the same sense of colour-matching she uses on her outfits. Some kind of anti-rainbow diet. Maybe her homeopath has told her she can't mix hues.

'Would you like some ketchup?' I ask. Arthur and Carrie nod.

'But she doesn't like tomatoes,' my mum interjects, utterly baffled by this turn of events.

'She still likes ketchup.'

I go to the cupboard, while Mum tries to compute what the hell just happened. A few seconds later and the kids' meals are covered with an obscene amount of ketchup. If this meal was reassembled afterwards it would basically look like a bowl of tomato soup with the occasional floating oven chip. I know I'm being a terrible parent, but I let myself off. This is meant to be my day off too.

'Are you OK watching them tonight if I go out?' I ask. 'I wanted to go to the pub with Ed.'

Before Mum can answer, Arthur interrupts. 'You're going out? I don't want you to go out.'

Carrie is having none of it either. 'I want Daddy to stay in. Stay in every night.'

'Well, that's not going to happen. Unless you want me to grow old and grey, sad and single, I've got to go out *sometimes*.'

'Old and grey, sad and single,' they both begin to chant. Before long it has become the most hilarious thing ever, my worst-case scenario future becoming a song of childhood before my eyes. Well, I guess it happened with *Ring a Ring o' Roses*. If those plague victims had realised the pleasure 'we all fall down' would bring to generations of four-year-olds, maybe they would have felt slightly comforted during their horrific and painful deaths.

'Old and grey, sad and single.'

Maybe not.

'Old and grey, sad and single.'

'So is that OK, Mum?'

'Old and grey, sad and single.'

'We're actually going round to Phil and Jenny's tonight for bridge.'

'Old and grey, sad and single.'

'So I'm afraid we won't be able to help.'

Arthur adds a topper: 'And stinnnnkkkyyyyyy!' Cue belly laughs all round.

Fucking great. This is my life.

Tuesday

The next morning, Mum reads to the kids from the remnants of my childhood library while I work in the room next door. The soundtrack of dated children's stories doesn't do great things for my concentration. Particularly as, to prop up the inane plotlines, all of them seem to have a sprinkling of casual racism: Tintin talking to pidgin-Englished natives, Topsy and Tim dressing up as gypsies; the highlight being them mocking up blackface with some cocoa power. Well, here's hoping they suggest that activity next time someone offers them hot chocolate on a play date.

I'm also spending ridiculous amounts of time in the toilet. Not due to any kind of problem – it's the only place to truly escape. I did a forty-five minute session today – all I needed was a wee. That said, I do now know what poutine is (a weird Canadian chip-based dish) and how I'd look as a pensioner... and man, apparently... thanks for that, FaceApp.

Still – I should probably cut down on the loo time. At this rate, in twenty years I'm going to be part of a major epidemic of Internet-related piles. From now on I'm going to become a more focused individual who doesn't waste his time on insignificant distractions, either in the loo or out of it. Huh?!? FaceApp has a new Hollywood filter.

I'll start after that.

Afternoon

Mum's feeling 'very tired' after lunch, so I take the kids to the playground. You've got to be considerate – I don't want her putting in a substandard performance tonight playing outdated card games.

It's weird being at the playground I used to go to as a kid. A few things have changed since the Eighties, but not much. Carrie and Arthur don't care either way – the locals have filled the paddling pool as it's freakishly hot. Twenty-two degrees – how that happens in October I have no idea. Maybe some heat has leaked out of my parents' house?

The kids strip their clothes off and jump in. I try to push them to keep their pants on, but by the time they're a couple of feet from the edge any illusion of control has disappeared.

'Come in the pool, Daddy!'

'No thanks, love.' *As much as I enjoy wading through a puddle of dilute child piss, I think I'll pass...*

I look around. It's mainly mums and nannies – there's just me and one other dad who looks vaguely normal. There's another dad here too, but he's got a tattoo on his face of... what I think are Peppa and Daddy Pig. Well, if you're going to make yourself unemployable, why not indulge a pre-schooler's two-year fad while you're at it? I might not initiate a conversation.

One of the nannies looks over and gives me a smile. I smile back. Just standard being-at-the-playground friendliness – I don't give it a second thought.

But then she smiles again. And I start to wonder... Does it mean something? I've been out of that world for so long, I don't know anymore.

I shake myself out of it. I'm being ridiculous. A month ago I wouldn't have thought twice about someone smiling – I was smiling at parents left, right and centre. I call to Carrie and Arthur not to splash too much, and the nanny looks over at them. She smiles *again* – that's right. I'm a great dad – she's impressed. Maybe she does like me.

Then suddenly, looking at Arthur, her face drops. She looks at me with a mild look of horror, then averts her eyes. I'm left with no idea of what's just happened.

I call Arthur over. No horrendous bruises – she's not thinking I'm beating him... I look him up and down... nothing... What the hell *was* she thinking? Then my eyes fix on something. Was she looking at... his penis?

I think it's always been there in the back of my mind that my son has a weirdly shaped penis. But it's something you ignore. Something you try not to think about. But now, looking around at a couple of other little boy penises (something I generally try to avoid) – I realise 'Little Arthur' is definitely... unusual. I mean, it's sort of normal at the top, but then it goes all weird and long like the stem on a wine glass. Obviously, it doesn't suddenly fan out at the bottom so you can stand it on a table but you get the idea. More like one of those disposable picnic wineglasses where the base comes off.

Specifics aside – it's an outlier. And then I realise: this woman must think he got it from me.

Now, obviously this doesn't matter, because I'm 150 miles from my home, and she's probably just being friendly. But technically I'm on the market now. Well, maybe not quite yet... but *eventually*. This could nuke a relationship. All it takes is for some potential date to catch a glimpse of the offending article, and mine will never get a look in. I've got about a three second window before they make the mental leap, and pulling out 'Little Tom' in the intervening period seems like it might do more harm than good.

'Let's get you dressed, Artie,' I say.

'But Carrie's still in the pool,' he protests. *That's 'cos Carrie doesn't have a weird penis.*

I get Arthur dressed, wrapping the towel round his body while I dry him so no one else can get a glimpse. The nanny still won't meet my eyes. God. I bet Sally's dad had a weird penis like this. That's where Arthur must have got it from. It must be a Livingstone trait. I bet her brother has it too. Unless it was Sally's grandfather. It could have skipped a couple of generations. Oh God – I'm falling down a rabbit hole of imagining my ex's family naked. My head is currently hosting the world's worst swingers' party.

25

It'd be good to find out though. For peace of mind. Maybe it starts weird in childhood but then turns into a normal one in puberty. The thin bit is just room to expand into. Someone was telling me German lederhosen do that. There are buttons ready to undo because they know you're going to get fat in a few years. Maybe this is the lederhosen of penises.

God, I have no way of finding out. If Sally does ever talk to me again, she won't be willing to ask her family. Her dad's dead anyway. I could push for the disinterment of his corpse, but it's been two years and the penis must be one of the first bits to go. Maybe I should send Arthur in to spy on the brother. Give him a weekend with his uncle and instruct him to have a look. *God*, I sound like a reverse bloody paedophile – try and get your uncle alone and have a look at his willy.

'Ok – pants on!' How to say this? 'Now, Arthur. You're becoming a very big boy now, so it's probably best that you always wear pants or trunks in the pool… You probably shouldn't let strangers see your willy.'

'Why not?' Arthur clearly isn't happy about this 19th century attitude towards nudity.

'Because a willy is a very private and special thing, and you only show it to people you know very well.'

'I don't understand. Why?' Oh God. I'm giving my son a complex.

This is bad. This is very bad. Why didn't I just keep my stupid mouth shut?

I scan my brain for ideas. 'I'll tell you why…' *Will you now?* 'The reason is…' *What exactly is the reason?* 'Because…' *We're waiting…* 'Because everyone else…' *Yes?* '…will be jealous.'
   What?!?

He pauses for a second to think about this. 'Because my willy is nicer than theirs?'

I pause for a second. 'Exactly that.'

Arthur seems pleased. Very pleased. Hmm! Excellent parenting! Problem solved. And all it needed was for me to give my child massive overconfidence about his genitals. As long as he doesn't start creating tributes to it in his art lesson, this has worked out well.

Really hope it does the lederhosen thing…

Wednesday – M40 Motorway

The kids are asleep in the back of the car. Great for music options but probably means they'll be up till midnight tonight. Still, I change *Best of Disney* for *The National,* and the mildly depressing music really lifts my mood. This is as close to grown-up time as it gets these days.

It's a relief to be on the way home. My parents are lovely, but given the chance, they don't leave the house all day. They're happy just sitting around in their ergonomic armchairs, reading a local paper or watching daytime television on iPlayer. They even watch it in the evening. Who watches daytime TV in the evening? It's like ordering beans on toast at a good restaurant. Actually, my mum might do that. As long as the sauce was rinsed off.

Is this what the future has in store for me? Sitting in a hermetically sealed room doing nothing but taking occasional breaks to eat beige food. These people created me. Unless the driven go-getter gene has the same generation-skipping quality of the weird penis one – this is my destiny.

They must have been driven in their younger days. They both started their own businesses. That's impressive. I haven't done that. I just sit in an office adding up bloody numbers. That is not what I wanted for my life. I wanted to be creative, to be exciting.

I used to be exciting in my early twenties. I was in a band for God's sake. Unexciting people aren't in bands.

And we were actually pretty good. Admittedly, some of the songs weren't 100% appropriate for the gigs. My uncle kicked up a right fuss when we played *To the Grave* at his fiftieth. It was meant to be a metaphor for stress, but I suppose I can see how it might come across as a specific statement about his remaining life expectancy. We even shared a bill with Coldplay once. About four hours earlier and they weren't that good then, but that is still factually true.

But look at me now. I'm nothing. My parents must have been hustling the whole time. I need to hustle. And to get organised. I mean, at least once a fortnight, I'm forced to re-wear some pants. This is not the kind of person I want to be: digging through my washing basket every other Friday trying to sniff out the best option. Like a bloodhound with an interspecies underwear fetish.

I need to make a change. I should start looking for a new job. Yeah. Make that bloody Sally realise what she's given up. A new start. A new me.

This is good. Right – I need to work out a plan of action. A list. A list is always good.

OK:

1. Get a new job and hustle.
2. Be more creative. Maybe restart band.
3. Do some visualisations. Everybody seems to do those who does well. Jim Carrey was all over them before he went all Eckhart Tolle.
4. Buy more pants. An extra three pairs should do it. It'll probably just mean I go longer between washes… Maybe put a clean pair in a bag in the bottom of the washing

basket, so I know it's time to do a wash when I'm forced to search it out. Could even put a laundry tab in the SAME BAG! THESE IDEAS ARE **GOLD**!

5. Stop being on phone when with kids. Don't want their memories of me to be of a man staring at his fucking handset. Hmm… May just lead to extra time in the toilet…

Service Station Stop

I take a break at the service station and treat myself to a Flake. I still don't understand how something so emasculating can be so delicious.

They should make a Man-Flake. That would be great. There's nothing essentially feminine about an elegant stick of crumbly chocolate. Maybe when you phrase it like that there is, but… They should think about making them look more phallic. That always works. Maybe not with food. Sure, we want our cars to look like a big cock, but when you have to put it in your mouth it probably takes the edge off the whole penis thing.

I can imagine the advert. All these men standing round on a building site, eating chocolate cocks. It can't fail. Particularly as bits crumble off as they bite in. Who doesn't want to eat a confectionery phallus that looks like it has leprosy?

Note to self: new job probably shouldn't be in chocolate design.

Thursday

A new job came up at work today. Completely freaked out. On the train to work I was doing my first visualisations, and now

29

something's actually happened. Probably a coincidence, but I may have to read Sally's copy of *The Secret*. Hmm – wonder if all this cosmic ordering stuff can differentiate between visualisations and dreams? Had a very vivid nightmare last night. Hopefully I haven't accidentally ordered up a sex session with a goblin dominatrix.

Anyway – so I'm talking to Carol about something, when she suddenly looks at her computer screen and gives this 'hmph' noise.

'Something interesting?'

Carol sighs. 'Just annoying. One of the creatives has been poached by Mother – I've got to suspend his access to the database.' Lucky him. No one ever poaches an in-house accountant. But my mind is ticking over… hustle, hustle, hustle.

'Um… do you know what they're doing about his job?'

Ten Minutes Later

I go down to HR only to have Layla tell me to get back to Accounts, but I'm not taking no for an answer, so I get in the lift to the upper floor, where the big boss is. I don't care if this works out. I feel empowered for the first time in… forever. Definitely since Frozen songs became the default structure of my thought patterns.

I head over to Jack Canonbury's office – Maestro J: the self-styled genius of advertising, and ask his assistant if I can have a quick word. She looks sceptical, but when I tell her I'm from Accounts, she perks up. That's the thing with us accountants – we don't waltz up and see the boss on a frivolous whim about 'becoming more creative'. We usually have something important and boring to say, and people respect that. She buzzes him on the intercom.

'Jack, I've got Tom from Accounts to see you.'

'Accounts… What did you say his name was?' says the Maestro.

'Tom.'

'Hmm… all right, better send him in.'

I enter the office. The walls are covered with various print ads and stills from TV commercials. Strange objects with no utility whatsoever adorn the shelves, from vintage typewriters to a strange taxidermy hybrid of a cat with a mouse head. In the centre of it all is a middle-aged man, trying to do tricks with a fidget spinner. Fucking hell, these creative people have got it sussed. As long as you come up with an idea every week or so you can do what the hell you want all day.

He doesn't acknowledge me for the first few seconds – Hmm – I'd forgotten how funny looking he is. Kind of like a weird little goblin. A GOBLIN. Oh God. I over-visualised. I'm going to have to goblin-fuck my way to a career change.

'Tom, isn't it? Accounts?'

'Yeah,' I say, flattered he still remembers me. Even if it is from the intercom about twenty-seven seconds ago.

'What can I do you for?'

'I don't know if you remember, we met once before.' He clearly doesn't, so I fill him in. 'About ten years ago, when I first came here, I originally applied for a job as a creative.'

He looks confused. 'But you're an accountant.'

'I am… but… I got my accountancy qualification as a sort of back-up, and you saw it on my CV and decided you needed an accountant more than a creative so you gave me that instead.'

'Oh. Right.' He's losing interest, and gets back to the fidget spinner. I've got about twenty percent of his attention. I reckon I have another thirty seconds to get this interview or I'm out of here.

'Well, I think I need a bit of a change. And I'd heard someone had left in the creative department, so I was wondering if I could get an interview.'

'FUCK!' he says, dropping the fidget spinner for the third time since I've been in there. 'Look you're an accountant – you still work here so you're probably pretty good – you should stick to that.' *Fuck you, goblin.*

Every part of me just wants to just walk out, but I have to try. I am here to change. I am here to hustle like a Midlands-based pensioner in their youth.

'I know, but… I've been doing this for a decade, and – Look, I've given a lot to this company. I'm not looking for any special favours. I just want a chance.'

'I can't work out how to do this bloody thing.' He's gone 100% fidget spinner. I'm fucked.

'Um… you just need to keep your fingers a bit flatter.'

'What?'

'When you chuck it from finger to finger.'

'Show me,' he demands.

I take the fidget spinner from him and spin it on my forefinger. And then I bounce it up into the air and onto the next finger of my right hand, onto the third, and then back again. I've never got it back again before.

'How'd you learn to do that?' he asks, intrigued. *I have a seven-year-old son who went through a fidget spinner craze about a couple of years ago.*

'Um… I like to mess about with things when I'm, er, thinking of ideas.'

'Hmm. Not just an accountant…' No, a newly single parent who can't afford regular babysitters, has already watched most of Netflix, and uses his son's toys to help pass the time. I'll probably be good at Fortnite a couple of years after everyone's lost interest. 'Tell you what – I'll give you an interview. You know it'll be a lot less money if you get it, though.'

'I get that.'

He nods and then goes back to the fidget spinner with slightly flatter fingers.

I leave his office with a massive smile on my face. Which seems strange, considering the words 'a lot less money' are still echoing in my ears. But I did it, I bloody did it. I'm so proud of myself. I'm being proactive – I'm not just sitting in a conservatory watching *Homes Under the Hammer*. I'm out here in the world, doing stuff. Making things happen.

As I walk back to the lift, I hear a voice from behind. 'Get your memo finished?'

There, behind me, is Stair Woman. I probably shouldn't call her that. Sounds like she's someone who stares a lot.

'Um… Yeah.' Deal with that witty comeback.

'Glad to hear it,' she says and starts to head into Canonbury's office.

'Sorry – I didn't know you worked here?'

'That's because you work in Accounts, loser,' she says, making a stupid face. I can't help letting out a little laugh. 'I'll keep an eye out for your next memo.'

I head back down to Accounts. I just got a job interview, saw Stair Woman (who I'm beginning to notice is kind of super sexy), and I didn't have to fuck a goblin.

The new me is working out pretty well.

Not that the old me fucked goblins.

Evening

Idea for a band: get together all the people Sally has slept with behind my back and call it The Cuckolds – if I'm the front man and they're all *literally* behind my back it has a nice poetic irony. Good PR angle too, plus might help me work through my issues

33

if I get all the fame and don't let the groupies anywhere near the rest of them.

Not sure if any of them play instruments. Probably put Gary on drums as he's not cool looking and there's less chance of him pushing to do baritone/soprano backing vocals.

Friday

Mark and Karen have invited me to a bar tonight. I've got this sneaking feeling they've set me up with someone. I've told them I'm 'open to things' but I've made it pretty clear I need a bit more time.

But maybe she'll be all right. Maybe I'll have fun.

I turn up at the pub exactly on time. That's one of the things about having to arrange childcare. Fashionably late is not something that's going to happen any more. You'd either have to purposefully ask the babysitter to come at the wrong time or wander around the streets for an extra fifteen minutes, neither of which seem particularly fashionable. Plus you'd end up doing bedtime, which is the main thing you pay a babysitter to get out of. Ironically, if you were actually taking your children with you, fifteen minutes late would be freakishly early.

Luckily, Mark and Karen also have children so they're there perfectly on time too. And alone. Phew.

'Hey stud!' Mark shouts.

'Hmm,' I grunt. I don't feel like a stud. Maybe one who's just been taken out of banging commission and is currently waiting to be turned into glue. 'Can we not say that, maybe?'

'Sure,' says Mark. 'Didn't really feel right, anyway.'

Karen offers a few sympathetic words and then they both start acting weird, like they're waiting for something to happen. I decide to confront them on it.

'Is someone else coming?'

Karen and Mark look at each other. 'There's someone we want you to meet,' she says.

I knew it. I bloody knew it. I said I'd try to be open about things, but I specifically said—

'Here he is now,' says Karen.

He? This is taking 'being open' further than I'd anticipated.

A man with a receding hairline and one too many buttons undone on his shirt approaches the table.

'This is Paul. He's single as well.' *What the hell is going on?* Is there something they think I don't know about myself? Is this why Sally left me – because everyone thought it was only a matter of time till I came out?

Paul reaches over and shakes hands with me.

'Um…' I'm trying to hide the fact I'm completely freaked out. 'Hi, Paul. Er, I don't know what they've told you, but I think they've got the wrong idea.'

Paul gives me a knowing smile. 'They told me you had broken up with your wife and wanted to meet new people.' What is this? Have I just Sam Becketted into a new body. I need to check a mirror to make sure I still have the same face.

I look Paul up and down. Do I find him attractive? No. Still not gay. Yeah, pretty confident on that. Don't think he'd be my type even if I was.

'Look Paul, you seem like a very nice guy, and I respect your sexuality, but I'm just… not gay.'

'What do you mean?'

'I don't fancy you. I don't fancy men. I'm sorry – these guys have known me for years – I don't know why they'd think otherwise.'

Paul looks at me, like he can't believe I'd turn him down.

Karen interjects: 'Paul…' she says, trying to stifle laughter, '…

is currently on the market as well, and we thought he might be able to give you an overview of the… current dating scene.'

'Oh… well.' I've dug myself so deep in this hole, I think I'm about to hit lava. 'That is… actually a far more logical interpretation of situation.' Paul doesn't look impressed. 'Lucky I didn't just go for your cock!' I joke.

Ice not broken. Paul looks like he may put an ice pick into my head.

Twenty Minutes Later

Everyone's moved on from the awkwardness, thank God. Amazing what buying a round of cocktails and gastro-snacks can do. People really do underestimate the power of duck scratchings and a Scotch quail egg.

Paul holds court. 'What you've got to realise is – it's all about the app.' I look sceptical. 'Look, old man – things have changed since you were last on the market – if you're not online, you're offline.' He laughs at this, like he hasn't just stated a basic tautological fact.

Don't get me wrong. I know he's right, but I don't like this. I remember when only weirdos met each other online. You could mock them for their great hook-up stories. 'Tell me again. Did you see her picture and think "she looks all right" and click on her profile? That's so romantic.' But now it's the other way round. Like approaching a girl in real life might be tantamount to sexual assault.

'First up you need to download Tinder.' Fucking hell, where else would I get this exclusive information? Thank God he's here.

'Put up a profile, put up a picture – choose a good one – picture's really important,' he continues.

'I'd heard about that – I'm in advertising,' I say with what I think is obvious sarcasm.

'Awesome. Then you'll know the deal. Bullshit, bullshit, bullshit.' Sarcasm not detected. 'No outright lies of course – just a nicely skewed version of the truth.' He looks at me directly, 'Hey – there's no Advertising Standards when it comes to love.'

A few minutes later and he's showing me his profile – complete with a full head of hair and a suit. Even his shirt's buttoned up. He's like a completely different person. 'See – it's a few years out of date, but it's me. If it was brought up in a court of law they wouldn't have a leg to stand on.'

'Sure they're going to know I've changed when they get there, but that's when I wow them with my scintillating personality. No harm, no foul. Might have brought a few back to my place as well.'

He leans in, like he's about to tell me his preferred brand of Rohypnol. 'Although if you want to do the same... might need to lose those grey patches.'

Grey patches? My fingers involuntarily stray up to my temples. I have, like, a one-inch grey patch on each side. He is missing the hair from the *entire top of his head*. I can't quite believe this. Unless... Maybe he's not bald... Maybe he just spotted a bit of discolouration in the fringe and decided to go full scorched-earth on his sumptuous mane.

Paul gets up from the table, but why should that stop the patronisation? 'Think up some good lines too. All about the text banter,' he tells me. 'Anyway, 'scuse me for a sec. Off to drain the main vein.'

'Great. I'll write that one down, in case I need to sign off on Tinder.' Karen puts her hand on my arm. She can see I'm angry. We watch Paul disappear into the loos, and I turn to Karen and Mark.

'*Really?*' I ask, incredulously.

'Look on the bright side,' grins Mark. 'At least we're not trying to make you fuck him.'

I shake my head, utterly unamused. 'He's a complete weirdo – I can't believe you'd think I'd need advice from him. This is not exactly good for my confidence.'

Karen looks at me. 'We don't think you need advice from him. We just thought that if you saw Paul can get dates—'

'…you might realise there's women out there desperate enough to go out with you,' Mark interrupts.

Karen smiles. 'We thought that might do *excellent* things for your confidence.'

Saturday

'I'm taking the kids this week.'

I'm woken by the first proper words Sally's spoken to me since she left. I've rehearsed this conversation a million times in my head. How I was going to approach it, keep my cool – poised, urbane, a latter-day Cary Grant: '*Ah Sally? How nice of you to call.*'

It does not come out like that.

'What the fuck, Sally? You haven't talked to me for six weeks and then you just call and say you're taking the kids!?' *Ah, Cary, how you've changed.*

'Are you recording this?' she demands. 'Because I didn't give you permission, so if you're recording it, that's illegal.'

'Of course I'm not recording this – you called me.' I'm also massively hung-over, which means I wouldn't have thought of it even if I'd wanted to.

'OK.' She calms down slightly. 'Well, my boss has invited me down to Cornwall for a few days with her family, so I need the kids.'

'Um… slow down. Where are you? I don't even know where you are.'

'It doesn't matter where I am. It's none of your business. I'm not taking them here – I'm taking them to Cornwall.' My head is spinning. Why do you pass the age of thirty-five and start getting hangovers from three drinks?

I head to the kitchen for a glass of water. 'Look – I just need to know what's going on. Where are you living? Are you with someone? Are you coming home?'

I immediately wish I hadn't said that.

'I'm not coming home.' Was I even hoping for that? I didn't think that was in my head. 'The rest of it, we'll talk about it when I'm ready.'

'For fuck's sake.'

'Look – I want to pick them up at eleven tomorrow. Is that OK?'

I don't have a choice. They're her kids too. Even if she did just fuck off and now wants to use them as an accessory while she schmoozes with the head of TV Commissioning.

'Fine. When will you drop them back?'

'Friday probably… I'll let you know.'

'But Arthur's got school.'

'I thought it was half-term. Fuck. Theirs must be different because it's a private school. Well, we can just tell them he's ill. I'll sort it out,' she says.

I'd be perfectly within my rights to tell her no, but I don't want to be the bad guy. Kids need to spend time with their mum. Given the amount Arthur seems to learn in a week's worth of school, I doubt it's going to hamper his education.

'OK.' There's a few seconds of silence, then we both hang up the phone.

I wander through to the living room, where Carrie is wearing no top, flying goggles and angel wings. Arthur is sitting upside down on the sofa reading a Spider-Man comic. This hangover is very much reminding me of every morning-after from my twenties. Hope the kids aren't on the pot...

'Guess what, guys. You're going away with Mummy tomorrow.' They suddenly light up.

'Mummy! Mummy, Mummy, Mummmmmyyyy!'

'I don't want you being weird with her 'cos she left and destroyed our family,' I mutter under my breath.

Even if it was at full volume the kids wouldn't have heard me. They're dancing round, like they've just heard the Good News from John the bloody Baptist.

It's so annoying, they've never been this happy to see me in their lives.

But at least I'll get a fucking break.

Sunday

With Sally turning up in a few hours, I have to get the kids dressed. Now this may sound pretty straightforward, only the last few times Sally's picked them up, she's seemed a little... judgmental – rolling her eyes at what Carrie's wearing and dropping her back six hours later in totally different clothes, her new outfit set off by a doggy bag containing her previous ensemble.

So this time I'm going to up my game. Show that it's not only love that I can provide. It's also style.

Now this may seem like a pretty simple task, but there's a problem; over-coordination runs in my genes. My mum's outfits are like a frame from a Wes Anderson film. And by that I do not mean cool and quirky. Bits of colour from one piece of clothing are reflected exactly in another. There's even a chance she may match the background. Now, whereas this looks brilliant in an indie film, it does not on a pensioner.

Not that I can judge. Before I met Sally, my clothes weren't much better. Sure, I didn't have a matching neckerchief and belt (for this I have the drabness of men's fashion to thank), but well... let's just say my get-ups didn't require separate wash cycles. I had a dream the other night where I found myself in a burgundy rollneck and scarlet/burgundy cords and woke up in horror. I think it was a dream. It may have been a memory. This is not something I can inflict on my kids.

Luckily for them, Sally dresses the kids REALLY WELL. They look fucking cool. When we were together this was great. Now it's also a bit annoying. But there's no reason I can't do it too. That I can't learn.

I open Carrie's drawer feeling like a monkey with an IKEA flat pack. I know I have everything in front of me that I need to make something good. I just have no idea how to put it together.

Right – there on the top, I spot a dress I like; it's dark green with small yellow birds. Yeah, that's a good one. I just need to find some tights to go with it, then I'm golden. It's October I'm pretty sure that's tights time. Carrie's next to me, expectant.

'Do you need to wear tights? Are you cold?' I ask.

'Really cold.'

I start to get a few pairs out of the drawer, then I remember – don't listen to your kids. Rule number one of parenting. Discount every opinion your child gives you. They have literally no idea about anything. Carrie's also standing next to me in her pants and the window's open, so that might affect things. Still – I'm going for tights.

'Let's put your dress on.'

I put the dress on her, and start surveying the hosiery options.

41

Right – there's grey, white, navy, dark green, light green, yellow, blue and a few others. OK – first – blue are out. That doesn't go at all. But then jeans are blue – they go with everything. Better keep blue in the mix. Dark green is pretty similar. I think that's too close. Light green might be good, but then grey and white are pretty neutral so they're probably good too. For fuck's sake.

'Carrie – do you know what tights Mummy normally puts you in with this?'

'Yellow.'

Of course – because of the yellow of the birds. That matches the tights but doesn't over-coordinate with the dress. That's perfect. Why didn't I think of it?

I pick up the tights and then it hits me.

What am I doing?!? This is 100% Granny Jan. Fight your instincts. If it seems right, it's wrong. If you're not going to reject everything your brain is telling you right now, you may as well buy her a bloody matching belt and neckerchief and be done with it.

'Are you sure Mummy puts you in the yellow?'

'Yellow matches the birds.'

'That's what I thought…'

I'm kind of frustrated. But at the same time, pleased. When you find out your wife's been screwing around, it's reassuring to see that your daughter's inherited the same genetic style disorder.

'Can you not actually remember?'

Carrie shakes her head. I'm on my own.

I hold the tights up one by one next to Carrie's dress. I literally can't tell what goes. I feel like one of those animals that can see contrasts but not hue. They all look *kind of* OK. But maybe they all look kind of bad too. I just can't bloody tell. How the hell does this work?!?

Then I have an idea: photos. I have hundreds and hundreds of photos. What good is our habit of documenting every second of our kids' childhoods if we can't use it to steal fashion tips from our estranged partners? This could work. And not just now. If I study them enough, maybe I could even start to understand the system – find patterns, formulate a theory. There must be rules. There are always rules. If people can find out how particles function at a quantum level, I must be able to come up with a basic algorithm for matching dresses with tights. Then I'd be completely independent. The kids could spend time with me and not be labelled 'the ones who dress badly'.

Invigorated, I pull out my phone and start swiping through the pictures. Forty back, there it is – a few months ago at Dan and Miranda's house. Dark green dress, navy blue tights. Jesus. Never would have gone with that. It doesn't make any sense. Navy and dark green. Madness. But it looks good. Maybe there are no rules. Maybe I'll have to let go of my aspirations of independence and just stick to copying the photos.

I pass Carrie the navy tights and she starts to put them on. I should help her, but I find myself just staring at the photo. It was only ten weeks ago – we're all smiling – we're with our friends – a happy family.

Then I hear a car horn outside. Sally's early. I look out of the window, and notice something. There's a man in the front seat. A bloody man. I can't believe she brought someone here.

'Are you all right, Daddy?' Carrie's still struggling with the tights but she's spotted I'm upset. It takes a few seconds for me to catch my breath.

'Yeah,' I nod. 'Yeah I am.' I smile at her reassuringly, but inside I'm fuming. 'Mummy's here, so it's time to go,' I tell her. 'But you know, I think you were right. Let's put the yellow tights on. Then we'll go down and see Mummy.'

Fuck you, Sally. Fuck you. She's my daughter too. And in my family, we dress badly.

43

Ten Minutes Later

'I'll text you when I'm bringing them back,' Sally says coldly.

The guy in the front seat doesn't get out. He's wearing a cap and just stares down at his phone to avoid being spotted. I nod an OK to Sally and she straps in the kids and they take off.

Going back into the flat, it seems ridiculously empty.

I wanted some peace, but this doesn't feel like peace, it feels like a vacuum. I chuck a coat on and head out, picking up a flat white from the coffee shop on the way. I need to walk to clear my head.

I head to the river. The footpath's full of runners. These days, strolling by the Thames feels like taking a golf cart onto a motorway; trying to maintain your calm, while panting office workers jog by you with numbers fixed to their backs.

Maybe I should start running. Everyone seems to do it now. They seem to get some sense of fulfilment from it. It's become the norm. Taking a walk by yourself is the weirdo thing to do. Am I stuck in the past somehow? Trying not to date online, travelling down the towpath in a way that isn't ridiculously unpleasant...

Someone runs past in the other direction with a backpack filled with flour, a packet of Homepride peeping out of the top. Even this doesn't seem strange anymore. If you'd seen this twenty years ago you wouldn't know what to think. 'Shit! There's an emergency at the bakery! If they don't get there fast there won't be time for the sourdough to prove!'

There are a few others walking. Mainly young couples and families. A pair of grannies strut by with walking poles, someone dressed in running gear strolls by wearing a medal... I'm assuming he's finished the run. Either that, or he subscribes to my kids' philosophy of what to wear at weekends.

I need to find someone... or something. If the kids are going to be taken away from me half the time, I need something to do – or at least someone to share it with. But online bloody dating... The fact I'm wary about it makes me into even more of a fucking grandad. Which makes me even more wary. For God's sake.

Back on our road, my neighbour asks me to watch her kids for a second, while she pops inside to get her bag. I know the son a bit – Jake. He plays with Arthur occasionally.

'Where's Arthur?'

'He's with his mum.'

'Arthur said his mummy doesn't live with him anymore.'

'That's right.'

'Is it because you have a whore?'

'I beg your pardon?'

'My daddy nearly left, because Mummy said he had a "whore", but then she forgave him and he came back.'

'Oh. No. I don't have... a "whore". Maybe one day I'll get a girlfriend, but she won't be... charging.' *Well done filling him in on the details, idiot.* 'Look, can you please not say that word in front of Arthur.'

He nods. 'How will you get a girlfriend?'

'I might try and meet someone on the Internet. I was just worrying I was too old, but I'm just being stupid.'

'How old are you?'

'What do you think?'

I love asking children how old they think you are. They always guess ridiculously young. In their minds everyone over twenty is hideously ancient, which means them saying something like twenty-five is basically them calling you a pensioner. But still, hearing those beautiful digits is sweet. For a moment you can pretend that this child is a genius, and you're only a few years past getting 'Think 21'-ed in Sainsbury's.

He considers the question for a second. 'Hmmmm… I don't know…' He's taking this very seriously. '…fifty, maybe…'

That did not go the way I planned.

'Fifty?' I say through a gritted smile. 'That's very old. I'm nowhere near fifty. I'm still in my thirties.'

'No, you're not.' You can't say that. That's an actual fact. But the little shithead is on a roll. 'My dad is thirty-nine and he looks a lot younger than you.'

Nothing like a bit of whoring to keep the wrinkles away.

'I'm sure your dad doesn't look that much younger than me,' I say.

'Your hair is white.'

I point to my two-centimetre square grey patches by my temples. 'These bits?'

'Yeah! You look like Santa Claus.' He laughs like he's just heard the funniest joke of his life.

'Can I have some good presents this year please, Santa? Ha, ha!' he continues, almost exploding with hilarity. You better watch it, kid, or you'll be hearing something about Santa that will turn your whole fucking existence upside down.

I force a smile, but I'm only one more comment away from ruining his childhood. His mum comes back just in time. Still, he may be receiving an anonymous note through his letterbox during Advent…

'Thanks for watching him. I always forget my bag or keys or something.'

'No problem,' I say. She goes to get in the car.

'Sorry… can I just ask? Your husband – does he look particularly young?' *It's probably him, not me.*

'No, just normal I suppose. Why?' *OK, it's me.*

'Just wondering…'

I go back into our flat and look at myself in the bathroom

mirror. Maybe I do look old. If I'm going to meet someone, I'm going to have to deal with this. Sure, a bit of grey hair at the temples has a certain charm if you're Reed Richards in a comic book, but in real life, maybe Reed Richards would just look like someone who kids thought was fifty.

For fuck's sake. I'm going to have to get my hair dyed.

Tuesday

I sit in the waiting room of the unisex salon feeling like I'm waiting for the executioner's chair. I've decided to take a long lunch hour after yesterday's attempted purchase of *Just for Men* was nipped in the bud by an orange-maned man in his sixties flashing me a wink in Superdrug. So I'm turning to the professionals. People who can be trusted. People who know what they're doing.

'Hi, I'm Emilio,' says a flamboyant man in his early twenties. 'If you'd like to come with me, we'll get your massage done, then we'll have a look at your hair.'

'Oh no,' I say, 'I didn't book a massage.'

'It's part of the service.'

While I'm pondering whether I've missed any connection between the two (maybe hair needs to be relaxed before it takes any colour), a girl with a bright green bob comes over and asks me to choose a scent.

I close my eyes, and get a noseful of aromatherapy oil. Hmm – to think I was dreading this. But this is actually all right. Is this what all women's haircuts are like? How the hell have they got away with this? They go and get their hair done and get a free massage in the process? It's amazing. What else do they get? Facials before a doctor's appointment? Reiki during a dental bridge fitting?

47

Still, I'm part of it now. I'm going to enjoy my massage. Maybe if I relax enough I can forget I'm about to undergo the most embarrassing experience of my life.

Post-massage, Emilio takes me to my chair.

'So,' he says, followed by an unconscious handclap that attracts everyone in the salon's attention. Thank God; I was worrying they hadn't noticed me. 'You want to get some colour?'

'Can you keep your voice down?'

'Oh, sorry,' he moves to a whisper, 'do you have a headache?'

'No,' I whisper back. 'I'm *massively embarrassed.*'

He laughs. 'Oh well; don't be,' he says, offering no possible reason why not. 'So, what are you thinking? A kind of rich chestnut?'

'I just want to cover up the grey bits.'

'Really? I like them – they're very cool.' They're cool if you're twenty-five, dickhead, but when they're a symptom of your rapidly decaying body, they lose a bit of their pizzazz.

'Well, that's the thing,' I reply, 'I'm worried I'm looking a bit too cool and I wanted to take the edge off.'

'Oh yeah, sure thing, man.' Huh – wow. He's got about the same level of sarcasm appreciation as Paul. 'Well, I'll just mix up some colour and then we'll get you sorted.'

He wanders off into his little room to do his mixology thing and then it suddenly hits me:

I'm by a window. Onto the street. A street that people walk down. In the place where I live.

This is not good. This is not good at all.

He comes back with his trolley, adorned with a couple of pots and brushes.

'Hey, I was just wondering if it might be possible to move to a different seat?'

Emilio looks confused. 'Sorry, no, this is my chair.'

'But there's another one free over there.'

'Yeah, but that's not my chair.'

And before I know it, he's started to comb in the dye. I can't hide. I can't run. I'd be left washing it out in a café bathroom, with one side of my hair a rich chestnut. This is happening. I'm getting my hair dyed in a public viewing gallery. I'm like one of those window prostitutes in Amsterdam. Well, not that much like them – only in as much as neither are positions I envisioned being in when I woke up this morning.

I shouldn't panic. No-one will probably walk past, and, if they do, it'll just look like my hair's wet. They'll just think there's a guy with wet hair about to get a haircut. He's been enjoying the hairdresser's complimentary pre-cut steam room. I'm sure some places have those.

And then Emilio picks up some foils.

I flinch. 'What are you doing?'

'I'm putting some highlights in. We'll blend it so it'll look more natural.'

I don't have anything to say. He's putting foil in my hair, in a public window. I try to concentrate on my breathing. That's what all the mindfulness idiots do, isn't it? In… out… in… out… Soon he'll be done. No one will have seen me. My hair will be dyed and this will all be a bad memory.

'Right – so I'll be back here in about thirty minutes and then we'll have a look at it.' Thirty minutes? That's half an hour. Maybe my hair wasn't relaxed enough by the massage. I had no idea it would be this long. I spill some coffee down a shirt, rinse it immediately and it never comes out, yet hair dye takes thirty minutes before it even bloody *works*?!?

I bury my head in some men's magazines – *Esquire, GQ, Men's Health* – thinking I'll be less recognisable in profile. Oo – maybe I *do* want to get a washboard stomach in just ten minutes a day.

Non-grey hair and a six-pack. Wait a minute. Ha. You have to eat *that*? Three hours of food prep is really going to eat into my Netflix schedule.

I chuck *Men's Health* to one side and start looking at some fashion stuff. There's a nice coat for only £3,200. Very reasonable. I don't know why the hell they put this stuff in a magazine that normal people can buy? What percentage of their readership is spending £3,000 on a coat?!? By the time you'd assembled an outfit you could put a down payment on a house.

I look at my watch – eight minutes gone. This is terrible. I'm still in the window and I've still got foils in my hair. Then I have an idea: the loo! I can hide in the loo! I raise my hand like a ten-year-old in a geography lesson.

'Is it OK if I go to the toilet?'

The woman with green hair looks at me, her confusion instantly becoming mockery, 'Um, yeah. Just make sure you wash your hands properly.'

I wander over to the loo, giving her what can only be described as a hate-smile. You may feel smug, but your hair looks stupid. Says the man with metallic dreadlocks. I go down the stairs to the basement and shut myself in the toilet. Sanctuary. Privacy. A bomb shelter. No Internet on my phone. I'm alone with my thoughts. Probably not ideal…

I look at myself in the mirror. What was I thinking anyway? Everyone's going to know I've dyed my hair. They've seen the grey patches. Their children think I look fifty. Shit. I'm going to have to buy a beanie. Yeah, that could work. Then I can cover it up during school pick-up and drop-off and at work, and just whip it out when I go on my dates. So to speak. Perfect. Those women will be new so they'll have no point of reference and just assume I'm a youthful-looking 39-year-old. Beanie it is. Actually, I think there was a nice one in GQ for two hundred and fifty. I might not be able to afford a £3,000 coat, but I can damn well up my beanie game if I'm prepared to cut a few corners on the kids' Christmas presents. Once word gets round there's no Santa, they'll have lower expectations anyway.

This is good. The transition period should only take a couple of months. After that I can go hat-free and people will begin to doubt their own memory. Maybe it won't be enough. I might need something bigger to distract them on the reveal. Hmmm… What about a dog? I could get a dog. Yeah, dog definitely trumps hair dye. 'Wow! You got a cockapoo!' No one's even going to look at my hair. If it's still a puppy I could probably sport a neckbeard with impunity.

I look at my watch. Twenty-nine minutes have gone. Cool. I head back to my seat. Where's Emilio? Any second…

With the time running out, I'm feeling better. Why should I be embarrassed? Look at all these women around me. Some of them are younger than me and they're getting their hair dyed. Why should there be one rule for men and one for women? It's fine. We're all human beings. If we want to live in a world where everyone is equal, I've got to take a stand and dye my hair. If anything, this is me making a statement of equality. Tom Cooper: hammering down the door of sexism.

I can almost hear the sounds. *Bang, bang, bang.*

And then I turn to the window. Pounding on the glass, a big smile on his face… is John. Pointing at the foils in my hair like he's just seen an alien spaceship.

He gestures that he's coming in, and a second later he's next to my chair.

'Ha! What's happening here then?'

'Just…' I've got nothing.

'Be interesting to hear what people think when I tell them about this in the office!' he beams. A little chuckle to himself and he wanders out.

I am a broken man.

Emilio comes back. 'Right let's have a little look at it, shall we? Hope I haven't left it too long.' He starts looking under the foils.

You have, Emilio. You really have.

Wednesday

I wear a baseball cap in the office today. My hair looks great, but I couldn't face styling it out. I think everyone assumed I was trying to look cooler now I'm applying to be a creative.

John's biding his time. He's clearly planning his next move. I need to find some kind of equivalent blackmail information…

Thursday

I'm trying to do my Tinder profile when Sally decides to drop the kids back twenty-four hours early.

'I thought you were dropping them off tomorrow.'

'No, today. It was always today.'

'Daddy, daddy!!!' The kids come running up the path. As much as I'm angry with Sally, it's awesome to see them. It feels like my real life is suddenly back.

'OK – well, when do you want them again?' I ask.

'I'll text you.' Or just turn up randomly at my door? 'I'm not sure what I'm doing at the moment,' she tells me.

I shrug and she turns away. Then she remembers.

'Oh, I told the school Arthur had norovirus. I've coached him on the story, so he'll be fine – they don't let you go to the doctors for that…' She suddenly notices something. 'Did you do something to your hair?'

The cap. I answered the door without my bloody cap.

'Um… it's for work. It's a sponsored thing. Everyone's getting their hair dyed for charity.'

'In a natural colour?'

'They didn't specify, so I went with natural.'

'Oh.' She looks like she's considering something. 'Well, it looks quite good actually,' she says. 'You look a lot younger.'

She heads back to the car. I notice there's no one else in the front this time. I hear screaming from the flat and go back in to drown myself in a sea of childcare.

I try asking the kids if there was a man with them on holiday too, but they won't give me anything. Seems like they've been coached on that too.

Friday

One of the mums was acting really flirty with me at school drop-off. I was just leaving and she comes over, saying she's heard about Sally and was I OK and if I ever needed to talk, while stroking my arm the whole time.

Nothing can ever happen though, as I've known her for three years and can't remember her name. Should never have deleted that bloody contact list the PTA sent round.

Saturday

I sit watching *The Leftovers,* regretting not booking Lacey to babysit and having to stay in for the second night in a row. Maybe it's good – I still haven't done my Tinder profile so this could be a perfect opportunity.

I look at a few people's example profiles on Google and I hate everybody. As a man, is it possible to write anything about yourself without sounding like a wanker? One of these idiots has even put 'consent is sexy'. No, it's not; it's a basic moral and legal necessity. What next? Not killing someone is mysterious? Hmm… a lot of people seem to use quotes. I try to think of something that seems relevant, but all I can come up is with random clichés. 'A bird in the hand is worth two in the bush'… it just sounds like I'm saying I prefer hand-jobs to group sex. I try and think of others. 'Two's company…', 'Too many cooks...' God; everything just sounds like I'm trying to hold back the flood of threesomes I'm assuming I'm going to be offered. I move to the photo. I can come back to the rest.

There're a few OK ones in my phone, but they've all got kids' elbows etc. over part of my face. I could try cutting them off on one side, but it's going to look like I have a facial injury like the guy off *Boardwalk Empire*. I take a few selfies but nothing is great. Jesus – this is so unfair. Why do you have to know a bloody professional photographer if you want to get a date now?

Then I remember FaceApp. They had that Hollywood filter. I put it on the selfie I just took. I look pretty good. Oh God; actually pretty good… This seems really wrong. But if that Paul guy can put up a photo with a full head of hair, why can't I put up a picture that looks exactly like me but a hundred times better than I've ever actually looked? Movie stars do it all the time. They look all great and airbrushed in the photos and then you see them in the actual film and you kind of overlook the fact that they don't look like that any more because they're 'in character'. It's still their bloody face. That's how I'll approach my dates – like I'm in character as a more average-looking guy to make myself seem more down to earth. It's totally wrong. It goes against all of my principles. I'm doing it.

By 2:00 am, it's all set up. A completely deceitful representation of everything about me, from my appearance to the level of wit they can expect from our conversations. And I start to look at some women. To look for a date…

Within seconds I'm loving it. I feel like a God, judging face after face with a single swipe of my holy finger. Not my type… you look like you used the Hollywood filter (*I'll date someone with integrity, thank you*)… you look almost exactly like my sister – swipe left. Super important I get that one the right way round… And… *ah, good evening, young lady; you, I believe, are worthy…* This is brilliant. It's like selecting items from a catalogue.

And then I realise… not only is this totally objectifying – some of these items might not want to be selected. It's like an Argos where every so often the toaster looks you up and down and decides it's not for sale. And right now, these people, real people out there in the world, might currently be judging me. Ten seconds later I've closed the phone, and I'm walking away from it like it's fucking uranium.

I swiped three rights. Oh God. Three people who can say no. I'm getting rejected and I haven't even left my living room. This is awful. Please let someone say yes. Please let someone say bloody yes…

Sunday

Having a 90% chance of total rejection and humiliation next time you look at your phone turns out to be an excellent way of cutting down on your Internet time. The kids keep asking if there's something wrong with my tummy as I don't seem to be using the loo like normal. God, I really do have a problem. Not that it matters today. My phone's currently on top of the wardrobe with the notifications turned off. It's also buried under a pile of clothes in case I see the light come on and start getting paranoid. This is going to be a day of being a dad.

Although sometimes I think I don't even have what it takes to do that.

In the afternoon we watch our weekend Disney film. The three of us snuggle up on the sofa and eat home-made popcorn. The film's great, except for when Mufasa dies and Carrie ends up crying for half an hour. I have to pause the film to comfort her.

'It's all right Carrie, it's all right. You don't have to worry. Daddy's not going to die.'

Carrie looks at me with utter disgust, shakes her head and points at the TV. Basically: 'What are you talking about, idiot? I don't give a shit about you: *Mufasa.*'

It's weird so many of these films still have parents dying. Is it really necessary? I get that a lot of them are based on 200-year-old fairy tales – back then parents probably popped their clogs left, right and centre. With that level of medical knowledge, I'm sure you couldn't swing an unanaesthetised amputee without hitting an orphan. Pre-operation of course. After that, the arc would obviously be smaller.

Point is: back then a stepmother probably made the whole thing relatable. But now… parents just don't die that much. Sure, it happens occasionally, but chances are their mums and dads will be around. Well, alive. It's always possible one of them might have fucked off after sleeping with four of their friends' parents.

But what really makes me feel bad is when Mufasa gives Simba advice.

All film and TV dads are really good at offering the kids life tips. 'Son, when you are older, all this will be yours. Remember these words.' And then they hit them with something badass that will completely transform their existence.

But me? I've got nothing. Less than nothing. Put me in *The Lion King* and it's suddenly a far less inspiring film.

'Simba. Come sit with me. I have something to tell you.'

Simba sits and looks up at me.

'What is it, Father?'

'One day all this will be yours. Listen to these words. They will serve you well.'

An expectant pause.

'Always remember,' I tell him sagely, 'when eating an ice cream, it is a mistake to bite off the bottom of the cone too early. There won't be any ice cream in there, and you'll end up with drips all over your clothes.'

Children all over the world find something useless planted in their subconscious forever.

Cut to later in the film:

Simba is older, I am dead. He goes to an interview for a low-level job in Scar's organization. It's not like he's going to stand up to him with me as an inspiration. On the way there he has an ice cream, but he stupidly bites the bottom off after his third lick. As soon as he enters the room, Scar laughs him out of his office, because he has mint choc chip on his tie.

My face appears in a cloud. 'You should have followed my advice about the ice cream.'

'You were right, Father. It was stupid. And, as you warned me, there was no ice cream in there.'

Maybe best that I leave it. Some people just aren't meant to give advice. We have Mufasa for that. I guess I should just sit on the sofa and listen. Maybe I can learn something from him too. And hey, if these idiot kids feel loved enough, you never know… they might just make the right decisions for themselves.

Monday

I check my phone for responses every five minutes for the whole day.

Nothing.

Even with the Hollywood filter.

Tuesday – Halloween

Trick or treating with the kids tonight. I never thought it would catch on here, but now I spend an hour every October knocking on the doors of houses with pumpkins outside, hoping the owners know the rules; I don't want to give some old lady a heart attack just because she bought too many squashes. After all, consent is sexy.

Afterwards, we head to a party at their friends' house. My kids' costumes are particularly uninspiring this year. Arthur's wearing his pyjamas with a Spider-man mask, and Carrie's an angel. I put some fake blood on her dress as a token nod to horror, but it looks more like she spilt something down her front. Although taken objectively, white dress/blood/wings – I've basically dressed her as a panty liner. Still, all the kids seem to be having fun. Only the host's kid, Theo, looks uncomfortable. He's wearing an Elsa dress. His dad's convinced he's trans after he caught him trying on his mother's bra once and now he's forced to choose his clothes from the M&S 9-12 Girls' range. I've heard him protest a few times, but his dad keeps telling him not to give in to societal pressures. The wonders of liberal parenting.

The kids eat party rings, cake and pumpkin pie, while the mums and dads neck Prosecco and pretend they're not getting pissed. Mark's there alone with Amelie, his daughter, as Karen's got a deadline tomorrow. We always joke that Arthur and Amelie will end up together one day. It's why I can't confide in Mark about Arthur's weird penis thing – don't want to nip his chances in the funnel-shaped bud.

I chat to Mark about various bullshit – bands, the kids, what we think of the new *Avengers* movie – when I notice Flirty Mum over the other side of the kitchen. When did she get here? I suddenly realise Mark might be able to help me out with some identification.

'Hey, that woman over there in the black jumper…' I point her out. 'Do you know what she's called?'

Mark shrugs. 'No idea. You're the only person in the room whose name I *do* know.' At least it's not just me. But Mark's curious. 'Why?'

I try to avoid the question, but Mark's having none of it, and keeps pushing. 'Nothing, really. She was just a bit flirty with me at pick-up, and…' I feel like a teenage boy telling his friend he fancies someone. 'She's divorced, isn't she?'

'Yeah. Think so. Are you not doing the online thing?'

'No responses. I contacted three women and none of them got back to me.'

'But you signed up?' he asks. I nod. Mark beams with delight. 'Right, let's see your profile.'

I don't want to, but eventually I give in. I hold up my phone and show him. And he laughs. Straight to my face.

'Bloody hell, mate. Are you wearing make-up?' Mark can't stop laughing.

I mumble a, 'No, it's the Hollywood filter,' but he's in full-on hysterics. This may explain the lack of responses.

'Nice photo.' A woman's voice interrupts from over my shoulder. Standing behind me is the black-sweatered beauty whose name I don't know.

'That's embarrassing,' I say.

'No, you look really good. Doing some online dating are you?'

'I just set up a profile. He pushed me into it.' I gesture towards Mark, who then decides to use this as an opportunity to screw with me.

'He should though, shouldn't he?' says Mark. 'Good-looking guy don't you think?' You *fucker*.

'He's not so bad,' says Flirty Mum. 'Although it's always possible he could find someone closer to home.'

I was right. That was a hint. That was a definite hint. I may have absolutely no ability to read women, but that was definitely a hint.

'Sorry,' Mark interjects. Oh, no, what's he going to bloody say now? You are no friend, Mark Baker, no friend at all. 'This is really embarrassing,' he continues, 'but I can't actually remember your name.' I take it back. Mark, you are a saint. You are a bloody saint.

'Oh, can't you, *Mark*?' She says, pronouncing his name like a pointing finger. 'Well, *Mark*, let me remind you.' She looks at me and shakes her head. I shake my head back. There's no point Mark falling on his sword if I jump on too. Besides, these martyrs like to go down alone. Anything else is just stealing their thunder.

'It's Claire.'

'Claire! Of course; sorry, I knew it, but then there's just so many names to remember these days…'

'You could have always asked me.' I say, flashing Claire a smile. She smiles back. Mark doesn't look impressed.

'Anyway,' continues Claire, 'we only popped in a for a few minutes, but I just wanted to say hi… Are you going to the parents' thing next week by the way?' I literally had no idea it was on.

'Um. Maybe… yeah… you?'

'Definitely. My ex is taking the kids so it's a rare opportunity to get pissed and go back to an empty flat.' She looks at me meaningfully. 'Anyway, see you there, or… at drop-off tomorrow.'

She wanders off, leaving me with my hero.

'You're a good friend.' I say.

'I know,' says Mark. 'Wouldn't do it, though.'

'Why not? She's attractive, right?'

'Nothing to do with it. Don't shit on your own doorstep. It gets messy and you'll just end up with more problems on your hands,' he says, his eyes drifting over my shoulder, 'Or… on someone else's wall.'

'I have literally no idea what that means…' I say, following his eyes to Carrie, who is under the kitchen table, crayoning on the host's feature wall.

'*Shit.*' I run over to Carrie and manage to extract her before anyone else spots what she's doing. 'Time to go home, love; let's get Arthur.' I find Arthur in the bedroom. He is currently swapping costumes with Theo. Maybe I should think again about the whole trans thing, Arthur looks pretty happy in an aquamarine gown. Besides, if he's going to have gender reassignment surgery one day, the weird penis thing just becomes moot.

Back at home, I put the kids to sleep, quite pleased that Arthur is already in his pyjamas. Maybe that was a good costume after all, it definitely sped up bedtime. And then my phone beeps. Probably Mark telling me how I owe him about twenty beers. I do.

There's a notification. Someone's messaged me.

'Sorry for slow reply – away with work. Liked your picture/profile. Want to chat?'

It's one of my right swipes. The one I liked the most. I stay up for another hour texting her. She texts back as well – it's important to make that clear so I don't sound like a weirdo – and at the end of it we agree to meet up. On Friday.

61

I've got a date. I've got a bloody date. And Flirty Mum likes me. Maybe I am a stud.

Wednesday

I go into work with a new sense of confidence. Sure, I'm an exhausted dad with slightly too much belly fat who's separated from his wife, but I'm also able to fool the occasional person into thinking I'm attractive. I feel so good, I don't even wear my cap. Give me what you've got, world – nothing can take me down.

Then I hear some giggling by the water cooler. I stop. Even a man who's on top of the world is going to feel paranoid to a soundtrack of high-pitched sniggering.

I head over. 'What is it? What's going on?'

'The hair,' says Annie, barely able to keep a straight face.

The cap. I should have worn the cap. Never get too cocky to underestimate the power of group mockery.

'Have you seen it?' she spits the words out in between hyperventilations. *Yes I've seen it – it's on my head.*

But she's not looking at me. She's looking towards where I sit. And there it is:

John. His hair a deep black with a Peaky Blinders undercut. Jesus, John. You wally. You bloody wally.

I start to smile, but at the same time I'm aware that this could have been me. I may hate the guy and sure, this is a better distraction than a cockapoo puppy, but we men with slightly less than natural hair have to stick together.

'He's probably just feeling insecure about getting older. Maybe someone made a comment about him being grey,' I say, trying to come across all mature.

'I wouldn't defend him,' says Carol. 'He's applying for the same job as you.'

He's what?!?

Fucking *JOHN*.

I walk over to my desk and throw my backpack on the chair with defiance. It falls off, but I think the throw made the point. Really hope my laptop isn't broken…

John looks at me, challenging me to confront him.

'Hey John,' I say. 'What's with the hair?'

'Keep your voice down. You say one word and I'll tell them about yours,' he says.

But I've got a bone to pick. 'That's not what I mean,' I say. 'I was wondering… *why* you got it done.'

John looks evasive. 'Just fancied a change, that's all. I can be cool too, you know. You don't have a monopoly on hair dye.'

I walk away and then do my Columbo 'one more thing' move. 'Only… I just wanted to check it wasn't because you were thinking of applying for a job – the same job as me. That would be kind of a dick move.'

John looks like he's just been caught with his actual dick hanging out of his fly. 'How did you know?'

'Word gets round,' I say. 'But hey – who cares? May the best man win.' Mature, confident, cool.

'Oh, and by the way,' I continue, gesturing towards the giggling throng. 'They're laughing because they think your hair looks stupid.'

Wednesday Night

The stress of the upcoming interview is failing to cancel out the stress of the upcoming date. I've got a date for the interview now.

They want me to come up with a way of pitching a popular product to a new market. Fuck.

Also, I'm now starting to think thirty-three is too young for the date. I mean, it's only six years, but what if we have nothing in common? What if we start talking about our childhoods and she's never seen *Dogtanian and the Three Muskehounds*? If she hasn't heard of *Cities of Gold*? It's probably fine, but if she starts reminiscing about Season One of *Peppa Pig*, I'll be out of there faster than Willy Fogg – which admittedly, by modern standards, probably wasn't that fast. I could probably circumnavigate the globe about seventy-nine days quicker than him if I bought a couple of plane tickets, but hey; I'm not an anthropomorphic lion. That's got to slow things down a bit at Passport Control. I guess we can talk about *Neighbours*. We'll have completely different casts in mind, but at least Karl will provide some overlap. He's always in it.

I'm proud of myself for standing up to John today though. That's the kind of person I want to be. Fuck John. He's never had any desire to be creative, he just wants to stop me from getting it. Well, I'm not going to let him. From now on, I'm the kind of guy who doesn't take any shit from anybody.

Thursday

Not taking any shit from anybody is not turning out well. I may have slightly embarrassed myself at school drop off. I may be slightly misusing the word 'slightly'.

We get to school about five minutes before the bell and Arthur runs over to join this group of boys when some kid just completely blocks him out. I try not to react, but inside I'm furious.

And then I recognise the kid. It's *Oliver*. Little shithead Oliver. Now let me be clear: I hate Oliver. I've always hated Oliver. He's the worst kind of little macho turd who'll spend his life bullying people and never develop the self-awareness to realise he's an arsehole.

Arthur goes back in. He's not taking no for an answer. Good on him. But then, Oliver *pushes* him. Right onto his ass. My child. I mean I'm *here*. I'm right here. You don't bully a kid in front of his dad.

I'm about to go over when I see who's in front of me: Oliver's dad. A sense of relief comes over me. He'll deal with it.

But he doesn't. He just stands there. Watching. Looking almost... proud.

I tell Carrie to stay put, and push through the lines of parents to the fray. No kid bullies mine with impunity.

'Ahem.' Someone coughs and grabs me by the arm. I turn round. 'Did you just push me?'

Holding onto my sleeve is Oliver's dad. The clan head. The paterfamilias. The patriarse.

'No. I'm just trying to stop my son being bullied.'

'Interesting,' says Oliver's dad as I try to walk away. 'You're feeling insecure that your son's lower down the pecking order than mine, so you decide to take it out on his father.' Bugger. Now I've got to deal with this.

'That's not what's happening,' I say.

'It's clearly what's happening.'

This little man is starting to annoy me. Well, technically not little. He's got about twenty pounds on me and quite a lot of muscle mass. He's actually pretty massive. And looks like a bouncer. But still, he is small of soul.

'If your son's acting like a bully,' I point out, 'it's your job to tell him how to behave.'

Oliver's dad laughs. 'It'll work itself out,' he tells me. 'It's part of life. Your son just needs to man up.' *Man up? What century are you living in?* But he's not finished. 'You know, like his dad.'

I know he's trying to provoke me. And I want to back down. But I can't. This is the new me. The me who doesn't take shit from anybody. I take the bait.

'Martin, isn't it?' I literally don't know how I know that.

'Yeah.'

I go down to a whisper. 'Well, *Martin*, you go and tell your son to back the fuck off. Or I go and tell him for you.'

'You want to tell my son what to do, you'll have to go through me.' He steps in to me. And, before I know it, I've stepped in too.

I don't know what's happening. For some reason I'm squaring up with someone in the playground. I have no idea why my body is doing this. Christ, I really hope no-one remembers. I may have a custody hearing to deal with in a few months.

'He's got to learn to stand up for himself if he wants to survive,' says Martin.

'Maybe you need to think about your own survival right now.' *What am I saying?!? Why are these words coming out of my mouth?!?*

I'm shaking from the adrenaline. Martin's built like a brick shithouse. But I can't back down. What is a brick shithouse anyway? A toilet. I'm not scared of a toilet. And what is a toilet full of? Crap. That's right. He's full of crap. He's not going to hit me. He's not going to hit me in the school playground.

I go forward to stop Oliver. And Martin pushes me. He actually pushes me. That's not allowed.

He must have done it without thinking. A glitch in the matrix. He'll be regretting it; it's no big deal. I step forward, and he pushes me *again*. Onto *my* ass. I'm on the floor. Oh *God*. Playground rules apply.

I look around. This is embarrassing. People are watching, but no one's doing anything. I'm being bullied. I'm being bloody bullied.

'It looks like someone else should've learnt to stand up for themselves at school,' laughs Martin.

Why are none of the teachers coming over? Why is no one coming? I've got to do this myself. I get back up. He pushes me down again.

'Stay down.'

I scan the playground, relieved that none of the hot mums are around. But Arthur's watching me. I don't think this is what it means to be a man, but I'm not having my son see his dad pushed down by a bully. I'm getting up again. God, I hope he doesn't give me a wedgie.

I make it to my feet. I have an overwhelming urge to punch him, but I'm not going to stoop to his level. Words are more powerful than the stick.

'Look – *idiot*. Let me tell you something. You may live in a world where pushing someone over is considered OK, but I don't. If this is the way you want to bring your kid up, fine. But you're not dragging mine down with him. I… and my son will be taking a higher path.'

And Martin just laughs in my face. Humiliating me in front of the whole school.

But I remember where I heard that laugh before… He was standing on the sidelines when I was playing tennis. I fell over, and he let out that same stupid guffaw. Dickhead wasn't even playing. He was just watching because he had a knee injury.

He had a knee injury.

I think for a second and take the only course of action available. I kick him really hard in the knee.

He goes down in pain. I stand there victorious. The hero triumphant against the dragon. I see his underwear slightly coming up above the back of his trousers and I'm tempted. Believe me, I'm tempted. But I'm bigger than that. At least in public. I've won. Even by your rules little/big man.

'Excuse me,' comes a voice from behind.

I turn round – it's Mrs. Winsley, Arthur's teacher.

'Did you just kick Mr. Rolph in the knee?'

'Um…' I stumble, 'Maybe… I… He pushed me over.'

She looks at me in utter disgust. 'I think you need to go and have a word with the headmaster.'

I trudge over towards the entrance of the building, feeling the disposition of a moody seven-year-old come over me.

'Daddy.' Carrie runs over and holds my hand. She looks up at me. 'That man was a nasty man. Good kick.'

I smile slightly inside. And then head into the school to get told off. Behind me Oliver and Arthur have stopped fighting and everyone's talking together… I think they might be taking the piss out of me and Martin. It's true, violence doesn't pay, but I'm pretty sure the headmaster can't give me detention after work…

I hope not. I've got to take Carrie to her swimming lesson.

Friday – Day of the Date

I spend the whole day stressing about the date – whether I'll look OK, whether she'll recognize me, whether I'll have anything to say. I manage to slip out of work at five, which gives me time to get home, have a shower, change and feed the kids before the babysitter comes and I head off to Waterloo.

And I'm feeling good. She may be a bit younger, but so what? She seemed really cool in her texts. Plus she's generous. Not only has she agreed to go out with me, she's also followed me on four different types of social media. Even if this doesn't work out, I'm going to look slightly less unpopular on Instagram.

But on the way there, the insecurity starts. A few weeks ago I left the house feeling vaguely confident, only to walk into a well-lit loo at a Mexican restaurant and be confronted with my actual face. Complete with eyebags, shaving foam in my left ear and a white eyebrow hair that had suddenly grown to about an inch long.

Anyway, point is, I now have to do supplementary checks after leaving the house. So when the suitably neon train carriage empties out at Vauxhall, I seize the opportunity. At thirty-three, Hannah might not have had to face this kind of thing before. She's still basking in those last few years of innocence before you realise your youth is over.

I turn on my phone to use the camera as a mirror and start to perform the examination. Not bad. A stray eyebrow hair is returned to the fold with a single sweep of the thumb. De-Norman Lamont-ed in a single gesture. Jesus – thirty-*two*. I wonder if she knows who Norman Lamont *is*.

I check my teeth – no bits of food. No weird eye boogers or dislocated facial sproutings. Looking good.

But then I see it. A single straight nasal hair protruding from my right nostril. And *long*. Like half a centimetre beyond the perimeter long.

I try to push it back inside my nose. But the hair's having none of it. It's thick. *Aggressive*. It pings back into place like a shatterproof ruler. Why do these freak hairs always seem stronger and more forceful than the others? The will to power. Maybe Nietzsche's whole moustache was his *übermensch* nasal hair fighting its way out of his nostrils.

I have to pull it out. Unfortunately, I don't have the required implements. A pair of tweezers and it's simple. Painful, but simple.

Although, for some reason if you pinch the top of your nose while you do it, it hurts less. What's with that? I suppose you're keeping your nose more stable, so pulling the hair puts less stress on the inside wall of your nose. *And to think I was worried about having nothing to talk about?!?*

I try grabbing it with my fingers, but can't get a grip. Why did I cut my damn nails earlier?!??! Hmm – still got a little bit of nail on my thumb – if I really dig that into my index finger with the hair in-between, maybe I could… No. Arggh. I need tweezers. I need bloody tweezers.

There's a Boots at Waterloo. But she's meeting me outside the gates… If she's late, it'll be fine, but otherwise I think the detour could create a bad first impression.

I have to get it out. I start looking through my bag for potential tools. Pencil? No. Highlighter? No. Wait – it's got a snap-on lid. Maybe I could trap the hair in it; that could work. I try it. Stupid thing keeps slipping out. They should deal with that. It the lid's not tight enough to trap a nasal hair, how's it going to stop the tip drying out? Oo – conversational gambit number two! If I can deal with this hair, I'm going to be a veritable raconteur.

I check my bag again… pencil sharpener… zip on my headphone case? For God's sake.

'You are now approaching your final destination.'

Fuck. Fuck, fuck, fuck. Maybe I can run along the platforms before I go through the barriers. If I can get straight to the other end by platform one and then slip round the back while she's waiting, I could do this. FOCUS. Keep searching. Nail clippers! OH MY GOD! I have nail clippers!!! Shit. We're pulling in. People can see me on the platform. Doesn't matter – I'm not going on a date with them. She won't be there. Actually, that woman's quite hot… NO! … *EYE ON THE PRIZE!*

I prop my phone/mirror up on my leg, ignoring the open

mouths of the audience of commuters heading home for the evening. I manage to grab one end of the hair between my left finger and thumb with the bit of nail. That's it. Then I raise the clippers… got to be careful I don't cut my nose…. Shit, the angle's all wrong, but if I come at it in sideways….

And then… Snip. It's gone. It's really gone. I did it. I BLOODY DID IT! Hey, lovely 33-year-old, I'm Tom, a man with no protruding nasal hair. Let's go and enjoy our evening.

I'm out on the platform. All the people who watched are behind me. If I don't look back I'm golden. I'm like Orpheus leaving the underworld, only with more willpower and a keen sense of shame.

I go through the barriers. She's there. She actually looks like her photo, only prettier. She's even prettier than her photo! She's looking at her phone. She hasn't seen me yet. Big smile. Lead with a smile, that's always good.

But then her facial expression changes. She hasn't noticed me, she's still looking at her phone – so at least it's not that, but she looks like she got some bad news. God, that's going to sour our date. And be bad for her too. I care about that as well. I'm not an animal.

Wow. It must be *terrible*. She's making a really weird face. I hope no-one's died. But she still looks pretty. Even when she's making a weird face, she looks pretty. This is great. I hope she's got a good personality. I hope she doesn't smell weird. She looks like she's going to smell great. This is awesome. Online dating is AWESOME.

Then she looks up. And sees me. The look of repulsion on her face doesn't change.

She clearly hasn't recognized me yet. That's fine. Must be the Hollywood filter.

'Hi, I'm—'

She cuts me off mid-sentence.

'You know you were just live on Instagram?'

It takes me a second to make the connection. I don't broadcast live on Instagram. I don't even know how to. I'm a bloody Luddite. I email, check the web, play a few games, but that's it! I still use my bloody phone as a mirror! As a *mirror*… Oh, God.

She holds up her phone. And there I am – a low angle shot of a 39-year-old man struggling with a stray nasal hair. Holding it taut with one hand. And then cutting it with nail clippers.

We look at each other.

A moment passes. Nothing else needs to be said.

I nod an acknowledgment and turn back towards the barriers. It's no big deal. Maybe she smelt weird. I probably should have had a sniff. She already thinks I'm a freak – be good to have known that it wasn't going to work anyway because she had a strange odour. Look on the bright side. It'll be good to have an early night. Still probably have to pay the babysitter full whack though. Lacey hates it when I get back early.

Saturday
9:00 am

I order a couple of desk lamps from Amazon without leaving my bed. My plan is to set them up in front of a mirror in the living room. Two of them pointing directly at my face with hundred watt bulbs, so I can't miss anything. I can't risk last night happening again. Sure, if I get a girl back I'll look like a teenager with his own YouTube studio, but if I get a girl back, I won't care.

I veg round under the duvet, while I let the kids watch cartoons. The idea of getting up seems horrendous – like I'll be re-entering a world that knows I'm a fool. Instead, I just sit there, looking at my phone, watching my life evaporate away one click at a time. Maybe I should I go back on to Tinder and try again – hair of the dog and all that – but I can't face it. I need time to regroup.

Thirty minutes later the kids are back in the bedroom.

'Can we watch some more?' I let them have another ten minutes so I don't have to get up. God, I'm a terrible parent.

But I try to forgive myself. Doing this alone is too much. I need some help. It goes through my head to call Sally, but I stop myself, because it wouldn't just be about the kids. I want to talk to her, to be back where we were. Being single sounds great when you're married, but that's because in your head you're a sex god who's secure enough to not need a cuddle when you get home… It's why *Hall Pass* is one of the uncelebrated great movies – all these guys get a free pass to fuck anyone they want and they can't get anyone interested. Well, maybe not one of the great movies, but not as terrible as everyone thinks. I wonder what it got on Metacritic…

I chuck my phone down and force myself out of the covers. I'm stewing in my own juices – a technology-savvy version of my bloody parents. I catch myself in the bedroom mirror. Yuck. Morning me is horrible.

I stand there, looking at my reflection – a fully-grown man in his pants. I'm pretty sure the only reason anyone considers pictures of men in their pants sexy is because it's better than the alternative. Once you've seen a man completely naked, pants seem relatively attractive. Maybe I should try to lose some weight. I'm not fat, but I'm not as thin as I used to be…

Is that really something women care about? I once had a woman tell me the sexiest thing a man could do was the washing up. I'm pretty sure that's bullshit. What was the sexiest thing a woman could do? Lie to a man to manipulate him into doing the

73

housework? Don't get me wrong – I think a guy should do his fair share of the chores, but there's a reason women buy calendars of firemen rather than *Hot Cleaners*.

Right – I'm going to get in shape. I drop down to the floor and do twenty press-ups. Well... three. The rest look like I'm dry-humping the carpet with slightly bent arms, but at least I'm moving. Jeez, that hurt. Should probably do some sit-ups too. It can wait till tomorrow – best to focus on a single muscle group per day. And I thought reading *Men's Health* in the hairdresser's was a waste of time.

'Can we watch one more?' Carrie's re-appeared at the door. Does ten minutes really pass that quickly? I need to get my act together.

'No.'

'Why not?' asks Arthur.

'Because we're an active, industrious family. We do things. We don't just sit around watching telly. We're going to have breakfast and leave the house.'

'Can we look at your phone?' asks Carrie.

'No, we're having breakfast.'

'*While* we're having breakfast,' explains Carrie, like I'm an idiot. Patronising little shit.

'No, we don't look at phones at breakfast.'

'You look at your phone at breakfast.' Hmm... should probably stop that.

'Not any more. Come on – let's go to the kitchen. No more phones, no more telly. This is going to be a day of getting things done.'

Breakfast

Eat my cereal. Really want to look at my phone. Eating is boring.

Playground

Still setting a good example. I manage not to look at my phone the whole time. Watching kids at the playground is boring.

Lunch

Fish fingers, oven chips and peas. I wonder what's happening in the news. I bet my phone would know. Probably need to do a quick toilet trip.

Pudding

Feel better after loo trip. I didn't actually go, but at least I informed myself about what's going on. Once again I'm a proper citizen of the world with his finger on the pulse of the information superhighway. Can't believe *Hall Pass* only has 34% on Rotten Tomatoes.

Afternoon

We all do drawing. The kids seem happy. I feel like I'm going to explode.

I can't take anymore childcare. I'm dying. I'm just bloody dying.

I'm not sure the world tells us the truth about being a man. We're meant to be OK with looking after kids and homemaking and all that shit, but I always feel like I should be out doing something else. Working, or… hunting an animal or something.

Maybe I need to start a project to take the edge off – it should be something properly manly – woodworking maybe… you need a lot of tools though; perhaps I could start with whittling and move up from there.

I could even fix up an old car, that'd be cool. Maybe a motorbike's cheaper. Jesus, could I get any more stereotypical? I'm one step away from signing up for a course on bull fighting. Actually, I wonder if they do those? I'd have to move to Spain, but that'd be a small price to pay – the Spanish women would see me as interesting, exotic. I'm sure decades of tourism have done nothing to erode our natural British mystique. I'd be like a modern day Hemingway. Maybe I *should* actually do some hunting. If I knew what it felt like to take a life, maybe it'd be easier for me to supervise a two-hour crayoning session. They'd be colouring in a lion, but I'd be remembering what it felt like to end one with a rifle. Jesus; what is wrong with me? I'm a member of the bloody WWF, and now I'm fantasising about shooting big game?!? I'm losing my mind.

God, I want to look at my phone.

Dinner

We have steak for dinner – seems a good way to ward off my desire to kill endangered species. The kids like theirs well done. It's almost as if they lack any primal bloodlust.

Still Internet-free.

76

Evening

I do the kids' bedtime, read them both a story and cuddle them while they go to sleep. They're a lot worse at sleeping since Sally left. Arthur had a bad nightmare yesterday. Even in the dark, I resist the temptation to have a quick look at Reddit. I'm awesome.

Five Minutes Later

I spend three hours looking at my phone while watching Netflix. Literally no idea on the content of either of them. Bliss. May not need to kill animals after all.

Sunday – Bonfire Night

Bonfire night is one of the great things about being British. The Americans have the Fourth of July, the French have Bastille Day, the Italians seem to knock out a few fireworks every bloody Saint's day – but do any of them have a massive fire with the effigy of a human being on top of it? No. That's why we're the best.

Interestingly, in real life they didn't actually burn Guy Fawkes – he was going to be hung, drawn, castrated and quartered, but then managed to jump off a ladder and break his neck on the way to the scaffold to avoid it. Strange that hasn't made it into the traditional celebrations. A nice stuffed Guy with detachable testes, one of the organisers walking round with a big knife ready to cut them off, then everyone looking disappointed when the Guy is thrown off a ladder with his balls still attached. Guess that would be more a summer thing.

We head over to Mark and Karen's for a drink beforehand, and then stroll down to the athletics ground where the main event's happening. The kids walk ahead, ridiculously excited. Carrie's sandwiched between Arthur and Amelie, while another girl, Tabitha, jumps around trying to get Arthur's attention. Karen's talking to Tabitha's mum, Harriet. Her husband died a few years ago of a massive coronary. When you hear about things like that happening, breaking up a family because you don't fancy someone seems almost ungrateful.

Crowds of people pour into the sports club. The way in is lined with stalls selling glow-in-the-dark paraphernalia and hog roast, providing a warm welcome to all who aren't Muslim, Jewish or have a phobia of the Eighties. I buy the kids a hot dog to share and get me, Mark, Harriet and Karen some doughy white rolls filled with pig, then we head down to the bonfire. Nikki Minaj is playing over the speaker system, requesting someone 'turn her on' over a pumping bass beat. It's funny that this is the soundtrack my kids' memories will be made to. I comfort myself in the knowledge that they have no idea what 'turning someone on' is. They probably think it's some experimental lyric told from the point of view of an electrical device.

We head closer to the bonfire and watch Mike from the sports club light it up. I don't know him, but he's always propping up the bar in our local pub and I'm pretty sure he's not qualified. It's crazy; there are barriers everywhere for health and safety, yet a guy who's 90% proof is in charge of the fire lighting. I'm also pretty sure he doesn't do athletics. Mike is basically a pyromaniac who pays a club membership fee and tolerates a year's worth of track events, so every twelve months he can set fire to something in public. But as it goes up in flames, I'm not looking at Mike. I'm not even looking at the fire. I'm watching Arthur and Carrie's faces as they slowly illuminate in the growing firelight. When I see their expressions it's like I can remember what it felt like to be a kid again. To not realise anything will ever change – it's one of those times you wish you could keep them like this forever.

A few minutes later and we're standing amidst the throng, waiting for the fireworks to start. Nikki Minaj has been replaced by Katy Perry, who at least doesn't want to be turned on. She's probably still got a bit of residual arousal from all that girl-kissing she did ten years ago. But it's not long till it fades out and the countdown begins.

'Ten, nine, eight…' Carrie tries to join in from my shoulders, but counting backwards is slightly beyond her at the moment.

'Ten, nine, ten—'

'Don't worry, love,' I interrupt, 'when it gets to "one" it starts.'

'Two, one,' concludes the announcement, and the lights snap out. Carrie pats me on the head to let me know it's time, and then the soundtrack shifts to classical and fire starts shooting into the sky.

I'm cold, but content. Even if I spend the rest of my life single, I've got these guys, and I love them. I look around and see the crowds to the left of me, families and couples, their heads backlit in the floodlight. They all look like they're wearing little haloes. Like a legion of happy angels looking up at the heavens.

The fireworks are surprisingly good. They start small, then move onto these cool ones that suddenly fill the sky with crackles and glitter, then there're these little red lights that shoot up in the air looking like a unit before suddenly splitting into four. You don't expect it, but then it suddenly happens out of nowhere and takes you completely by surprise.

I look over to Karen who's standing to the right of me. I haven't talked to her all evening. I give her a smile, but she just looks back at the fireworks. I haven't really thought about it, but I guess she's been acting weird all night. She doesn't seem to want to meet my eye.

'Are you all right?' I ask her.

'I'm fine.'

'You're acting a bit strange.'

She hesitates for a while, but then decides it's probably better to talk. 'I saw Sally yesterday.'

Suddenly the crowd erupts as the first big rockets fill the sky.

'What? When?'

'She called me and we went out for a drink.'

I try to act cool. 'Oh, right. How's she doing?'

'Fine. She's fine.' She looks down at the ground. There's something she's trying to avoid telling me.

'Look, I think there's something you should know…' She hesitates some more. 'She's seeing someone.'

The crowd 'woo' at a particularly spectacular explosion.

It's not really a surprise. I knew that. I'd seen someone in the car with her. This is fine. 'Just the one person?' I joke.

Karen's laugh is pretty subdued – she's got more to say. 'I don't know about that. But this… this sounds more serious.'

The crowd lets out an awestruck 'ahhhh'.

I don't know why she's telling me this. It's Sally's business who she's with. I knew she'd been seeing someone. Having it confirmed doesn't change things. But Karen is speaking like there's something I'm missing.

'He's Canadian.'

I shrug. 'So what?'

'He lives in Canada.'

I'm trying to work out what she thinks is so important. 'That's great. A long-distance relationship – I'm happy for her,' I lie.

Karen looks at me with sympathy plastered all over her face. She doesn't realise I've already taken this in. 'She's planning to move to Canada with him,' she says.

'OK…' I suddenly realise what this means for the kids. She'll

80

hardly ever see them. Fucking Sally. I never knew she was this selfish. 'Well… I mean… it'll be weird for the kids. But… I can't make her stay. I don't see how anyone would be happy with their kids that far away from them, but…'

Karen's just looking at me.

And then it clicks. She's moving to Canada. Of course she won't be happy with the kids half a planet away. She wants to take them with her.

The crowd bursts into rapturous applause. Like they're celebrating the fact I've finally overcome my idiocy.

The world just fades out. It feels like a glass wall has appeared between me and reality. I can vaguely hear Pomp and Circumstance playing in the distance, but I'm suddenly alone in this mass of woolly hats and scarves.

My kids. Away from me. To *Canada*. They don't even have Bonfire Night.

The rest of the fireworks are a blur. As we walk home, I'm blank. The kids are super-excited, running ahead and jumping up and down with their luminous wristbands, and light-up electric windmills, but they're in a different place. I want to be with them, but I can't. Suddenly everything is overshadowed by the fact that this might be the last Bonfire Night I ever spend with them.

Halfway home, Carrie gets tired so I pick her up and she falls asleep with her head on my shoulder. Arthur walks alongside, talking to Amelie about the sort of inane shit boys talk about to girls they like. I can hear Carrie's breathing in my ear. I hold her as tight as I can, like somehow that's going to keep her from being taken away from me.

I try to pay attention to this moment, to what's happening around me – it may be the last one like it I ever get. But my head is just filled with thoughts – of the future, of what went wrong – but not of the present.

And to think I thought the worst thing that could happen tonight was third-degree burns.

Monday

In my lunch hour I call a lawyer Carol recommended, and fix up an appointment for next week. I can fight this. I'm being reasonable, she's not. Surely that counts for something.

I can see John working on something in his cubicle, he covers his screen up as I walk past. Shit. He's doing prep for the interview. It's this bloody Friday. I'd almost forgotten in the last eighteen hours with all this Sally crap.

I realise I'm going to have to block it out until I meet with the lawyer. I won't know where I stand until then anyway. It can wait. I've got an interview this week that won't.

Evening

The kids are in bed by 7:30 so I sit at the kitchen table trying to come up with ideas. I've got four days to work out how to introduce a product to a new market; that should be child's play. All right, creative brain – work your magic.

After ten minutes of staring at my computer, I start walking round my flat looking at various things and thinking how I could sell them to my parents. iPads, laptops – they've already got all that. All I can think of is making the screens and keys bigger on everything so they can see them – but then a phone becomes a tablet, a tablet becomes a laptop, and before you know it you've marketed them a desktop, which is what they all bloody use anyway.

The parents thing is a dead end, so I move onto myself for inspiration. What am I finding difficult? Work/life balance... looking after the kids... Hmm... Could I make childcare more appealing to men? That's good. What about... a pram that looks like a race car? Yeah. Maybe food preparation equipment that looks like hunting gear – a jungle knife or something. A hair wash jug that looks like a pint glass. Jesus, I'm basically describing the contents of a men's novelty Christmas gifts catalogue. What do kids need? Child seats in the car. Could I market that to adults? For when you're so drunk a seatbelt just won't do... My GOD. My head is so full of shit, it could fertilise a botanical gardens.

This is impossible. I need to sleep on it. That's how creativity works. My subconscious will internalise the problem and I'll wake up with an idea. Sounds good. I'll have something by morning. Might try that new season of *Mr Robot* on Amazon.

Morning

Nothing. Shit.

Tuesday Evening

Another brainstorm session. How do you come up with ideas? I type 'how to be creative' into Google. Ah. This is more like it.

1. The thirty circle test – draw thirty circles and then make as many into drawings as you can in one minute.

OK, that sounds doable. Go.
Sixty seconds later, and I'm looking at what are basically three

faces. Crying, smiling and sad. I've basically just drawn some emojis. I check my phone. They're actually in the same order they come up in on the keyboard. My creativity is on fire. Maybe that wasn't my exercise. Bugger. What's next?

2. Doodle… OK, I'll try that.

Five minutes of doodling and my second piece of paper has some more circles, a few triangles, and two drawings of penises. I don't even remember doing those. I want to think I grabbed some paper Arthur used earlier, but the cocks are straight as an arrow and don't come in at the end, so it's looking doubtful. I look at the page; this is not good. The nearest thing to an original idea is that one of the penises is inside a triangle. It looks like the Highway Code's warning sign for 'flashers crossing'.

I've got nothing. Literally nothing. I'm not even engaging with the problem.

I distract myself by going on Tinder. Turns out the idea of abject humiliation on another date is actually better than doing what I thought was my dream job.

Don't panic. It's OK. Still two days. At least I've prepped my subconscious for some sleep creativity again. I'm good at that.

Maybe I should watch something more fun. *Mr Robot* was probably too serious and de-creativated me. I wonder what that *Russian Doll* show is like…

Wednesday Morning

Still nothing. *Russian Doll* was pretty good. The main actress was a bit annoying, but I got used to her by the third episode. I call it the 'Russell Brand effect' – if you get exposed to something enough, eventually you'll forget how irritating you found it in the first place.

The whole alternate realities thing was a bit of head fuck though. It got me thinking about me and Sally. What could have been... That said, I comfort-ate a multipack of Flakes while watching, so the blood sugar peaks may have caused some kind of mild hallucinations. Worth it though. Whatever reality you're in, that is a delicious chocolate.

Wednesday Evening

After a panicked lunchtime phone call, my parents have come down to help with the kids while I prepare. I have to admit I'm impressed they're already here. That said, there's a good chance they may have been motivated by my mum's interest in *Stylist Live* this weekend. I'm sure if I paid attention to the Kensington Olympia/Royal Albert Hall calendars I could actually get semi-regular childcare. Add to that David Essex's tour schedule and I might be able to stop sending Carrie to nursery.

I'm being sarky, but I'm grateful. They've really come through for me this time. Sure, it's probably also a reflection of their massive disappointment in my career, but I'll give them this one.

Mum and Dad put Arthur and Carrie to bed while I go for a walk to try and clear my head and come up with something. As I walk round the streets, there's a hint of winter in the air. England may be cold and miserable a lot of the time, but sometimes it's magical. The sky's clear apart from a few clouds illuminated by the moonlight. There's still the occasional firework going off in the distance as people use up their leftovers from Sunday. Sometimes I feel jealous walking past all these houses I'll never be able to afford, but today they're just a

85

picturesque stage set for my late night ramblings. They're looking down on me, willing me to succeed. It feels like something could happen. Something revolutionary, something… creative…

Suddenly something pings. Unfortunately it's my phone rather than an idea. One of the women I Tindered has messaged me. I can't think about that now, so I send back something polite asking if I can message her next week as I've got this interview and she messages me to not to bother then. She must have been really enthusiastic. Still – I've got to think of this idea.

An hour later and I'm back home. I feel like I've been on the cusp of something the whole time, but I've still got nothing.

The kids are in bed, and Mum's cooked me some dinner.

'Any good?' she asks.

'Nah,' I shrug.

Dad's in the other room, watching a film from the 1930s on the TV's YouTube app. He always complains the flat's too small for them to stay in, but then doesn't leave a six by two foot area except for when he's either eating, sleeping or using the loo.

'Thing is… I'm just not sure I can do this, Mum. I'm not sure I'm that creative.'

'Of course you're creative – you were always coming up with stuff when you were little – doing your little drawings of superheroes and monsters and things.'

'Thanks, Mum, but I don't think a sketch of an owlbear is going to cut it this time.' She looks at me encouragingly. 'I know you believe in me, but maybe this just isn't the right way for me to go at the moment.'

'I'm sure you can do it, if you want to. Something will come to you if you sleep on it.' How much time am I going to have to spend asleep? This building will be covered in fairytale vines by the time I bloody have something.

86

My mum plonks some jar-made chicken tikka masala in front of me. It's nice being looked after, even if the food is disgusting. I feel a bit like a kid again, but that's OK every once in a while.

'It'll be cold, but Dad was hungry and I couldn't keep it warm. You should get a hostess trolley, you know.'

I look at her with incredulity. 'Of course I'm not getting a hostess trolley. No one my age has a hostess trolley.'

'I don't see why not.'

Do I really need to spell this out? 'Because they're massive ridiculous things that only old people have. If I got one in here, it'd take up half the kitchen.'

'Well what do you do when you have a roast?'

'Have slightly cold vegetables. It's really no big deal. I'm sorry Mum, but no one of my generation is ever going to buy a hostess trolley.'

No.

You'd have to completely resell it to a new market.

'Mum – you're a genius.'

I pick up my lukewarm curry and head to my bedroom kissing her on the way out. She seems genuinely proud. 100% pleased with herself with absolutely no idea why.

I sit on my bed for the next three hours writing up a pitch for the modern hostess trolley. Slimline, stylish, and energy efficient. It also has Bluetooth speakers and an optional teppanyaki griddle top for all your grilling needs. Perfect for the aspirational foodie hosting a dinner party. I actually want one. I change the name to 'The Host', so it doesn't seem sexist (although it's *The Maître d'* by the end of the evening – hmm – maybe I could add a voice that tells you the seating arrangement) and at one in the morning, I press 'save' for the final time.

I've done it. I've come up with an idea. It might not get me the job, but I did it.

And even if things do go tits up, at least I'll have done better than John.

Thursday

My printer's run out of ink again, so I'm printing the presentation out at work. What is it with printers? All I ever do is print black and white and suddenly I'm out of cyan. I mean, I know I'm an outlier in not wanting my black to have a cyan tinge, but really?! I bet if I printed out an entire page of cyan I'd randomly run out of yellow.

Anyway, I'm standing by the printer waiting for my masterpiece to appear, and I'm desperate for the loo. Someone's printing out what seems like a client's entire correspondence with our company, communications so old they look like they've been scanned from microfilm. I've got a sneaking suspicion that any second now, the machine's going to start belching out smoke signals.

This is going to take forever. I decide to make a break for the toilet while I'm waiting.

The men's is occupied so I hover outside. I've got a feeling it might be John. He always takes about twenty minutes. Then Annie comes out of the ladies' and I keep waiting. She just looks at me like I'm mad.

'Why don't you just pop in here?'

'Umm…'

'It'll be fine.'

I think for a second; she's right, it'll be fine.

'Thanks, Annie.'

This is all above board. I've been given permission. Anyone raises it, I've got the perfect get-out. I don't know why we can't

88

use it anyway. It's sexist. It's offensive. A bit of congestion and a few units of alcohol and their lot are all over ours.

Then I go in. I see why they don't let us use it.

It's lovely. The surfaces are clean, the air is fresh, there's a full roll of toilet paper, the handwash even has soap in it. Luxury. There's a bloody pot pourri for God's sake. It's like peeing in a spa.

Anyway, I understand why women don't want us in here. But surely there should be some kind of process for exceptions? For people like me. Some kind of application. It'd be like immigration. If people share their values they can take some kind of naturalisation oath:

I hereby declare, that I renounce all allegiance to the men's bathroom, of which I have heretofore been a user, and I shall support and defend the values of the women's toilet. Those of cleanliness, hygiene, and not peeing on stuff. I will contribute to a kitty for the pot pourri and not use the facilities for anything other than a number one unless I get really, really desperate. I swear this on the Bible and any volume that might serve as a really good toilet book.

That's when I hear someone outside. A woman. She's waiting to come in.

'Why don't you just use the men's?' a passing female voice says.

'Why don't I just go and bathe in a puddle of raw sewage?!?' they laugh.

This is not good. The weakness of the Annie excuse is beginning to reveal itself. What if this woman doesn't know Annie? Anybody could just make up the name of someone and say they gave them permission. And 'Annie'? It sounds so generic. Maybe I should change it to something more unusual? Aphrodite.

That's good. No one in their right mind would make up 'Aphrodite'. Maybe she'll just think I'm a guy who's not good at making stuff up... *Really? Did Zeus come and put the seat down for you?* I should just go with 'Annie'. I'm not in a rush. I've got time to think this through.

'Are you going to be in there much longer?' Shit.

'Just a second.' I reply, realising I just put on a high voice. Why did I put on a high voice?!?

This is awful. I want to tunnel out of here, through into the men's. I could come out of the other door, and act like 'who made this weird hole in the wall?!?' Then again, even if it was doable, I'd be going at it with the plastic spoon I nicked from Pret to eat my yoghurt. At best, the hole would only be an inch across by the time they kicked the door down. Not only would I be hogging their toilet, it'd look like I'd used disposable cutlery to carve out some kind of makeshift glory hole.

I'm going to have to face this.

I wash up and unlock the door. That's a powerful tap. They've even got better water pressure than us.

Right – I'll start with a high voice and transition down like there was a problem with my throat. This kind of thing must happen to Gary all the time.

The door opens, and I'm face to face with Layla from HR. Probably the least friendly person in the building. Stick with the plan.

'Oh, hi – the men's...' COUGH, move to normal tone. 'The men's isn't working.' *Isn't working?!? Don't improvise!* God, I just made my story both factually inaccurate and 100% verifiable. 'So Aphro— Annie – said it would be OK to use this one.'

Cue John coming out of the men's. The sound of a flush echoing behind him. Fucking John. Layla looks at me and raises her eyebrows.

'Must have got it fixed.'

Layla shakes her head, and goes in. She spots the toilet seat. Fine droplets of liquid all over at it.

She looks at me in disgust.

'No. It must have been the tap. It has unexpectedly good pressure.'

She shakes her head and looks at me with contempt. Then shuts the door.

I stand there for a few seconds in shock, then go back to the printer, shamed. My thing still hasn't come out.

And it doesn't seem like it's going to. Where's my presentation? I wander round the office trying to find out who's got the tome that was printing out before.

It's on Carol's desk.

'Hey Carol. You didn't pick up my document by mistake did you?'

She flicks through the document at breakneck speed. She really is good with her hands.

'Sorry, no. By the way, the offer's still open if you're interested.'

'Thanks, Carol. All that kind of stuff's on the back burner with the interview at the moment, but… good to know.'

Where the fuck has my stuff gone? I go back to my computer with the slight suspicion that my life has just gone full *Leftovers*. Where the fuck did it go? I guess I'll just have to print it out again…

4:00 pm

A memo comes round from HR.

'There has been an incident with a man in the Accounts Department using the ladies' toilet.'

I'll tell everyone it was John.

'I won't mention any names, but let's just say it was not John. Please note: anyone caught using the opposite sex's toilet in future should be reported to HR for disciplinary action. Even if they do have Annie's permission.'

Two minutes later, Annie turns up.

'Thanks for dropping me in it,' she says.

Should have gone with Aphrodite.

Friday – Day of the Interview

I feel like an utter dick standing in front of my wardrobe, wondering what to wear. It's an interview – I should probably wear a suit and tie… but I'm meant to be creative. Do creative people wear suits for interviews? Why does no one tell you the rules? I decide on a suit, but with a more casual shirt. It's got flowers on – when did you last see an accountant in a shirt with flowers on? Well, last Friday when I wore it jacket-less to my disastrous excuse for a date, but *generally*…

My dad is sitting at the breakfast table in his dressing gown, and Mum's making a second cup of tea. She's been up since 6:00 am working on her hair so she'll be ready to walk the kids to school. Mum's focused on trying to find the teabags, but my dad looks up from his iPad and notices what I'm wearing.

'I thought you had your interview today?' he asks.

'I do.'

'Then why are you wearing that?'

'I'm going for a creative position.'

'Creative?'

'Yeah.'

'What's creative about wearing a shirt with flowers on?'

When you put it like that, you've got to admit he has a point.

'Creative people do things like that. They don't just… wear suits and ties. They put their own twist on things.' My dad rolls his eyes.

My mum's waiting for the tea to brew and has a few thoughts of her own. 'I'm with your dad. Although if you are going to wear it, you could at least put a matching handkerchief in your breast pocket. You're not exactly coordinated at the moment.'

'I don't have a matching handkerchief.'

My mother sighs, exasperated. 'Well, you've got to think ahead when you're buying clothes. Otherwise you'll end up in situations like this.'

'Send me a photo of your shirts and I'll try to find something at *Stylist Live* at the weekend.'

'It'll be too late then,' I smile politely.

'Well, if you're not going to get this job, it's all the more reason to be better prepared for next time.'

Sometimes, I feel my parents are a little too smothering with all their support.

'I'll take some photos of your wardrobe after I've dropped the kids off so you don't have to worry about it,' she continues. Well, that's actually happening then.

Then dad tags in. 'I just think if you're applying for a job you want to look like you're taking it seriously.'

The worst thing is – I don't know if I agree with him or not. Maybe I shouldn't be applying for this bloody job. I'm clearly not right for it.

'You know what my advice is? Novelty socks.'

'I beg your pardon?'

'Novelty socks,' repeats my father. 'That's what I put on when I want a creative day. You still look businesslike, but if you meet someone else who has a bit of creativity, you can cross your legs and flash them the fun.'

'And you're suggesting I try to get a read on the interviewer, and if he seems like he's up for it, I introduce him to Bart Simpson.'

'Exactly.'

I shake my dad's hand. 'Thank you.'

'No problem.'

He watches me as I leave, presumably on my way to pick up some novelty socks from my drawer. But I'm on my way out.

'Make sure the kids are there by 8:50.'

I kiss Carrie and Arthur goodbye as I head out the door, truly grateful to my father. What he just did was better than any advice from Mufasa. That's the great thing about parents – let them talk enough and they'll say something truly ridiculous. Something that reminds you to disregard every single other thing they've said beforehand.

Work

After an hour of accounting to get me in the mood, I head up to the top floor for my interview. I'm waiting outside the boss's office; they're running late. Whoever's in before me must be doing all right. That's not a good sign. This is a zero sum game – their success is literally my failure.

At 10:20, the previous interviewee emerges from the office. And… it's John. How the hell did John's interview overrun? Did he actually do *well*? This makes no sense. And what in God's name is he wearing? He's got what I think is… an Ed Hardy T-shirt under his blazer. Where the hell did he dig that up from? Are the early 2000s making a comeback? Well at least his dress sense is letting him down. I think…

Jack Canonbury follows John out of the office and pats him on the back.

'Great interview, awesome to hear your ideas – and love the T-shirt. Feels like an ironic twist on… irony. And impressed you knew I knew him. Excellent research. Great guy. Utter dickhead, but… great guy.'

John tries to hide his confusion; he clearly didn't intend any of this – but it's nothing compared to what I'm experiencing. Excellent research? Great interview? Awesome ideas? John hasn't got a creative bone in his body. I once checked his Facebook page and, under 'Interests', he'd just written 'Eating, sleeping, drinking'. Essentially, a list of the basic requirements to maintain life. I was half expecting to see 'oxygen'. I should be confident – it just means their standards are lower than I thought. This is good news.

'All right,' says Maestro J. 'Who's next?' He points at me. 'You.' He clearly recognises me, but has no idea what my name is.

'Tom,' says his secretary.

'Of course – Tom. The other accountant. Fidget spinner extraordinaire. Who could forget Tom?'

I go into his office, only to come face to face with the other person he's interviewing me with. The cool girl from the stairs. Shiiiit…

Suddenly I feel like an Ed Hardy-level dick. I'm about to spout all this pre-rehearsed crap about myself in front of a woman I fancy. I didn't even realise I fancied her. What a terrible time to have that revelation. And now I feel like I'm about to go to speed-dating with a written statement in front of me, at the same time as doing what's probably the only interview for a creative job I'll ever get. This is awful. This is bloody awful.

'You know Amanda?' asks Jack.

'Um… we've met. We've never actually been introduced.'

'Hi.' Amanda gives me a smile.

Jack sits down at his desk. 'Well, I have to admit I was sceptical about having accountants in to interview for creative positions – kind of me doing my bit for charity – but I have to admit that last guy really impressed me.'

John?

'Kind of dull during the general stuff, but then he came out with this amazing idea about a hostess trolley for hipsters.'

Oh God. That's my idea. John stole my fucking idea.

'Utterly unworkable, but it was *creative*. And that's what we're looking for here. Springboards – lateral thinking. There are no bad ideas. Bad ideas lead to good ideas.' *Bad ideas like printing your stuff at work so your arch-enemy can nick it?*

Fuck. I've got nothing. I've got absolutely nothing. I'm fucked. I'm absolutely fucked.

'Well, let's hope it wasn't a fluke – maybe you accountants are more than just numbers…' He smiles, and then a second later he's lost in a reverie. 'Numbers… numbers game… there's something there…' He turns to Amanda, clicking his fingers to himself so rapidly they don't make any sound, like he's an ideas machine that's just been turned on. Maybe this is what Nikki Minaj was singing about? I'm seeing Maestro J go full-on creative in front of my eyes.

'Accountants aren't numbers… number of accountants…'

I'm not like this. Why am I applying for this job? I don't do weird finger clicks when I'm thinking. Suddenly the idea solidifies in his mind:

'Finding the right accountant is more than just a numbers game…' He turns to Amanda. 'Write that down in case we ever get a pitch for an accountancy recruitment firm.' That wasn't actually so great. But Maestro J is on a roll.

'Numbers… Pi. Pi, pi, pi. r^2. Pis are… Pies are… Pies are squared. We market pies by changing the shape to a square and hitting them with that bad boy as a slogan. Boom.'

Amanda writes it down dutifully, and then suddenly, temporarily drained of genius, JC's back to me.

'So, why don't we start with the idea. Introducing a product to a new market. What have you got?'

I sit there in silence, utterly lost for something to say.

'Um... I...' Should I try doing the finger-clicking thing? Maybe that would help. More likely, it'll look like I'm taking the piss. I put my hands behind the chair and try a quick one... nothing. Shit.

'Come on.' Jack is losing interest.

'I've got a few, I'm just trying to think of which one would be the best.' My mind is completely empty. Blank. Buddhist monks spend years trying to get to this state; it took me three minutes of interview questions. I find myself staring at a Flake wrapper in JC's bin. I could eat about twenty of those right now. Jack interrupts.

'Look, Tom, if you haven't got anything, that's fine, but maybe we should just end this here,' he says. Amanda's looking sympathetic as JC continues talking. 'We're busy people and... maybe this isn't the right job for you. Right job... write job. W.R.I.T.E. – jot that down too – might be useful.'

'I think I can remember it,' says Amanda.

Jack shrugs, then looks at me. 'Sorry to break it to you, Tom, but some people just aren't creative. Some people are just... accountants.' I sit there unable to move from my chair, like a deer in a creative job interview. JC flicks his fingers twice in the direction of the door. 'Out you go then.'

I stand up. I've made a complete and utter fool of myself. And I've blown it. In front of this woman I fancy as well. I've blown my one chance at a new life. Probably ever. I'm going to head down to the vending machine and eat so much chocolate my body fat percentage hits triple figures.

Chocolate.

I suddenly turn around, and find myself starting to speak.

'Chocolate. We all love chocolate. There's a cliché that women love chocolate, but men love chocolate too. Chocolate is universal. It's... human.' Wow – I sound like one of these idiots. Do I have an idea? I think I have an idea...

But Maestro J is unimpressed. 'There's plenty of chocolates for men. Yorkie, Mars...'

'That's true,' I continue. 'But what is the greatest chocolate of all?' I reach down into his bin and pull out the wrapper.

'*Flake*. Crumbly, delicious, and marketed 100% at women.' Was that it?

'I'm listening.' He's buying it... he's actually buying it...

'You know it's delicious. *I* know it's delicious. But how many men would be confident enough in themselves to eat something that's meant to be accompanied by candles and a bubble bath?'

JC sees this a massive compliment, like he's somehow transcended all gender identity. Like he's one step away from qualifying for the pronoun 'zie'.

'Not many,' he says. Behind him Amanda is smiling... This is working... this is actually working...

'That's why my idea is this...' I hold the wrapper aloft. 'The Man Flake. Still crumbly, still delicious, but twice as thick, and marketed exclusively at men.' *Don't mention making it phallus-shaped. That was definitely a bad angle.* 'It's like three Flakes fused together, and we call it...'

'Yes?' He's on the edge of his chair. *What the hell do we call it?*

'...Quake!'

Jack Canonbury almost jumps out of his seat. 'Quake – I love it. Are you man enough to handle... the Quake? I can see the ad now: a workman biting into it – the building he's doing demolition on collapses behind him.'

'Exactly the kind of thing I had in mind.'

'The building's standing there like a massive phallus.' Well, better than people eating one I suppose. 'You too, can be a massive phallus.' Never a truer word spoken. JC looks amazingly pleased with himself. 'Bit of psychology. Power, subconscious, all that. And then you throw it back at them. But can you handle it? No? The building falls. *Impotence.*'

Amanda stifles a laugh behind him. I just about manage to keep a straight face.

He pushes the button on his intercom. 'Hey, Jill; set up a phone call with Cadburys. I've got something for them.'

'OK, interview over. I'm on a roll. I need some space – ideas are coming.' Maestro J's shifting into creative overdrive. 'Amanda; see me back here in twenty minutes for the next interview. Don't knock – just walk in quietly in case I'm in the middle of something. I'll notice you when I'm done.'

I walk out of the door, closely followed by Amanda. Did that actually go all right? I think so. Although it is possible he thought every idea I came up with was actually his.

Amanda shakes her head. 'He's like this. When he gets on a roll, he can't be interrupted.

'Well, I guess his ideas are what keep this company going,' I say.

Amanda's eyebrow raise holds back a tide of ssepticism. 'He hasn't had a good idea in ten years. Also, he should probably have realised your 'Quake' idea breached pretty much every new ASA gender stereotype guideline.'

I wince a little. But Amanda's smiling.

'You did well… obviously I can't give you any official feedback because I'm your interviewer…' She smiles, clearly finding her new role pretty hilarious. 'But let's just say you didn't completely embarrass yourself.'

'Do you think I have a chance?'

'If it was up to me. But unfortunately you'll have to just wait on the whims of Maestro J – advertising genius, M.D. and passing acquaintance of Ed Hardy.'

I laugh. Amanda smiles and heads off.

'Hey…' I call after her. She turns around. 'Would you like to…'

I pause. What am I doing? If Flirty Mum was watchamacalliting on my own doorstep, this would be like doing one in the hallway. We might be working together – you can't just go about asking people out at work. It'll make everything weird. She might even end up being my boss or something…

'…um… follow me on Twitter?' That cover up may have been worse than real-life following someone. 'I could follow you back, and if I have any more amazing chocolate ideas, you'll be the first to know.'

She pauses for a moment. Is that disappointment, or is she just thinking I'm an idiot?

'Why don't you tell me directly, so I can feel special? Besides, if you get this job, JC's not going to want you putting that gold up on social media.'

And then she's gone. Amanda. A woman I fancy. A woman I can't possibly ask out.

I spend the rest of the day at work avoiding any conversations, for fear that I'll just beam at people like the village idiot. John keeps stealing glances at me, his eyes a mixture of triumph at his interview sabotage coupled with a massive fear that I know and might mention it.

At 4:45 pm, I see him hanging round by the water cooler talking to Annie. Carol's desk is just round the corner, so I go over for a quick chat.

'How did it go?' asks Carol.

'Really well, thanks,' I say, smiling.

'You managed to come up with an idea?'

'Yeah – a couple actually. I originally had this thing about marketing hostess trolleys to younger people, but then...' – I'm pretty sure John can hear me – 'I found that someone had already done it on the Internet, so it was just going to look nicked.'

'Oh gosh; that's terrible. But you managed to come up with something else?'

'Oh yeah; something far better.' I pause for effect. '...which was lucky because JC said he was going to Google all the ideas to make sure people hadn't just stolen them. Phew!'

'Phew,' echoes Carol. She smiles at me, and I head round to the water cooler.

I walk straight into John and act all surprised. 'Oh – hi, John. How'd your interview go?'

John's mouth is slightly open. He struggles to regain a bit of composure, mumbling, 'Um, yeah... good thanks.'

'Glad to hear it.' I smile and head back to my desk. He may have screwed me on the interview, but at least he's going to spend his evening searching the Internet for a non-existent website on hostess trolleys.

And people talk about pettiness like it's a bad thing.

* * *

I consider joining the rest of the Accounts department for an after-work drink, but I'm interrupted by an email from my mum. I know it must be serious, as any message of this length has involved thirty minutes of trying to find letters on her iPad keyboard.

'*How did interview go? One of mums at school asked if you were going to parents' drinks tonight? Are you? Dad and I can babysit if want?*'

101

The bloody parents' drinks. I'd completely forgotten they were on. I should go. What are the chances I'd get free babysitting on the same night? Plus Flirty Mum – strike that: Claire (she has a name now) – will be there. Maybe it'll be fun. Maybe I'll enjoy myself. And I deserve a night off. I can stress about everything else in my life tomorrow.

I wait a few minutes before replying, so as not to rub Mum's face in it that two-line emails can be written in under a minute. 'Thanks SO much. Love to go. Interview went great – idiot from work nicked my idea but managed to come up with something better.'

My mum replies immediately. Which basically means I'm entering the Tube ten minutes later when I get it.

'X'

Evening

I arrive at the pub about thirty minutes after it starts. Mark texted me on the way to let me know he and Karen weren't going to make it, so I'm flying solo. I look around for Claire, but she's not there, so I end up talking to some random dads for the first twenty minutes – they're discussing cycling gear, which is something I have literally no interest in. Still, better than standing round like some plonker who doesn't know anyone's name.

'They're completely puncture-proof,' says Dad 1/possibly Adrian.

'Tell me that when you've ridden on them for six months,' retorts Dad 2/possibly Billy. He bursts out laughing. Everyone else bursts out laughing. I try to join in but just end up with a strained expression on my face like I'm trying to inflate a tyre with the power of my mind. Luckily no-one's noticed and the conversation continues.

'Plus they're clinchers, aren't they?' says Dad 2/Billy, 'I prefer a tubeless – I just think they provide better protection. I just got some Vittorias. They're excellent.'

Everybody nods at this. It does sound pretty convincing.

'What about you, Tom? What are you packing tyre-wise these days?'

'Well… good question. The clinchers are definitely good, but tubeless…well… who needs a tube, eh? They're tyres, not Smarties – know what I mean?'

Everybody nods to this very seriously. I clearly made a good point. I thought it was a mildly amusing joke. Apparently not.

The conversation continues, and I quickly finish my pint. I've managed to time it so everyone else's glasses are pretty full, so I don't have to offer anyone a drink. I'm not being stingy – I just don't want to have to come back to these people.

At the bar, I manage to infiltrate a group of mums. They're talking about binge-watching Netflix shows. This is more like it – something I can cope with. Before long, I'm actually having an OK time.

But every so often I see one of the individual mums looking at me. Quite a few of them are doing it – like they're interested, keen to get me alone. I'm single now and suddenly I'm a target. A target who can give them something their husbands can't.

Gossip.

This is the first official 'social' since the break-up, and from their point of view Sally just seemed to vanish, so everyone's in the dark and keen to get something juicy.

Like a tigress hunting its prey, a particularly aggressive mum, Camilla, sees an opportunity and manages to break me away from the group. Cornered, separated from the pack, she starts softening me up, ready for the kill.

'How are you?' she asks, all full of sympathy.

'I'm good,' I say, smiling and nodding.

'No, I mean: how *are* you?' she says raising her eyebrows twice in succession in case I hadn't got her implication.

'Oh, you mean about Sally?' Like I didn't know.

Her nostrils flare almost imperceptibly. The tigress has smelt blood.

'I kind of want to have a night off from thinking about it,' I explain.

'I completely understand,' she says. She doesn't – that would involve her not continuing to talk. She tips her head to the side and looks at me with doe eyes, like she's one of my kind. 'So what exactly happened?'

'Oh, you know – the usual.'

'And is she with someone?'

I pause. She tries to prompt me with what little she does know.

'I heard she had a thing with Gary, but apparently he's trying to work things out with Sam again.' She looks at me like this is all for my benefit. 'It's good to talk about these things, you know.'

I've had a pint and a half. And I do want to talk. But I know if I say anything it'll be all over the pub in twenty minutes. That's the thing with grief and misery. When you talk about it, it feels good. When other people talk about it – it feels like they're passing round a Polaroid of you wearing nothing but novelty antlers.

'I've got to use the loo,' I blurt out. I have to escape. Hopefully she won't give chase. The fact she doesn't is the best argument I've ever heard against unisex toilets.

As I walk away, it's like I can feel her behind me shrug and mouth 'nothing' to the other mums. In my head, they all perform cartoon 'drat' gestures.

In the toilet, I find myself at the urinal next to one of the dads – I think Dad number 2/Billy. 'All right, Tom. How's it going?'

'Good, thanks.'

'Saw you got waylaid by the women – rather you than me, mate.' Normally, I hate this kind of sexist shit. But following the Camilla conversation, I'm unusually agreeable.

'Yeah.' For once in my life I'd rather be spending my evening talking about cycling.

'Hey, meant to ask – what gym do you go to?' Hmm… maybe being gossip prey wasn't so bad.

'Oh. I don't really. I do sort of… bodyweight stuff at home.' Bent arm pelvic thrusts a week ago and a set of sit-ups sometime within the next month.

'Oh, right. Sounds good,' says possi-Billy, nonplussed. He nods my way, zips up, and leaves without washing his hands.

I head out of the loo and over to the pile of coats. I shouldn't have come here. It's time I went. I should nip this evening in the bud while I still have my dignity intact. But then I feel a tap on my shoulder. Bloody Camilla isn't going to leave me alone.

I turn around.

It's Claire.

'Not going, are you?'

'Um… no,' I say with my coat in hand. 'Just getting my…' I reach into the pocket and pull out the first thing I find. '… Nando's loyalty card.' It was that or an old tissue.

'You can't put a price on loyalty,' she jokes, in a way that doesn't actually seem that bitter. 'Thought I'd missed you. I only just got here.'

'No – I've been here for a while. I didn't think you were coming.' Damn. That sounded far too much like I'd thought about it.

'Just a few hassles with my ex. Divorce, eh?'

'Yeah… Divorce.' I'm not sure if I should ask her what happened. I don't want to end up pulling a Camilla, but she might want me to. 'Is everything all right?'

'He's an arsehole. I don't want to talk about it.' Music to my ears.

'Sure. Well, I was just heading to the bar,' I say, flashing my card.

'I don't think they take Nando's.' I look down at my hand. And, yeah – not my debit card. I pull out my wallet.

'Do you want something?'

'That depends…' she says looking me in the eye, über-serious. 'Are you trying to get me drunk?'

I go to protest, but she stops me.

'"Yes" is an acceptable answer.'

Slightly Later

The next few hours pass by in a blur. It turns out getting Claire drunk might not actually be on the cards for tonight. She clearly has a lot more tolerance than me, and four drinks in I'm wasted, whereas she's barely hitting her stride. Not that it matters; we're having a great time. I tell her about JC's reaction to my Man-Flake and she thinks it's hilarious and tells me about how her ex is so homophobic he once threw away five bath towels after they went pink in the wash. We're talking, and laughing, and it's fun. Actual FUN.

As we chat, we're touching each other on the arm in that way you only can with someone new. Feeling out the boundaries, crossing invisible barriers and it's just so… *exciting*. Nothing's going to happen, but it just feels amazing to have someone *interested* in you. She's really attractive too, but obviously a parent at Arthur's school, so obviously this can't go anywhere, but, God… I really want it to.

By 11:30 pm everyone else has drifted out of the pub, and we're sitting on a sofa with her legs draped over me; incredibly inappropriate at a parents' drinks, but only a couple of them saw, so only everyone will know by 9:15 am Monday morning. The barman's looking annoyed with us, so we stumble out of the pub laughing, and I offer to walk her home.

We walk through the moonlit streets holding hands and fooling around, being stupid. And before we know it, we're outside her place.

She looks at me. And then towards her door.

'So… do you want to come in?'

I hesitate. I can't. But maybe I should. I mean – it's not as bad as it would be with Amanda. It's not like Claire and I work together. We just live close. And Arthur goes to After School Club most days so we'll hardly ever overlap at pick-up anyway. Plus, this is not my own doorstep. It's her doorstep. No one ever said anything about doorsteps in general. That would close off most of civilized society. Unless I'm going to focus on women who live in barns, the doorstep thing really shouldn't be an issue.

'No-one's home. It's a rare opportunity,' she says, smiling. And it is. I don't have to get back for a babysitter. I don't have work tomorrow. Her place is free. It feels like this is meant to happen. Like it's fated.

'So are you coming in or not?'

'Yeah,' I say, my mouth making a decision before my brain. 'I am.'

She takes my hand and leads me inside. The moment the door shuts we're kissing and touching each other and two minutes later we're snogging on the hall floor and I've got a teenage-level boner. I manage to get my foot caught in the shoe rack and flick eight pairs of kids' trainers everywhere, but even that doesn't wreck the moment – we're far too into it for the occasional light-up shoe in the back to undermine the mood.

She reaches down and starts feeling me through my trousers. She looks me in the eye and smiles and says, 'Well, that's a nice surprise.' Admittedly, it's the most impressive I've probably been in the last few years, but I still don't think it's going to take anyone's breath away. Maybe she didn't think I had one. Still, I go with it. Maybe her ex was particularly small, so average seems impressive. Maybe Sally spread rumours I was impotent, so she is genuinely relieved.

I'm not going to say it isn't weird kissing this woman. I'm incredibly turned on so there's no place in the world I'd rather be, but she smells different, kisses different... I didn't think I was going to kiss anyone but Sally for the rest of my life, so this is strange, alien – but I reassure myself that's to be expected.

She suddenly stops. We're both breathing heavily.

'Give me a second.'

'Sure,' I say.

'Make yourself at home.' Claire indicates towards the living room.

'Do you have a loo?' I ask.

She points me towards it and disappears into the bedroom.

I head to the bathroom, completely high on alcohol and pheromones. It strikes me I don't have any condoms. Maybe she does. There's a garage just down the road if not. God, these are things I haven't had to think about for the last decade. I'd kind of forgotten buying condoms was a thing. I'm pretty sure I didn't do the deed with Sally since she had an affair, but who knows? Shit, I may have an STD that says 'aboot'.

I find the bathroom, and go to shut myself in. But before the door's fully closed, I spot something through the gap. A bedroom door opposite. And on that bedroom door I can see a couple of wooden letters: E R.

Something inside tells me to leave it at that – maybe the room's occupied by the Queen or 1990s-era George Clooney. But curiosity gets the better of me. I need to know. I open the bathroom door to reveal the six wooden letters on the kid's room opposite. Six letters that make me question everything that's happened tonight: 'Oliver'.

My boner collapses faster than the tower in JC's Flake advert.

I shut myself in the bathroom. This is not good. She's Oliver's mum. Claire is Oliver's *mum*. I hate Oliver. Stupid bullying little shit Oliver. And Claire... made him. Yuck. That means she loves him. That means this whole place is... Oliver's. Oliver goes to this bathroom, Oliver's worn those light-up trainers... Oliver's slept in her bed. Everywhere I go tonight, Oliver will have been before me. That came out cruder than I meant it to.

But that's not all. If she's Oliver's mum, then she used to be married to... Martin. And I hate Martin. I hate him even more than Oliver. Why would someone who married Martin want to have a thing with me? It makes me question who I am. Martin and I are like two different species. It's like finding out your partner previously had a thing with a sheep. Who wouldn't start worrying that their back hair was white and slightly curly?

I've got to get out of here. I can't be involved with this family. What if I fell for her? If we got married? I'd be living with *Oliver*. I'd have to see Martin every time there was a kid transfer. My *kids* would have to live with Oliver. Arthur would get bullied at HOME. Leave. Leave now. But that's not even the half of it. What if she wanted to have another kid? With me. It might come out all... Oliver-y. I'd hate it. I'd hate my own child.

I exit the bathroom and head down the corridor towards the front door. I hear Claire coming out of a bedroom behind me.

'Going somewhere?'

I turn around. And she's standing there in a sexy little lace teddy, leaning against the door frame. And she's wearing stockings. Actual stockings. I've only ever seen those once before in real life. I can't *not* look. It'd be like turning your back on an animal on the WWF's endangered list. You might never get the opportunity to see it again, so you'd better make the most of it.

I have to go. I hesitate. There's no way I can stay. But… wow.

I have to spit it out. 'Is… Martin your ex?'

'Yeah,' she says, her body language changing, 'you know him?'

I can't hold back. 'I hate him. I think he's a thick loathsome dick with an attitude problem.'

'Well,' she says, 'so do I, so that makes two of us'. I'm tempted to admit I hate Oliver too but I doubt that'll get the same reception.

I stand there, unsure again. My erection is most definitely back. She hates Martin. But does that make it all right? I have to leave.

But I can't. Claire, standing in front of me dressed like she is, is sapping away my will. I find myself moving towards her. I'd have to be tied to a mast not to. I doubt even Odysseus would have resisted if all he had to stop him was a bedroom name plaque.

We go into her bedroom. There are condoms by the bed. Phew. Then I notice they're Durex XL. That's not good. Why has she got those? Oh God. Maybe they're Martin's. Maybe he's not just a thick, loathsome dick. Maybe he has one.

I try to reassure myself. Hopefully this is a good sign. It might just mean she's an optimist. A good, positive attitude is definitely a plus in a relationship. I should be positive too. Maybe they'll be more comfortable. Like normal ones but with a bit more room to move around. I've been thinking of moving from a skinny to straight leg jean recently, so how is this different?

But a millisecond later, Claire kisses me and starts to unbutton my shirt. And after that, I'm too turned on to care.

Saturday

I'm woken by my phone vibrating with a message. I look round the room, completely spaced out by being in someone else's house. Claire's asleep by the side of me. I pick up my phone – twenty missed calls – all from my mother. I must have silenced the ringtone. There's also a message: 'WHERE ARE YOU? NEED TO LEAVE. GOING TO MISS EARLY ENTRY TO STYLIST LIVE.'

Shit. It's nine o'clock. I grab my jeans from the floor and chuck them on. I manage to get my leg trapped and fall over. Ouch. Maybe a straight leg would be better. The noise wakes Claire up.

'Going already?' she says looking up at me sleepily seductive. 'I mean, last night was great, but that doesn't mean your services aren't still required.'

I'm torn. Me having sex for the second time in six months is definitely more important than Mum getting to her fashion show ten minutes early. But Mum's really come through for me this week. I should probably leave. Even if I could have sex really quickly.

Another pro-leave point is that I've just realised how stinky I am. I'm pretty sure when I was younger I didn't smell this bad in the morning. You can kind of ignore it when you're on your own/married, but confronting a stranger with the reality of 'morning you' seems tantamount to assault.

'I'm really sorry – I've got to go.'

She looks disappointed. Did I accidentally just do a 'treat 'em mean keep 'em keen'? Maybe that's good. That's the kind of thing men do. I mean, I am one, but still… I bet Martin did it all the time. He can't have kept their relationship together with his scintillating personality. I want to explain my actual reasons, but talking about being considerate to my mother may undermine my newly-created aura of rugged independence.

111

I give Claire a quick hold-my-breath kiss and head out. 'I'll call you later.'

I walk down the corridor towards the front door. I would have really liked to have hung round and had breakfast with her and stuff, but maybe that's a problem. Maybe I'm too nice to keep women interested. That could have been what went wrong with Sally. That said, Claire broke up with Martin and he's one of the biggest nobs I've ever met. God – I hope not literally.

A shudder goes down my spine as I walk past Oliver's room. I'm tempted to go back and knock a letter off, but maturity prevails and I walk out of the front door, into the cold November air. Besides, the best thing I could think of changing it to was 'Liver'.

I can't help but feel that maybe everything's going to be all right. I might have a new job, a new woman. This might be the start of a new life. And Claire even seems to think I'm a proper man. A mature man. Maybe I'm becoming one.

'Olive'. I could have changed it to 'Olive'. Damn.

Afternoon

After a telling-off from my mother, I spend the rest of the day with a smile on my face. I can't stop myself from grinning. At one point Arthur asks me if there's something wrong. But there isn't. I'm just… happy.

I keep thinking about last night. It was awesome. I am officially sexually active. And Claire seems great. There are a few times in the day that Amanda pops into my head too, but I shut it down quickly. That's a no go. I just slept with Claire. I'm not going to be thinking about someone else the next day.

Mum and Dad come back just after five, laden with bags, and

Mum proceeds to show us a full season's worth of matching outfits. Carrie seems particularly taken by them. But even the coordinated shirt/pocket square combos Mum's bought me can't take away my buzz. She's going to have to try a lot harder than that.

I'm so golden, I even agree to stay in with them for the evening and play Scrabble. And that's when everything goes downhill. I try to wriggle out of it.

'Why don't we just watch a film or something? You can play Scrabble tomorrow when you're home.'

'We're going out for bridge tomorrow, so if we don't play tonight, it'll mess things up. It's only three weeks until we decide who gets the Cup.'

'The cup?'

'The Scrabble Cup. Look – if it's any later, we'll be paying extra for the engraving. The village tennis tournament's on and the engraver'll be completely chocker. Before that, we can do a deal for cash. Dad organised it.' Somehow we've skipped over why a cup is getting engraved in the first place.

'How much is it?'

'£7.50. It's normally ten.'

'I'll tell you what. I will give you £2.50 to not play Scrabble. Heck, I'll make it £3. You could even turn over a profit.'

'Don't be ridiculous. We don't need money.' *Then why are you getting a cash deal on engraving that costs a tenner?!?*

I decide to change tack. 'OK, well; what if I win? Am I in the running?'

My mum pauses. And almost successfully represses a laugh.

'Let's cross that bridge when we come to it.'

* * *

It's 9:00 pm and I'm sitting down playing Scrabble with my parents. This is my post-intercourse Saturday night. Sitting with the two people who sired me, playing a game I don't like. If there's a way to take the edge off your just-had-sex buzz, I've found it. Dad starts with the trash talking.

'Right – let's see if you've got any better at words since you've got older. Hopefully, you'll come up with gazumples of them.'

Mum and Dad both think this is hilarious. 'Gazumples' is a word I once attempted to put down at the age of twelve. It has since fallen into family folklore. I don't even know what I thought it meant.

We start. First turn, Dad clears his whole rack.

'KEYNOTE. Fourteen points – and a double word score. That's twenty-eight. Plus fifty for putting all my letters down. That's seventy-eight. Oh, just realized double letter under the K: eighty-eight.' *What the…?!? I don't think I've ever got eighty-eight in a full game.*

'That was a good one, love.'

'Thanks, love.' Less of the pleasantries. You people make me sick.

My turn. I manage to put down an A, a B and an S above KEYNOTE. The A is above the T, the B is above the E, the S on its own. Boom – I just made three words at once. ABS, BE and AT. It seems I *have* got a little better at words.

'Eleven points.'

'What? I just made three words.'

'Three low-scoring words,' Dad mutters under his breath.

'There's one of those double letter things under the A'.

'Oh, you're right. Twelve.' Mum spots the deflation on my face. 'I'm sorry darling, you'll probably do better if you don't try to do anything clever.'

Then Dad pipes in. 'I'm not even sure "abs" is a word.'

'Of course it is – it means "abdominals".'

'Then it's an abbreviation.'

The peacemaker intervenes. 'Let him have it. Otherwise he's just going to make a fuss.' *Yes, let me have it.* It's twelve points. What kind of person would argue over that? Hmm… maybe the kind of person who'd negotiate a £2.50 cash discount on getting a fake trophy engraved.

'Fine,' he mumbles. Somehow my Dad's passive-aggressiveness takes the sting out of being patronised by my mother.

Mum's go. She puts an E at the bottom of the AT, an L at the bottom of BE, and then continues it to spell ELIXIRS.

'Sixteen, plus fifty for putting all my letters down, and eight for the ATE and the BEL. Seventy-four. Not as good as Dad's but I had rubbish letters.'

Yeah, rub it in. Then it strikes me.

'Bel's not a word. It's two Ls.'

'It's not that kind of bell, dear. It's ten decibels.'

I go online. She's right. How does she know that? God, I hate Scrabble players and their stupid little three-letter words. Any three letters they've got on their rack is a bloody word. UJK: A springtime hat worn by a Cossack. GBY: the left testicle of an ageing goat.

'For God's sake,' I mutter.

'Well,' says Dad. 'Maybe if you spent a bit less time thinking about your abs and a bit more reading a dictionary—'

'Really, nothing to aspire to.'

'It is if you want to be good at Scrabble.'

I don't. I don't even want to be *playing* Scrabble. Besides, I have no abs, so who looks stupid now?

By the end of turn two, Dad's on 120, Mum's hit 134, I'm on 22. This is exactly why I don't play. I've got better things to do with my free time than being emasculated by my parents. Then it strikes me; there must be some kind of app or website for this. Something that gives you words if you type in the letters.

It feels slightly wrong, but deep down I convince myself it's not. They may be better at word games than me, but I am a man of my time. I have the weapon of technology. If you were attacked by a bear you wouldn't hesitate to use a Kalashnikov just because the bear didn't know how the trigger worked.

I excuse myself and go to the loo, desperately trying to remember my letters.

The door locks. Google Search – there it is: scrabblecheaters.com. That's not actually the name of the website, but if someone hasn't snapped it up I'm buying the domain first thing tomorrow.

I type in the letters – seven letter anagram. There it is. I look it up, find the meaning, and I'm ready to go back.

I don't even bother to flush the loo on my way out.

'Right, my go,' I declare as I reach the table. After a bad soap opera-level performance of 'hmm… I don't know what to do,' I drop the bomb. Seven letters descend onto the board like an MC with a mic. QUINATE. Boom. Sound of reverb. I'm out of here.

A silence fills the room and it almost feels like my gazumples are growing back.

'Quinate? That's not a word.'

'I think you'll find it is. It's a salt of quinic acid.'

Dad raises his eyebrows.

'I've been reading a little organic chemistry recently.' All about the follow-ups.

'Well, that's surprising.' Mum's getting involved now too.

'I'm trying to be a more well-rounded person.'

'No, it's surprising it was in a book on organic chemistry. Quinic acid is not an organic compound.' My mum did a degree in biochemistry sometime around the invention of the motorcar,

116

and every so often pulls out a science fact. It's her one area of expertise: an island of knowledge in a sea of ignorance and uninformed opinions. I change the subject.

'OK, let's look it up then.' I pull out my phone, careful to make sure I've closed scrabblecheaters.com and start to type in 'quinate'. Dad is having none of it.

'You can't use the Internet. It's the Wild West out there. Everything's a word on the Internet.' Yeah, like fucking '*bel*'. 'We'll use the proper dictionary.'

'I don't have a dictionary.'

Dad shakes his head like I'm being ridiculous, 'We brought ours.'

He goes to his bag and pulls out a dusty hardback tome that is their official Scrabble dictionary. Not *the* official Scrabble dictionary. *Their* official Scrabble dictionary. A cloud of dust rises around it as he puts it on the table, like it's been pulled out of Gandalf's bloody library.

'You can't use that,' I protest. 'It's completely outdated. It wouldn't have the word 'computer' in it.'

He turns to C to prove a point.

'Computer: A person who computes.'

'OK, well, iPhone then.'

Mum interjects, 'That's a proper noun.'

'I don't care that it's a proper noun. That's not my point. The point is – just because Scrabble was invented in bloody 1938,' another fact from the Scrabble cheaters' website, 'it doesn't mean you need to use a dictionary from the bloody period.' Hmm… 1938. Right before the War started. Coincidence?

'Look this is the official family Scrabble dictionary, so if it's not in here, it doesn't count.' He turns to Q.

'…no, not in here. Therefore: not a word.'

I can't take any more. This is a farce. I think about flipping the table, but I remember it was actually quite expensive and I may have to sell it if we end up moving to a smaller flat. Instead, I stand up, managing to maintain a minimal level of dignity.

'Sorry guys; I'm just really tired from looking after the kids and the parents' night out. Think I'll get an early night. Hope I haven't messed things up with the trophy.'

'That's fine, love.'

Mum smiles and I head straight to the bedroom, so I can get in three hours of stewing before I go to sleep.

At 11:00 pm I get a text, which I assume is from Claire. 'Enjoyed last night. Shame you couldn't stay.'

I text back something flirty, hoping to God I'm right. It's also possible I just sent an erotic message to one of the cycling dads – I should have gone with something about rubber so both possibilities would have been covered.

We text back and forth for an hour or so. I'm relieved she's got in touch – I realised this afternoon I didn't have her number. I was thinking of dropping a note through her door but it seemed a bit stalker-y. She must have got mine off the parents' contact list. Maybe if this thing turns serious, I can ask her to forward it to me.

She asks what I'm doing tomorrow and I say I'll call in the morning. Maybe we could meet up? I've got the kids but maybe she's got hers too. How much better would that be? Having someone I fancy at the playground with me.

But then I remember it's Oliver, and suddenly I'm not so sure...

Sunday

I wake up in the midst of a full on D-Day attack from the kids, who've been sleeping on the floor of my room due to my parents'

118

hostile takeover of their bedroom. After an hour of stories I manage to redirect them towards Mum and Dad for a bit while I put some breakfast on. I'm making French toast as I want Arthur in a good mood. I've got something I want to chat to him about.

In the kitchen, I notice my parents' dictionary still out on the side. I figure if I take my parents in some tea, I can undo my behaviour last night, so I browse through the archaic entries while I wait for the kettle to boil. This thing really is a joke. I mean, it's from 1973: it lists 'flares' as 'fashionable wide-bottomed trousers.' A few more random entries later, and I find myself in the Q section. Q. As in 'quinate'. And I suddenly have the desire to check whether it's actually there.

I feel ridiculous – it's not like my father would lie. He's a grown man. That'd be like… going into the toilet to get Scrabble words from the Internet.

I turn to the page. And there it is. In black and… musty-smelling yellow. Quinate.

I can't believe it. My *dad*. What a bloody role model. I've got to remember to never be like this with my kids. Especially in bloody Scrabble. I need to set a standard of behaviour that is inspirational and aspirational. I need to be bigger than this. I will still take my parents tea.

Although I might leave my dad's bag in. He hates it when it overbrews.

After Breakfast

The whole family are in a maple syrup and white carb-induced stupor. That's the thing with French toast – it's delicious at the time, but it's no way to fuel a morning. No wonder the French have got such a weird culture. If your whole country is in a low blood sugar delirium by 11:00 am, it's only a matter of time before you come up with post-structuralism and MC Solaar.

My parents are packing their bags with assistance from Carrie, and Arthur's on the sofa playing with his Batman, who seems particularly sluggish today. Maybe French toast is his kryptonite. Get the Joker to introduce that into his diet and suddenly Gotham is a lot more vulnerable to crime. Still, it seems like a good time for Arthur and I to have our chat.

'Hey Artie. How you doing?'

He makes a noise like a zombie that's overindulged on brains.

'Just wondering… how are things going with you and Oliver? You seemed to be getting on a bit better after I… fought his dad.'

'I don't like him. He still pushes me at break time,' says Arthur.

'But he's got better, yeah? He's not as bad as he was.'

'He's worse. He spat at a teacher the other day.'

'God, that's…' I'm a bit lost for words. Jesus, why do I want to shag this awful kid's mum?!? 'Do you think maybe he's just a bit… misunderstood? Perhaps he just isn't good at making friends, so he bullies people to make up for it.'

'He's got loads of friends. He's friends with the other bullies.'

'Right. But I guess… he doesn't really have a positive male role model… like you,' says the man trying to manipulate his child into seeing an idiot with a hot mum. 'His dad's a bit of a…' – *dick* – '…silly…' – *dick* – '…billy.'

Arthur thinks about this. 'I don't know what a "positive male role" thingy is, but his dad is definitely a dick.'

'Arthur, don't say that.'

'You said it.'

'I thought it; I didn't say it.'

'Not now. Before.'

'Oh.'

'You always say it.'

'Well, I shouldn't. If Daddy had a daddy, he'd be telling him off all the time.'

'But you do have a daddy – Grandad.'

'That's different; he's a…'

'Dick? That's one of the people you say it about.'

This conversation isn't going as I hoped. And my expectations weren't great to begin with. I move onto my closing statement.

'Well, look. I think maybe the best thing we can do is to go to the playground today, and invite Oliver to see if we can't patch things up between the two of you.'

'Why?'

Because he's got a hot mum. 'Because we should try to deal with problems head on rather than just ignoring them.'

'But I don't want to!'

'Well, we're going to.'

'Fine,' says Arthur, meaning exactly the opposite. He throws down his toy in frustration and storms out of the room.

God; that was worse than anything my dad ever did. What happened to a standard of behaviour that was inspirational and aspirational?

I notice Dad standing in the doorway with a couple of packed bags.

'Any other names you call me in front of my grandson?'

'Nah. You'd probably lie about whether they were in the dictionary.'

Afternoon

With my parents packed off back to Birmingham, we head down to Battersea Park to meet Claire and Oliver.

Arthur's still in a foul mood about the whole thing, but Carrie's just happy to be out. We're late, due to it taking twenty minutes to find a parking space, so when we get to the café, Claire is looking a bit annoyed and Oliver is throwing stones at a pigeon.

'Sorry we're late, I couldn't find a space.'

'I was beginning to think you'd stood me up.'

There's a flicker of forgiveness on her face. I go in for a kiss on the cheek, but Claire leans her head and a second later we're snogging. It only lasts for a couple of seconds, but when we stop the kids are all looking up at us with their mouths open.

'What did you just do to my mom?' asks Oliver.

You don't know the half of it kid. You don't know the half of it.

We get some coffees and head down past the boating lake. Apart from the odd looks we're getting from the kids, it almost seems… romantic. Kind of like when you see married couples in films and they're not worrying about paying their bills and their kids' behavioural problems and they look like they've slept properly for more than two nights in a row. The weirdness from the kids quickly disperses when they see the playground. It's been about six months since we were last at this one and they've forgotten how epic it is.

A few seconds later and Arthur and Oliver are discussing what they want to go on first. They decide to climb up this weird slope-like thing and they run off with Carrie trailing behind.

'See, it's not so bad is it?' says Claire. It's really not. It's not bad at all. It's kind of great.

She grabs me and starts to kiss me again. Maybe this is how it always is at the start of relationships. Not that I'm complaining. I really like kissing her. It's setting off something in my body that just makes me instantly turned on. I feel like a teenager again. Albeit a teenager who has to keep breaking off mid-kiss to check his children aren't doing anything stupid.

'Come on,' she says, grabbing me by the lapels and dragging me up against a wall and into a snog.

I break away. 'We need to watch the—'

She shuts me up by putting her lips on mine, so I start kissing her neck and she arches her head backwards.

'I like that,' she says, clearly excited that I'm taking the lead as I pull her towards me and twist her round. I haven't the heart to mention it's 100% motivated by me trying to keep eyes on Carrie, who's two metres up a climbing frame.

As it starts to get dark, we go and get the kids some pizza from the café. It's freezing cold, but we sit outside because it's nicer. Arthur and Oliver argue a bit, but when the pizza arrives harmony is restored. It's only 4:30 pm so I invite them all back so the kids can watch a movie.

We head back towards the cars, chatting and holding hands. In my head I'm starting to fantasise about where this could go. Could this actually turn into something serious? I hardly know this woman, but we're getting on great. Sure, Arthur and Oliver have been butting heads pretty much non-stop, but there've been moments where they seemed OK. Could Claire end up as my girlfriend, or… more? Could she be the kids'…

'Mummy!'

It takes me a second to register that it's Arthur and Carrie that have shouted it. Surely they can't have bonded with Claire that quickly?

I turn round in the direction they've run and there she is: Sally, bending down and hugging them. She looks up and sees me. She's obviously as surprised as I am.

'Oh, Tom…' she says. 'What are you doing here?'

'Just taking the kids to the playground.' I notice a guy hovering behind her. 'What about you?'

'I'm…' she says, but Claire comes up and takes my arm, stopping Sally mid-sentence.

'Sorry,' I explain, '…do you know Claire?' This is really awkward.

'Oh. Yeah. From school. Are you two…?' She seems tense. Even… *jealous*?

I'm about to say something non-committal, but Claire beats me to it. 'Yeah, we are.' She kisses me on the cheek as if to provide a visual aid. I'm not even sure what Claire thought Sally was going to say. Going out? Shagging?

'Oh, right,' says Sally. Hovering guy is edging closer. He's keen to get involved, but Sally's more interested in what's going on with me and Claire. 'I didn't think you'd be seeing anyone yet.' What's she talking about?!? It's been over two months since she left. She was seeing someone mid-relationship.

Sally's shadow decides to step forward. 'I'm Austin,' he says in what I assume is a Canadian accent. It sounds the same as American to me, but how would I know? He puts his hand out to shake. I don't take it.

'We've got to go,' says Claire, breaking the tension. 'We're going back to watch a movie.'

'Oh right. To your place?' Sally asks Claire, trying to make it seem offhand and casual.

'No. To… your place,' says Claire, far more pointedly than is necessary.

Sally winces slightly like she's just been winded. Claire takes my arm and starts to turn me away.

'Come on,' I say to the kids.

They hug their mum and I hear Sally say to them, 'Don't worry – you can come and live with me soon.' I start to say something, but stop myself. Now's not the time. I'm seeing the lawyer on Thursday. After that, I'll know where I stand.

As we walk away, Claire looks up and smiles at me like I should be pleased. I mean, I sort of am. But I don't know. Maybe I'm just a big pussy, but I don't feel good making Sally feel uncomfortable. I like having the moral high ground. Claire can clearly see some reticence in my face. She nudges me.

'And don't worry about that guy she's with – you're far hotter than him.'

Thirty Minutes Later

Back at the flat, we chuck the kids in front of *Trolls* and run into the bedroom. Everything's a bit of a blur so although I'm pretty sure it's the Justin Timberlake movie, it may be some new HBO series about people who are just really mean on the Internet.

I put a chair under the door handle and we jump onto the bed. I like how aggressive she is. Biting and grabbing with this general attitude of *'yeah you want it'*.

One thing leads to another, and suddenly it's condom time. And then I realise… I might not actually have any. Damn. I really should have thought about this beforehand. Even if there is a packet, I probably should've written XL on in Sharpie to maintain the façade.

I go through the drawer like a madman. It's not like being twenty anymore. Back then I could have walked to the garage and back without so much as a mild softening, but now I'm on a timer. An elongated condom hunt is death to a 39-year-old erection, so I find myself going back for kisses intermittently to boost it between searches. Socks… old iPhone… quick snog… Calpol… some euros… brief stroke of the bottom… pot pourri… kids' bum cream… twenty second full frontal naked embrace to counteract the presence of Sudocrem. And then… condoms! Actual condoms. I notice there's a '2016' at the end of the date, but that's probably OK. Condoms don't go off. It's just to keep people buying new ones… every five years…

I hold an out-of-date Durex above my head, triumphant, rip open the packet and try to get it on. God, it's difficult. I can't remember having this trouble the other night. Must have been the XL bit. I mean, sure, it was like using a pillowcase as a sock, but the whole putting-on moment flowed a *lot* better.

Sober sex is far more stressful than the other night's drunken escapade. After the initial high, I start to worry about how well I'm doing. Is she enjoying it? I literally have no idea – she's making noises – that's probably a good sign. That said, they're not that dissimilar to the ones I make now when I'm picking something up off the floor. I hope people don't think I'm approaching orgasm every time I lean over to do up my shoelaces.

'Are you… enjoying this?' I ask, hesitantly.

'Shut up and keep going.'

I tell myself not to worry. She can't be that loud anyway. There are kids in the next room. This might be the noisiest she's ever got. Maybe I'm nailing this. Metaphorically as well as literally.

But maybe I'm not. Maybe it's the quietest. Maybe she's famed in the neighbourhood for her volume. Shit. Now I've got an image in my head of Martin having sex with her wearing industrial-strength ear defenders. Eugh. Just concentrate on what you're doing. It feels great. Concentrate on that. She's enjoying this. It's good. You're doing well. That's better. I'm getting close. She seems to be getting close too. Finally starting to relax, I close my eyes. And hear a scream.

'Ahhhhhhhh!'

But it's not from her. I think it's… Carrie. Shit. I pull out and jump into my trousers, just remembering to pull off the condom at the last minute. I can hear Carrie crying. Arthur too. I head towards them, buttoning up my fly on the move. There, in the living room, is Carrie, hiding behind the arm of the sofa. Arthur's standing in front of her with his head… bleeding. And opposite them, a Sith lightsaber in his hand, is Oliver, smiling.

Any fears I had of coming in here with a semi are gone. The sex seems like a memory from a long time ago in a galaxy far, far away and I'm fucking furious.

'What happened?' I say, half shouting.

'O... O... Oliver,' Arthur stutters out. 'Oliver spat at Carrie, and I... I... I told him it was naughty and he pushed me and I hit my head on the table.'

I go to look at Arthur's head – it's not too bad, but I haven't heard him stutter for about three years. Fucking Oliver.

'What's going on?' says Claire, entering the room.

'Oliver spat at Carrie and pushed Arthur into a table.'

Claire turns to Oliver, and speaks with a tone of mild displeasure. 'You shouldn't spit, Oliver. That was a bit naughty.'

I go apeshit. 'A bit naughty?!? Spitting at a three year-old girl? It's bloody psychopathic.'

'Look, I'll deal with my kid in the way I see fit.'

'That's fine if they're calling each other names, but Arthur's got bloody... blood pouring from his forehead.'

'Well,' says Claire, 'maybe Arthur needs to toughen up a little.'

Did she just say that? I can't believe she just said that.

'Toughen up?' *Fuck you, Claire. Fuck you.* 'You're as bad as your bloody ex.' This seems to hit her where it hurts. But she's really disappointed me. I can't believe I was having sex with this woman two minutes ago. 'This whole thing was a mistake. I want you both out.'

'Fuck you, Tom. At least my husband didn't start bloody crying every time one of his children got hurt.'

'Fuck off, Claire.'

'You fuck off.'

'Right that's it,' I tell her. 'I'm not having my daughter spat at and my son assaulted in their own house. Get out.'

'Gladly. Let's see how cocky you are when you've had to do this

127

for a year and a half,' she says defiantly. 'And *Trolls* is a shit movie anyway. Come on, Oliver.' She grabs their stuff and heads out.

I hear the door slam, and suddenly it's just me and the kids again. Claire and Darth Oliver are gone. It feels like they were never there. A hallucination, rather than a memory.

I give Carrie and Arthur a hug and Carrie looks up at me questioningly.

'Did she "fock off", Daddy?'

'She did,' I tell her. 'But please don't ever repeat that, love.'

Monday

It's weird being back at work. The last forty-eight hours seem like a dream. Especially as everything here just seems so… normal. Now the interview's behind me, I'm just an accountant again. I'm back at my desk, inputting numbers into spreadsheets, planning when to make my next cup to tea to split the day up properly. If someone told me I'd imagined the whole new job/Claire thing, I might actually believe them. Sure, John's still got his stupid haircut, but apart from that, the world is as it was. And after a few days of absolute craziness, it's sort of reassuring. Life goes on.

An hour into my day and I'm bored. I keep thinking about Amanda; wondering if she'll come down here. I can't tell if it's because I want to see what's happening with the job or because I just want to see… her. I remember I had a dream about her last night. A sexy one. To start with it was with Claire, but then she turned round and it was Amanda. Then Oliver appeared twelve feet high wearing a Darth Vader cloak and told me to 'be a man' repeatedly while hitting me with a baguette. I have no idea why my subconscious decided on that rather than the straightforward lightsaber. Maybe it was a hangover from the French toast.

Anyway, I thought I had to protect her from giant, evil Oliver, but then he started saying that Amanda was his mother, not Claire, and I woke up in horror with dribble on my pillow. Good night.

Claire texts at 11:00 am to say sorry, but I ignore it. It can't work between us. I have to put the kids first. I don't think she's pushing for anything serious, but I have to think of Arthur.

Work's pretty light, so I find myself surreptitiously checking Facebook and descending down random Internet holes. Ten minutes in, I realise I'm reading about the Pharoah's servants being smeared with honey to attract flies away from him, with no idea how I got there.

What am I doing? These are the best years of my life. I'm sure Isambard Kingdom Brunel wasn't sitting around wasting his life at thirty-nine. No, he'd already completed the Great Western Railway and a number of bridges and tunnels. Oh, yeah – I was on a building kick, which led to the pyramids, which led to ancient forms of pest control.

At 4:30 pm, I'm called up to the top floor. I'm pretty sure that's a good sign – they can't give everyone rejections face to face. But maybe they're being nice because I'm an employee. Letting me down gently. They don't want to lose me as an accountant – not when I can multi-task between Sage 300 and Google Chrome with so much fluidity.

I step out of the lift and scan the floor. Amanda's nowhere to be seen. Damn. Maybe she's avoiding me because she doesn't want to be there when I get the bad news. I start towards JC's office, and there, sitting outside, is John. I suddenly realise he's been away from his desk for the last half hour. I'd just assumed he was doing another one of his epic toilet trips, but no, he's been up here. Waiting. He clocks me too. He looks as nervous as I am. JC appears and beckons him in – he's smiling. Does that mean he's got it? Surely if you were about to tell someone they haven't got a job, smiling would be incredibly inappropriate. Then again, he's JC – maybe he just thought of an idea about how to market Hula Hoops to choirs. 'Hoop-lah' or something like that… It really is a lot easier when you're doing it JC's way round.

They disappear into JC's office and I head to the sofa. His assistant barely acknowledges me, like she doesn't want to make eye contact. I don't think I've got it. They're giving it to John. God. This'll probably be the only time I'm up here until I retire in thirty years' time. I'll be sixty-eight years old, and octogenarian JC will give me a watch that'll probably have an eye or something. 'It's a watch that watches. Creativity, right?'

And I'll realise I've wasted my life.

Maybe I don't want to be here anyway. I look round the floor. It's just the same as downstairs, really. People sitting round desks looking at computers… I mean some of them have beanbags rather than chairs but – actually, that's not a computer; it's a PS4 – still… it's *kind* of similar. I see some people in a glass-fronted side office with a flip chart with a mind map and some drawings on it. So what? We have flip charts in Accounts. Occasionally. But these people look different. I think… they're laughing. All of them. That doesn't happen in Accounts. Not usually. There was that one time when Eamon wrote '7' but said '11'. That was funny. The whole department was in hysterics for about ten minutes. We dined out on it for weeks. 'Hey, Eamon! See you after your six-day weekend!' Because eleven minus a five-day week leaves six. Classic accountancy humour.

God, I need to get this. Especially as… what's that? Crap; they've got a pool table. And… an original *Dragon's Lair* machine? Oh my God. I mean, it's a completely ridiculous game where you just move a stick at the right time and it decides what video you watch, but it's also awesome. These bloody 20-year-olds are probably all ironic about it, but they don't know what it was like to see a miracle unfurling in front of your eyes at seven years old. If I had this job, I could play it every day. I could laugh. I could sit on a bean bag. I could lose at pool on a semi-regular basis.

I pick up a copy of *i-D* from the coffee table to distract myself. I don't know who reads this magazine. I've seen it around, but have literally no idea what it's about. Someone's always got one eye closed on the cover like they're aspiring to be a pirate. I go to open it, but then stop myself. What if I don't like what's inside? The magic would disappear. Sure, it looks cool, but for all I know it actually might be *about* piracy. 'Ah haaar! When you're a pirate you don't needs to carry no *ID*.'

Then it strikes me – I'm in the same position with this job. All I've ever seen is the outside. It looks great, but the reality will probably disappoint. Not getting this job is fine. I can buy a bean bag – they're only like thirty quid. Hell, I could probably even buy a *Dragon's Lair* machine. I'm sure they're not more than twenty grand. If I put away fifteen quid a week, I'd have one to play throughout my retirement while wearing my weird eye-watch. I'm never going to be able to afford a house anyway; at least that would give me something to aspire to.

John comes out with JC. He's grinning so toothily I'm worried he's going to eat me. The little hope I had deflates like a balloon three days after a kids' party.

John looks at me evilly as he heads past to the lift. Then JC goes back into his office and shuts the door. Really? I have to sit here and wait before he tells me I haven't got it? He should get it over and done with. It's bad enough not getting a job, but pull it off like a plaster.

I sit there, depressed. Maybe it's not so bad. At least, I won't have to see John any more. That'll be great. I'd rather it was because he'd failed and I'd succeeded, but the end result is the same. And I can ask Amanda out now. Why not? She seems cool. She *might* say yes. But what if she's got horrible kids as well? They might be worse than Oliver. God, she might not even be single. She might have a boyfriend – a husband. Maybe I should just tell JC I quit. Just get out of here and try to find something else. But then I'd have no job. Things are about to get very financially sticky with the divorce and everything, so I guess I'm stuck. I'm fucking stuck.

JC comes out, and beckons me over. I follow him into the office, trying to keep it together. I need to take this on the chin. Maybe the Family Oliver is right. The Coopers need to man up a little.

'Take a seat,' says JC gesturing towards a bean bag. I may as well enjoy this while I can. I descend into the beany mass. Hmm – comfortable. JC drags his office chair over and sits on it. Great. Now I just feel stupid.

'So – how did you think your interview went?' says JC from on high.

'I think it went…' I pause. Should I sound confident here, or like it was the worst thing I ever did? Does this still matter? Am I still being interviewed? 'It went… OK. I was pleased with my idea, but maybe I should have gone with another one.'

'Like what?' asks JC. Why did I just say that? I'm an idiot. I'm a bloody idiot.

'Um… well, I think I'll save those for if you give me the job.'

'Ha! Like it.' *Phew.* 'Right, I suppose you want to know if you got it or not?'

'Yes, please.'

A look of seriousness comes over his face. 'We've decided to give the job to your colleague, John.'

It's amazing how hope holds on until the very last second. Like a man hanging from a cliff with a single finger. I bet, even in that situation, you'd still be thinking 'maybe this'll work out…' But then you drop, and suddenly it's all over. You're splatting on the ground in under ten seconds. You may as well accept it.

I stand up to leave, 'OK. Right. Well… thanks for giving me the opportunity.' Should I tell him John nicked my idea? I may have the truth on my side, but I'll look like a right petty little liar.

I'm mid-thought when JC laughs. At the man not getting the job. Now, I'm not great at social situations, but that seems rude. It seems really rude.

'I'm offering John *and* you the job.'

'I…' I'm lost for words. 'But there was only one job. I thought there was only one job.'

'You both really impressed me. So, I decided to get a bit…. *creative.*' He says it like he's just invented a fully conscious A.I.. 'You're both going to have a six-week trial period. And at the end of that, I'll make a decision.'

'That'll be… Christmas,' I stutter.

'Will it? November… Yeah I guess you're right. Ha. You accountants! Always with the maths! Hey, maybe we should give the announcement a bit of a Christmas theme. Tell you what – when I've made the decision, we'll give you both a present – and one of them… will be empty. I like that. Too harsh? OK. Then… one will contain a calculator and the other will contain a copy of my book: *Adver-ties.* Have you seen it?'

He holds up a copy of his book – it's tie-shaped. 'Every page gives you a few tit-bits on how to come up with ideas, be more creative etc. Great gift for a new advertising creative.' Something suddenly strikes him – he dictates a voice memo into his phone. 'Idea for sequel to *Adver-ties*: *"Tit-Bits"* – similar book, but shaped like tits. Possibly get it so they both fit together and it looks like the person with the tits is *wearing* a tie… Where was I?'

'Umm… presents with a calculator and a book in?'

'Oh yeah. Sorry – I'm on one at the moment. So: the person with a copy of my book gets the job, the one who doesn't gets a calculator. Bad news: but on the upside – at least you get a calculator. Y'know, to do your accounting on.'

'We have those downstairs.'

'This'll be a home one. So you can do some adding up in your spare time too.' We accountants love that. Well, when we're not busy laughing at Eamon misnaming numbers.

'Well, that's great news,' I say.

'It is, isn't it?' replies JC. 'Anyway, you start Wednesday. We'll give you a day's gardening leave tomorrow so you can go and get a new outfit.' Right, well, that's a new source of pressure. And a day's probably about right. Like I can afford a garden on what these guys pay. I'd be pushed to afford a bloody window box.

'Be here at nine on the dot,' I say.

'Creatives don't start till ten. But hey – you can get an hour of accounts in before you start. Should keep you happy. ' Why does he think I'm trying to get this job, if accountancy is something I do for fun?

But this is good. I've got a trial period. In six weeks I'm going to find out whether I'm an advertising creative or not. In a more demeaning way than I imagined humanly possible, but hey…

There's still hope.

Tuesday – Gardening Leave

It's nice not having to rush to drop the kids off at school/nursery. I saunter down to Arthur's school at 8:50 rather than my usual frantic drop-off at half past. Andy, my boss, has been good about overlooking my fairly consistent 9:15 am arrival since Sally left, but if I end up getting this job, I can saunter in every day. Ten am start. Maybe I can fit in a work-out and a coffee beforehand. I can get fit and drink cortados before I've even done anything. Wow; the life of a creative.

As I get closer to the school, I start getting paranoid that I'm going to bump into Claire. I still haven't replied to her texts. I know I should talk to her, but I need a few days to cool off. Still, she deserves a response.

As I enter the playground, I see Martin just ahead of me with Oliver in tow. I don't think I've ever been pleased to see him before. But at that moment, his weirdly pointy bald pate reflects the sun and it feels like a beacon giving me the all-clear. Claire is not in attendance.

I bump into him again on the way out.

'Hey… you,' says Martin. 'Arthur's dad. Did you go to the playground with my ex?'

'Umm…' I'm slightly worried he's going to hit me, or return the knee kick, but Carrie's on my shoulders so it seems he's unlikely to attack. 'Yeah. We just hung out for a bit.'

He looks at me from head to toe to see whether I'm a threat or not. I lift Carrie down from my shoulders. As much as I don't want to get hit, I'm not using her as a human shield. His eyes return to my face. He seems to have finished his assessment. I can't tell what conclusions he reached.

'Well, bit of advice,' he says, laughing. 'Don't try and bang her. It'll only be disappointing after this.' Then he grabs his crotch.

I can't quite believe he's doing this in front of Carrie. 'You do realise my daughter's right here?'

'She doesn't understand.'

'She's three, not blind. You just grabbed your crotch.'

'He didn't grab his "crott", Daddy; he grabbed his *willy*.' Thanks for clarifying that Carrie.

'You're right, love. I get confused sometimes.'

'Does he need a wee?'

'Um…' Martin looks furious at this. 'Yes, love, I think he does.' I make a face to Martin as if to say – thank God we got out of that one. But inside I'm thinking – *way to go, Carrie. That's the way to diss a fully-grown man who thinks he has a big penis.* Who actually probably does have a big penis.

'Well, Martin, you should probably pop along to the bathroom, before you accidentally grab your willy again.'

He looks at me, threateningly. 'If you didn't have your kid with you…'

My fear at his threat is completely undercut by Carrie's response. 'Would he do a wee in his pants?'

'I think that's what he means, Carrie. Yes.' Kids eh, Martin? *Kids.*

Martin walks away, pissed off. Why do I feel only a three-year-old could take him down in a way that he'd understand? Either way I came out on top. Maybe Carrie is pretty damn smart. Maybe Montessori's worth it after all.

After nursery drop-off, I head into town to get myself a new outfit. I went up to the creative floor at the end of play yesterday to scope out what people were wearing. I took a few mental notes from people's outfits. The aim today is to mash up a few of those to assemble a creative get-up of my own. I think I was also hoping to see Amanda again as well. I'm embarrassed about that. I'm sure she barely knows I exist, and I'm making excuses to try to catch a glimpse of her. Shameful. She's probably married. And from tomorrow I'll be with her every day. I don't want to end up as some seedy guy who keeps staring.

I go into Urban Outfitters and try a few things on. It's embarrassing. I look like a middle-aged man going to a fancy dress party as a teenager. I need something a little more… grown up. Sophisticated. I try Zara but don't fit into anything except an extra large, which hangs off me like I'm Carrie wearing one of Sally's dresses. This is horrendous. And exactly the kind of task Sally could have helped me with. Maybe Claire has a good eye. I could give her a call... I shake myself out of it. I'm just feeling lonely and insecure – she's not right for me. Her kid's a bully. I need to do this myself.

I walk round Soho for a bit to check out the media people for inspiration. I see some moustachioed dude about my age in a jacket that seems like the type of thing I saw yesterday... In a fit of desperation, I ask him where he got it from. Selfridges apparently. Christ. That means it's expensive. I head down to Bond Street to check out the damage.

I wander into the ground floor and spray on some random fragrance. Everyone does that, don't they? I'm pretty sure it doesn't mark me out as some pauper who just pops in for free smells? The shop assistant looks over and suddenly I feel like a homeless person looking for an alternative to showering. I shuffle off up to Menswear feeling ashamed.

After a few minutes, I find the jacket. £375. For God's sake. Worse thing is, it's one of the cheapest on the rail. How do people afford clothes like this? I um and ah about what to do. There's Christmas coming up. I can't have the kids thinking Santa's become suspiciously stingy now their parents have separated. But at the same time, I have to look the part for this job. I don't want to fuck this up and be depressed for the rest of my life. A happy parent is a good parent.

I try the jacket on over what I'm wearing. It looks amazing. I try not to think as I take it to the till. It's nearly 400 pounds. I feel sick, but I push through and hand it to the woman. She scans the ticket and starts to fold it. But then she notices something.

There's a mark. On the back. No one could see it, but there's a mark.

She turns to her colleague. 'There's a mark on this – should I offer a discount?'

'You can do 25%.'

She turns to me. 'Any good?'

I nod a little too enthusiastically. That's £281.25. I do it a lot quicker than her machine. Sometimes it's OK being an accountant. It's still extortionate but it's less extortionate. I'm getting a bargain. She turns to her friend. 'Can you authorise it if I put it through the till?'

Her colleague comes over to OK the discount, while she absentmindedly touches the mark. But then something happens. It comes off. With a single brush of her fingers. She presents me with a massive smile – good news! She turns back to her colleague. 'Don't worry about it. It was just some fluff or something.'

The nausea comes back with a vengeance. I see the £281.25 on the till disappear and £375 appear in its place. Suddenly, I can't breathe. It feels like I'm having some kind of panic attack.

'I'm sorry. I can't do this,' I suddenly blurt out. Like, really loud. 'I can't do this. It's too much. It's just too much.'

I move away from the till, sort of edging backwards, slightly bent over with one hand ahead of me – a sort of 'don't hit me anymore' retreat posture. All the other shoppers stare at me. And not sympathetically. More like my presence has polluted their hallowed environment. The guy behind me flinches away, trying not to touch me – like if he does, he might catch poor.

I get out as quickly as I can. As I walk away from the building, the smell of aftershave tester hovers around me as a reminder. Like I'm walking in a cloud of embarrassment. I didn't actually check what the aftershave was called. Maybe Calvin Klein now has a range called *Shame*.

I head down towards Chinatown for a cheap lunch. There's a good sushi place that's always full of Japanese people, which is probably a good sign. That said, if I was in Spain, I doubt the English Café full of red-skinned Brits would be the place to go. Still, I feel deflated. My gardening leave isn't turning out as I planned. So far I've done the equivalent of killing off a cactus.

On the way, I pass the window of some Soho boutique. It's shutting down, and in the window – is a jacket. Not the same as the one the guy was wearing. But similar. And there's a sale mark on it. I go in and it's £100. There is a God. Well, not for the guy whose business is failing, but for me. I get the jacket and the guy bundles in a couple of shirts (which seem vaguely reminiscent of the type of thing from yesterday's scouting) and some Edwin jeans that feel incredibly uncomfortable and tight, but apparently will loosen up over the next few days.

I wear the jeans out with the goal of being able to bend my legs by work tomorrow and goose-step over to lunch. I think they have a counter where I can eat standing. No one ever said being cool was easy.

Evening

I manage to book a babysitter in, as Mark and Karen have offered to take me for a drink. I think they assumed I'd get the job straight out. Now they probably feel they can't cancel. But hey – small victories… After all, they might be the only ones I get.

Karen and I take the train in, as we're meeting Mark after work. I've decided to abandon breaking in the jeans in the name of actually having a nice time.

Karen's more interested in the fact that I got off with Claire. She's all 'see where it goes' to start with, but when I tell her about the Oliver situation she's as on the fence as me. I tell her there's this girl I fancy at work, but she thinks that's a complete no-go as well. In my mind, Claire and I have already stopped seeing each other, but Karen thinks I should send a nice 'thanks but no thanks' text to draw a proper line under it. She helps me phrase it so that I only look like a bit of an arsehole. A world of doubt hits me as I press send, but I've got to think of the kids. It just can't work.

We find Mark at the bar, still in his work clothes, the end of his rolled-up tie peeking out of his jacket pocket. He's already had a few beers, so is probably more affectionate when he greets me than necessary. It's only a week since we saw each other, but he treats me like a long-lost cousin.

'Tom!' he shouts across the bar, coming over with his arms spread wide. He hugs me and then winks at Karen. 'Hey, babe.'

'And I was worried you might be drunk by the time we got here,' she says, kissing him.

'I've only had three,' he says, slurring slightly. Maybe all us lightweights need to start some kind of society. The 'only had' club. If the number is above five and you can still answer the question, you're out.

'Well, you've missed some excitement,' says Karen. 'Tom got off with Claire.'

'On the way here?'

'No, the other day.'

'You didn't?!' he says, surprised. 'I said you were a stud. You going over after this for a booty call?'

'Oliver hit Arthur so it's not going anywhere.'

'I always knew you were a player.'

'I'm not a player. People don't ask their female friends to help them phrase texts to avoid upsetting people if they're players.'

'The good ones do.'

I shake my head, but Mark still thinks he's hilarious. His friend, Ranj, comes over. I've met him about seven times. He never remembers me.

140

'Hey,' says Ranj, offering his hand. 'I'm Ranj.'

'Tom,' I say, shaking it. 'We've actually met a few times.'

He makes an awkward not-ringing-any-bells expression.

'We're celebrating Tom getting a new job,' interrupts Mark, clapping me a little too hard on the shoulder.

'A trial period for a new job—'

'…and also him being a playahhhh.'

'Playahhhh,' repeats Ranj, like this is a thing they do. I love Mark, but when he's with his work colleagues he does become a bit of a wankahhhh.

'So you're good with the ladies, are you?'

'I'm really not.'

'Ask Claire, the hot mum he's just been banging,' says Mark. I give Karen the evils for sharing this with her husband while he's drunk.

'Hot mum. Nice,' says Ranj. Not really. I'm a dad. When it comes to mum-banging, we're the major perpetrators.

'I like your style, Tim.'

'Tom.'

'Whatevs, Mister *Name*.' How was that a response? 'You can be my wingman. This old married dickhead's cramping my style.'

Mark laughs like being called a dickhead is a Wildean epigram.

'Come on,' says Ranj, dragging me inappropriately towards a bunch of twenty-something girls, 'Let's go meet some ladies.' Karen's laughing now as well. They have well and truly landed me in it.

Ranj introduces himself to the women, and I hover on the periphery, embarrassed. I suddenly remember Ranj describing himself as a pick-up artist when I met him before and realise he's ignoring the prettiest girl in the group, which was one of his moves – giving her the 'negs'. I say hi to her, but she appears to be giving me the 'negs' as well. She's clearly come in from Hackney and is so cool she can barely tolerate my presence.

'So you're one of these City wankers are you?'

'No, I work in advertising.'

She nods, sneering, as if to say 'sell-out'. I try to make polite conversation. 'What do you do?'

'I run a gallery,' she says, like it's obvious.

'Oh, great. That sounds really interesting.'

She shakes her head, like I'm a child pretending to know what galleries are. 'We display contemporary art,' she explains. 'It's kind of like what you do – only for people with souls.'

I think that was a diss. But if she thinks she can out-perform me when it comes to dissing Tom Cooper, she's got another thing coming.

'Actually,' I tell her defiantly, 'I don't do that side of it at the moment. I'm in accounts.' You've just been diss Top Trumped. Her face drops, like she's realised the person she's talking to is not only naked, but a member of the Tory Party.

A millisecond later my defiance has faded into insecurity and I'm explaining myself, desperately trying to get her approval. 'But… I've just been given a trial period doing creative stuff, so that's really exciting.' She looks at me like I'm waxing lyrical about a spreadsheet, and I actually feel worse.

There's a tense silence, then she turns away. I mean, I felt like a spanner before, but now I feel fucking horrible. Not that Ranj has noticed; he's still got his back to both of us. I wander over to Mark and Karen, who are talking to a woman in her fifties from Mark's office.

'The stud strikes out,' says Mark. *Thanks, I needed that.* 'Hey Tom – this is Stephanie. Stephanie this is Tom: a newly-single man about town.' Stephanie perks up and gives me a look up and down. She must be single too.

'Nice to meet you, Tom,' she says in an accent that sounds like money. 'So what do you do?'

'I've just, um, got a new job actually. Well – a trial period for a job, as a junior advertising creative.'

'What do you pull in for that?'

'Erm… probably a bit less than I do now,' I reply, laughing. And it's like I suddenly vanish from her field of vision. I mean, for God's sake – she's clearly rich. Why is she only interested in men that are as well? I'm fifteen years younger than her; she could at least pretend I might be an appropriate trophy husband.

I'm suddenly depressed. Not that either of these women are my type – I'm not cool, or looking for a sugar momma, or even that attracted to either of them (the twenty-something gallery owner a bit, if I'm pushed), but the lack of interest reminds me how awful it is being single. I've been a bit spoilt recently – single fish in a coupled-up pond. I mean, how many single mums and dads are there at school? Not that many. I thought Claire and me wasn't going to work because of our kids being at the same school. More likely that's the only reason she gave me a chance in the first place.

I look over and Ranj is now talking to the cool girl. She actually seems interested. God, why do women always seem to fall for idiots?

I end up talking to some other people from Mark's work. They seem nice, but we don't have much in common. They're talking about an office fun run. To me that seems like an oxymoron – two words only paired together because they contain the same vowel sounds. If I'm going to start exercising I need something that presents itself a bit more honestly. Maybe I should find a sport that rhymes with 'unpleasant'.

I'm staring off into space, when I notice someone over the other side of the bar. She really looks like Amanda. Like, almost identical. It takes me a few seconds to compute that it *is* her. What the hell's she doing here? We're not that close to the office. I suddenly get super worried. This is too much of a coincidence.

What if she thinks I followed her here or something? I get really paranoid. Maybe I should slip out before she notices me. But then she turns around like she's felt my gaze on her. And we're looking straight at each other.

There's a weird expression on her face. Somewhere between surprise and worry. I was right. She thinks I'm following her. This is awful. I'm going to end this evening with a restraining order from a work colleague. She excuses herself and comes over.

'What are you doing here?'

'Just having a drink with my friends.'

I point out Mark and Karen, but they put their heads down like they don't know me. Thanks for not wrecking my creepy vibe guys. Ranj walks back from the bar with a couple of drinks, biting his bottom lip and pumping his head to the music. It goes through my head to get him to back up my statement, but any association is probably worse than being a suspected stalker.

'We're celebrating me getting the trial period,' I explain. 'I think they thought it would go one way or another. Which would have made celebrating a bit more appropriate.'

'It's worth celebrating. Before you came in he'd basically decided on John. His crazy hostess trolley idea was just up JC's street.'

'Must have been a pretty good idea,' I say, somewhere between a compliment and a boast.

She rolls her eyes. Probably won't tell her it was mine then.

'Anyway, I'm really pleased for you,' she says. Then suddenly her face takes on the worried look again it had earlier. 'Look, can you not tell anyone you saw me?'

'Um… Sure. Why not?'

'That guy I'm with – he's a headhunter for another agency. They're offering me a job.'

'Oh. Course. Your secret's safe with me.' And then I realise what this entails. She won't be at work any more – which means this might be one of the last times I see her. 'How long till you leave?'

'End of the week – I'm going to tell JC tomorrow. I didn't want to hand in my notice till it was confirmed. He'll probably put me straight on gardening leave. I mean who has a bloody garden on the salary they pay? There's only so long you can spend working on a window box.'

Great minds.

"Window box leave' does seem to be rubbing salt into the wound...'

She laughs. Now the cat's out of the bag, she seems more relaxed. 'Look – I'd better get back. This guy's a bit of a sleaze, but I should probably keep on the right side of him.'

She looks over at the guy she's with, and he notices we've caught him staring. I take an instant dislike to him. Looks like the feeling is mutual. He gives me a hateful little sneer before turning away. Amanda takes it as a cue to get moving.

'Are you going to be here for a while?' she asks.

'Yeah.'

'Cool – if I can get away, I'll come over and have a drink.' She suddenly hesitates. '...If you want.'

'That'd be good,' I say, faking nonchalance. 'If you want, you can meet my friends... who are still pretending not to know me.' She looks over at Karen and Mark, who both look off in random directions like they've both spotted a different rare bird...

By ten o'clock things are a lot more fun. Now Amanda's here, I've got a great excuse not to be pushed towards any more random women, so I'm actually enjoying myself.

And I'm gradually realising what great news this is. She's out of the company. That means I can ask her out. She might say no, but at least there won't be any 'what ifs' anymore. I suddenly feel horrendously nervous. What if she says no? What if I screw it up? It'll be like Victoria Batty in the fourth form all over again. Well, if she lives with her parents and I shout 'wrong number' when her dad answers, only to have him 1471 me back and ask to speak to my father. At least Mum and Dad aren't staying at the moment.

The guy she's with really does look like a sleaze ball though. She's shifted position, and I keep seeing him putting his hand on her leg and her taking it off again, but I can't see her face. I'm sure she can handle it, but I really want to go over there and tell him to fuck off. I'm not trying to be possessive – I just hate these people, because, you know, a lot of us men – we're all right. But a few bad apples want to force their way into women's pants and suddenly we all look bad. Great. Now, I've got an image of a woman with an apple in her pants. Thank God no-one can mind read. I'd look like a pervert with a fruit fetish.

It's half ten when I notice Amanda's gone. I must have missed her leaving. Shit. She probably gave me a wave and I ignored her. Ranj comes over to say bye, and leaves arm in arm with the gallerist. Everybody's talking, which allows me to check out of the conversation for a while. And I suddenly realise I'm jealous.

I can't remember the last time I felt jealous. I don't think she'd be into that guy or anything, but the images fill my mind with the vividness of a girl with an apple in her pants. I never felt jealous with Sally. Not since we were first going out. Maybe I should have. Even when I found out she was with someone else, it wasn't the major emotion. I was more just angry. I guess the whole thing just happened so gradually I was sort of expecting it. But this…

'Hey, Space Cadet.' Mark's talking to me.

'What?'

'Time to go. Let's grab an Uber together.'

'Um… yeah. Are they closing up?'

'Not for a bit, but some of us are starting new jobs in the morning.'

I laugh, despite myself. But yeah – probably shouldn't turn up with a massive hangover.

We get up to go, and head towards the door. I feel a bit disappointed. It's ridiculous – I had no idea I was going to bump into Amanda tonight, so how can I be annoyed she's gone? I'll see her tomorrow at work anyway.

'Hey,' comes a voice from behind, 'I thought we were having a drink.'

I turn around. And suddenly Amanda's there. I put on a grin so wide I wish my face had an undo function.

'I thought you'd gone.'

'I popped out with *Matthewww*.' She says it like it's the most ridiculous name in the world. 'Anyway, I've packed him in a cab, so now I'm back. It'll be nice to have a drink without some dickhead's hand on my leg.' A little shiver seems to go down her spine. 'So are you sticking around?'

'I am indeed.' Karen notices what happening, and flashes me a smile before dragging her drunken husband out. 'What do you want?' I ask.

'I'll get it – I haven't had to pay for anything all night.'

A couple of G & Ts later and we're having an amazing time. Amanda's mainly regaling me with tales of JC's 'creativity'. It's not doing good things to up my respect for my new boss, but it's pretty hilarious. I really want to tell her about John stealing my idea but it seems a bit below the belt. I'll tell her when she's actually left.

It's really weird. I literally have no idea if she likes me or not. Well, clearly she likes me – but maybe just as a guy she wants to hang round with. Probably that. But it's OK – there's nothing wrong with fancying someone. As long as I keep my hand off her leg, I'm still one of the good guys.

147

At 11:30 pm we notice the pub's pretty much empty. There's just us and a few of the twenty-something girls, probably bitching about their friend going off with Ranj, and then I remember: I was meant to be having an early night.

'Dammit. I should go – first day tomorrow,' I say, possibly sounding too regretful.

She looks like she'd like to stay too. 'I'd cover for you, but I don't think I'm going to be in JC's good books by five past ten.'

We head outside and stop a taxi. I do the gentlemanly thing and offer it to her. Probably sexist, but she doesn't seem to mind. We say goodbye with a kiss on the cheek, but end up talking some more. It's one of those goodbyes that seems to go on and on, like we haven't quite got to where we want to yet.

The taxi driver opens his window and tells us to hurry up and we hug one last time before she gets in. It lasts far longer than necessary. We split holding hands and just looking at each other. I'm pretty sure this is not just work colleague behaviour. I try imagining myself in this position with JC. Yeah, definitely seems weird.

I find myself moving towards her. And she's moving too. It's not something either of us have planned. We always think we make our decisions, but sometimes something else just propels us, that we don't even see coming. It's such a strange moment, that second just before you kiss. Where you're getting closer and you think the other person is too, but you're hesitating and it's like the world is moving in slow motion.

Beep! The taxi driver honks his horn, and suddenly the moment is broken. What a fucking arsehole. But maybe it's for the best. I should take this slow. Maybe she doesn't want me to take it any way at all.

'I'd better go,' she says.

'Just in case I don't see you tomorrow; could I… get your number?'

She smiles and pauses for a second to give a sense of drama. Then she nods her head. I pull my phone out and she starts to give me the digits.

'07789 124...'

She pulls her phone out too to get mine.

'Six...' Then suddenly she pauses. 'Oh shit.' I look up from my phone, two thirds of her number in my keypad. She's reading a message. 'Shit, shit, shit, shit. That bloody dickhead.'

'What's going on?'

'Matthew just texted me. The job's gone away.'

'At 11:30 at night?'

'He must have known earlier. He was just trying to get into my pants. Damn it.'

'I'm so sorry.'

She shakes her head with an ironic smile, as pissed off at being suckered as about losing the job. 'I knew I shouldn't trust him, but I didn't think he'd go this far,' she says, shaking her head once more.

Then it's like she sees me again, and suddenly we both realise what this means. We're still working together. We're still colleagues. She might be my boss.

'I'd better go,' she says.

I nod, and she gets in the cab. Before it drives away, she looks at me one last time. I want to think she's allowing herself to imagine what might have been before she goes, but I don't even know.

The car drives off into the distance, and I watch as our little window of opportunity closes forever.

Wednesday

I arrive at work at 9:15 am to do my forty-five minutes of accounting. I'm not sure if JC meant it seriously, but I don't want to screw things up if he did. Not that he's ever been down here – he'd probably worry his creativity would disappear if he came within twenty metres of a spreadsheet.

The new jeans are still ridiculously stiff, so sitting at my desk is proving a bit of a challenge. I've got a normal pair in my bag in case I can't take it anymore, or someone suggests I sit on a bean bag. I'll have to do a quick change in the loo, or I may never get up again. I'm getting a few looks from the rest of the accounts department, but that's probably a good sign. The outfit's come together pretty well. Subtle plaid shirt, nicely-fitted jacket and a bit of raw denim. I didn't even know what raw denim was till yesterday. Maybe that's why it hurts so much. Maybe it's better once you've cooked it…

I go up to the top floor and get ushered over to JC's office. John's waiting outside on the sofa. He clearly didn't get the accounting memo. I choose to stand. No reason.

I'm dreading seeing Amanda. She's probably mortified after last night. I don't know whether to mention it. No. I'll leave it to her. She's above me. I'll act like it happens all the time. Like it's no biggie. Do I wish it hadn't happened? No. I just wish it had happened more. That everything else had been different.

'Welcome, accountants!' JC intones as he appears from his office. He's clearly trying to sound like a Roman orator, but I'm pretty sure Sophistry 101 didn't involve cracking up at your own wit. 'OK – for the next six weeks I want you to *forget* you're accountants. The only time I want to see you around numbers is at the Christmas party.'

We both look a bit confused.

'Musical numbers,' he explains. Oh, right. Maybe his creative days *are* behind him.

'So...' I enquire, 'should I not actually do the hour of accounting before I come up here?'

'No, you should still do that,' he clarifies. Great.

'OK,' he continues, 'you're creatives now. So you need to *think* creative.' Is he actually saying anything here? ''Cos creativity *is* as creativity *does*.' That would be a no. 'Nice outfit by the way,' he says looking in my direction. And all is forgiven.

'But being a creative is not easy. So – you're each going to have a mentor who's going to show you the ropes. You'll be working super closely together, so your success is their success.'

Please don't let it be Amanda, please don't let it be Amanda.

'Ah, here's one of them. '

We turn round, and, sods law, there she is: Amanda. Fuck.

'Your first mentor. Or should I say Wo-mentor.' Amanda smiles. Uncomfortably. But who's mentor is she? Mine or John's? JC should really have opened with that. Fucking tor-mentor more like.

'John... you're going to be with Amanda.' Thank you, JC – I could kiss you. I could actually kiss you. Actually, no, that would still be weird. 'Tom – you'll be with Doug. He'll be here in a sec.'

Doug – I don't know him. Hopefully not an arsehole, but at least he's not the woman I nearly snogged yesterday. Things have worked out OK. I'll still see Amanda around the office, but at least we won't be forced together every single day...

Then JC spots someone at the door. 'Here he is now—' JC stops in his tracks mid-sentence.

I turn round to get a first glimpse of my new mentor, desperately hoping he's not more than ten years younger than me.

And then I see why JC has stopped. Doug is in the doorway. He's about thirty-two (acceptable), seems friendly (good) and is smiling warmly (good again).

Unfortunately, he's also wearing the exact same outfit as me. Same jacket, same shirt, same jeans. Well, the shoes are different, but this was never a shoe-lead ensemble.

I suddenly realise what's happened. My scouting the other day must have had a little too narrow a focus. The reason that all the items of clothing had melded into one was that they were all from the same person. I basically copied my new mentor's outfit.

Doug is looking at me, mortified. It's not helped by JC bursting out laughing. John is watching on, a victorious sneer on his face. I look over at Amanda. She's trying to keep a straight face and be sympathetic, but she can't, and she breaks down into laughter. I feel smaller than I've ever felt in my life. Well, apart from round the jeans. A small person probably would probably be able to bend their legs right now. Maybe I should ask Doug how long they took to break in.

'Well,' says JC, still sniggering. 'Looks like you two may be a little *too* well matched. We want Jobs and Zuckerberg, not Gilbert and fucking George. You know what – I think maybe we should do it the other way round. John, you go with Doug; Tom – you'll be with Amanda.'

Fuck.

'Unless you two want to be able to coordinate your outfits every morning?' says JC, laughing.

Doug walks out of the room, a look of disgust on his face, and John follows him like the sidekick to an evil mastermind. I accompany Amanda into her glass-walled office, and we sit down and look at each other.

'I know I'm the best mentor, but you really didn't need to go that far.'

We both start laughing. I feel utterly ridiculous, but at least I'm laughing. Maybe being a wally is a good way to break the tension. That said, I really wish the walls weren't see-through. I can see the story spreading around the floor in whispers and Doug fuming at me. Maybe I should take a notepad out later and stand next to people jotting down what they're wearing. If I'm going to be the office joke, I can at least try to own it.

It strikes me – maybe now's a good time to bring up the elephant in the room. The fact that there's an identically-dressed rhinoceros might take the edge off.

'About last night…' I start.

'It's forgotten.'

'Cool,' I say.

We nod together in rhythm. That's what I wanted. But is it really? To forget what happened? To just sweep it all under the carpet? I get an image of Carrie during our last game of hide and seek where she tried to conceal herself under the living room rug. Is that what this is? A Carrie-sized issue in the middle of the floor? Sure, we can walk around it, pretending not to see it, but if we do manage to ignore it, it'll trip us up at the first opportunity.

But she's the boss. If she wants to forget it, I have to forget it. At least for the next few weeks. When I fail to get the job, maybe I can broach it. Fuck. Why does life have to be so complicated?

Thursday

The last day and a half has been an improvement. I went out at lunchtime yesterday and bought a shirt from M&S to change into and since then the whole thing's been plain sailing… Even Doug's starting to warm to me. Well, his sneer seems slightly less pronounced.

But now I'm on my way to the lawyers. To talk about Sally. I'd almost forgotten about the whole custody thing with work stress/Amanda, but now I'm back to real life.

And I need to find out if Sally can take the kids.

The plastic sign outside the shop doesn't bode well, particularly as it's broadcasting the words: 'Legal Ease'. I'd only got the solicitor's name so I didn't realise I was engaging a law firm with a pun-based moniker. I specifically decided against using Just Us and Folk Law for those very reasons.

I go inside and a moody receptionist looks at me, asking if I've got an appointment with a tone that suggests I haven't.

'Yeah. It's Tom Cooper. I'm seeing Ms. Statov…'

'Oh, right,' she says, looking disappointed that she can't tell me to fuck off. 'RHONDAAA!!!' She lobs the words into the back room like a grenade. 'It's for you!'

Rhonda comes out of her office. Well, at least she looks a bit more professional. Grey trouser suit, neatly coiffured shoulder-length hair, matching accessories. My mother would approve.

'Mr Cooper, very nice to meet you,' she says, offering her hand, then stumbling a little. She regains her composure pretty nicely, but smells like Sally's aunt at four o'clock on Christmas Day. For the record, the bouquet I'm referring to is not the scent of turkey.

'If you'd like to follow me into my office.' I do as instructed, making sure to give the doorframe a slightly wider berth than her lead would suggest. Maybe she's superstitious and likes to touch wood at the start of a new case. With her face.

We sit down either side of her desk. I clock a Bearobics calendar on her wall. That's probably good isn't it? Having a lawyer with a sense of humour? I'm less reassured by the fact that it's on the wrong month. Maybe October just has the funniest picture.

I tell her about the situation and she nods sagely, only saying, 'I'm sorry, I didn't get that,' once after a prolonged speech. It's good news. She may be an alcoholic, but unlike my spam filter, at least she's functioning. Well, let's wait till the end of the appointment. She might still offer me something for my erectile dysfunction.

'Well, it sounds like a fairly straightforward custody issue,' explains Ms. Statov. 'Sorry, can I ask how you found me?'

'Oh… a colleague recommended you.'

'Ah,' she says, disappointed. 'I was hoping it was the sign. We just changed the company name.'

'Well, everyone loves a good pun.' When engaging professional services.

'Anyway, what were we talking about?'

'My divorce. Look – I just want to know whether she can take the kids to Canada?'

'Hmmm… well, obviously it would be disturbing for the kids' routines, so that would favour not. I mean, the only leg she'd have to stand on would be if she can provide them with a better life than you. That's the only thing I can see her arguing. But… if she doesn't say she's planning on moving abroad, she may try to push for sole custody. Then, when she gets it, she can do what she wants.'

So, her only hope is lying. She wouldn't do that. But then I remember I was pretty confident she wouldn't start screwing people behind my back…

'Look – you don't want to take this to court if you can help it. It'll be messy and expensive. But, if you can cut her off at mediation, she'll realise it's not worth pursuing it.'

'Should I try to get her to bring up taking them to Canada?'

'Doesn't matter. It's 'without prejudice'.' I look confused. 'Off the record. You just need her to try and see reason.'

'But that's not fair. She did this. She's the one that went off with someone else.'

'It's irrelevant. The only question is – did it affect the kids?'

'Well, they knew she had a lot of… 'friends'. They saw her kissing some of them.'

'That might help. If it could be shown she wasn't a good role model…

155

Would you be willing to have the kids go on record?'

I hesitate. I didn't want to bring the kids into this. But if it's better for them overall… no. I don't want them losing respect for their mother. Outside of this, she's always been really good with them. I don't have a choice.

'No, I wouldn't. I wouldn't want to get them involved.'

Rhonda nods. 'Well, that shows you're a good person. You're clearly a good father.'

'Thanks.' Maybe there's something about being nice in English law.

'But, to be frank: *legally*, it doesn't mean shit.'

And that's how our appointment ends: with me worried, powerless, and staring at a picture of a grizzly bear wearing sweatbands; the smell of alcohol serving to remind me that I could really use a fucking drink.

Friday

With the stresses of life threatening to overcome me, I decide to lose myself in work. Unfortunately, that currently consists of using the photocopier/Nespresso machines. If you can 'lose yourself' in that, you probably don't have much going on to begin with.

Doug and John seem to be getting on like a house on fire. I saw them playing *Overwatch* together earlier on a couple of beanbags. I tried to make conversation, but John was pretty keen on keeping me out of the magic circle.

'What are you doing?' I ask.

'Playing this cool new game.' Anyone who calls something a cool new game probably isn't that cool. Plus I'm pretty sure *Overwatch* has been around for a few years. 'You probably wouldn't understand,' he says, as his character does a slick flip of his guns and then falls into a hole only to get shot by about six other people. Doug finds it hilarious, but John clearly isn't impressed.

'He distracted me.'

Me and Amanda are getting on well too, but there's definitely an awkwardness between us. Not much chance of us killing strangers together on bean bags, if you know what I mean. Not that I'm complaining about my new situation, but I'm not getting much chance to be *creative*. And in terms of actually getting this job, being more creative than John is the best hope I've got.

It's the afternoon when everything changes. JC assembles the whole creative team in the conference room. He has a big announcement.

We sit around, waiting. Everyone's on their phones until JC walks in. I feel like a bit of a plonker, having left mine on my desk. Although the rest of them are probably all checking emails and I'd just be looking at funny dog pictures, so maybe it's for the best.

'Great news,' JC enunciates. 'Detergent. In two weeks time we may have one. They've dropped their current agency and are giving us a shot. We're pitching a new TV ad middle of next week.'

Everybody looks at each other and suddenly claps. Amanda nudges me when I don't join in. I join in.

'Which means we've got four days to get some ideas together. They've come to us, so they clearly want something modern, edgy, ironic.'

Amanda looks wary, and whispers to me. 'Things never happen this fast – something must have gone seriously tits up with their last guys.'

JC notices, seeing her lack of attention as a massive affront. 'Amanda… do you have a question?'

'I do, actually, if now's an appropriate time.'

He seems annoyed that she hasn't just rolled over and shown her stomach. 'Oh, OK, shoot.'

'Who were they with before?'

JC pretends not to remember. He doesn't do a very good job of it. 'Erm… Ham Hock, I think.' Amanda flashes a knowing smile, and JC quickly changes the subject.

'Anyway, it's shooting the week after, so all I can say is: get to it. There'll be a breakdown in your inbox any second…' – he presses send on his iPhone – '…now.'

Pings echo round the room, and suddenly everyone's getting up and heading to their desks/the pool table. They all seem to understand what's happened, but I'm completely in the dark.

'Ham Hock's Ian Scargill's company.' I'm none the wiser. 'The guy who's been in the papers?'

I think for a second. 'The one who kept masturbating into his female employees' bags?'

'Yeah. So what do you think?'

'I can't really see the appeal.'

'I mean about the campaign.'

Awkward.

Amanda smiles. 'Pleased to hear it, though. Nice to know I can leave my backpack round without you getting excited.'

Hans joins us in the office and we start to brainstorm ideas. We come up with some good stuff about 'staining your reputation' but come to the conclusion they probably don't want edgy at all. They want nice, safe, and not masturbating into handbags.

By six we've got a few possibilities, but nothing solid.

'Can you work tomorrow?'

'No, I'm going to Germany tonight,' says Hans. Amanda turns to me.

'Erm…' I hesitate. I've got the kids. I suddenly realise that

Amanda might not even know I *have* kids. For some reason I don't want to mention it. And I don't think it's because of work. 'Give me a second.'

I go out into the floor reception and phone my mum. They're coming down to stay tomorrow night before we all go down to my cousin's wedding on Sunday. Maybe they can do it earlier? Mum texts back straight away. I see the little dots appear and then five minutes later her reply materialises. 'Sorry, no, have hair appointment.' I thought that was Friday. Damn, she must have traded in some favours to get that moved one day closer to the wedding.

Maybe I can bring the kids into work. No. How the hell would we get anything done with Carrie there? Then it suddenly strikes me – maybe I can try Sally? I mean just because she's gone, it doesn't mean I can't ask. I have to work for God's sake; why's it all up to me? Two minutes later she's texted back. 'OK. I'll pick them up tomorrow at eight.'

I'm a bit taken aback. It worked. Why didn't I just do that before? I didn't realise I could. If she's going to take my kids halfway across the world, the very least she can do is a day of weekend childcare.

I go back into the office, beaming. 'I can work!'

Hans looks at me like I'm a weirdo, but Amanda seems pleased.

'I don't think I've ever seen anybody so happy to be in the office at the weekend before.'

She clearly doesn't have children. If she knew what that was like, she'd definitely understand.

Saturday

The handover to Sally goes fine. Austin's not with her, so that makes things a bit less uncomfortable. She's got Monday off, so she offers to drop the kids back that evening. I was kind of hoping to take the kids to the wedding, but I decide it's better just to go with the flow.

We don't say anything as we load the car. But once the kids are in she asks the question that must have been on her mind.

'So… are you still seeing that Claire woman?'

I hesitate. 'I don't feel comfortable talking about this stuff with you.'

She thinks for a second, annoyed that I haven't given her a straight answer. 'Well, I know it's none of my business,' she says, 'but I think you could do a lot better than that.'

Then she gets in her car and drives off. And that's it.

It's really weird. I don't know if she was being nice, or trying to take me down. Claire was great. If she hadn't got that awful kid, maybe it could have gone somewhere. Maybe not – I didn't know her, but I'm pretty sure I wasn't too good for her. But even if it's just some underhand attempt to insult a rival, it's nice having Sally couch something in affection. It makes me sad. Sad to think that that just used to be standard. Whereas now it's something I can hardly get my head round.

I get into town just before ten. It's cool being in town on a Saturday. There're a few people going to work, but none of the shoppers are in yet, so it feels kind of peaceful.

The office is pretty much empty too. There's someone on the downstairs reception but the rest of the building is ridiculously quiet. Amanda's already there.

'Nice of you to join me.'

'Sorry – have you been here for ages?'

'About three minutes.'

We get straight to work. With no one else there, the office feels like a playground – like an abandoned amusement park that you've managed to break into after closing. We're chatting about ideas, and playing table football and pool, but we're actually coming up with things. Maybe being creative *is* fun.

At noon we're back at the desk writing some things up, when John and Doug come in. Suddenly, it feels like work again. Like we found our little creative Eden, and suddenly we've been made aware that we're wearing nothing but fig leaves. Although seeing Amanda in fig leaves might almost be enough to make me forget it wasn't the most flattering outfit for me.

I can see John and Doug laughing at what they've come up with through the glass partition. I get paranoid that they're doing better than us, but maybe they're just playing it up to make me feel insecure.

Doug: I can't think of anything. You?

John: Nothing, but Tom's looking so guffaw like I've said something brilliant.

Both: Ha, ha, ha!

By the end of the day, we've got our pitch together. The slogan's 'As Clean as your Conscience' and it's about this little naughty boy character who keeps getting dirty. As much as JC thinks these washing powder guys want edgy, I think he's dreaming. When was the last time you saw an edgy washing powder advert? Apart from one of those accidentally racist ones where the washing powder manages to turn the person in it white.

It's been dark out for a few hours when my phone beeps with a message. It's Mum: 'WHERE ARE YOU?'

I suddenly realise it's seven o'clock and I'm meant to be letting my parents into the flat. Plus, if Mum's had time to send a text she's probably been there since six.

'Shit. I've got to go,' I suddenly blurt out. 'My parents are outside my flat.'

'No problem – let's call it a day,' says Amanda. 'I reckon we're good anyway. We just need a few hours tomorrow to rehearse the pitch and then we'll be ready.'

'Tomorrow?'

'Are you busy?'

'I'm driving down to my cousin's wedding in Dorset. Well, getting a lift with my parents.'

Amanda thinks for a second. Then has an idea. 'Dorset?'

'Yeah.'

'Why don't I come down with you?'

A vision of my Dad offering Amanda creative tips while we sit in the back seat comes into my head. 'I don't think a car journey with my parents would be that conducive to rehearsal.'

'I could drive us. My parents live down there. If I pop in to see them, it might mean I can get out of Christmas.'

'Um… Are you sure? That sounds like a major ball-ache.'

'One of the advantages of being a woman. Ball-ache really isn't a primary concern.'

I look sceptical, but Amanda's clearly a lot more spontaneous than me. She seems quite taken by the idea. 'Come on – why not? We need to get it done and I've already cancelled my plans. Maybe a road trip would be fun?'

Maybe it *would* be fun. Definitely better than listening to my dad suggest what socks to wear for our presentation. I'm hesitating, but I desperately want to say yes.

'OK,' I nod. 'Let's do it.'

Sunday

My parents leave the house at 7:00 am to allow for coffee and food breaks, having been up since five making snacks and filling thermoses. I don't know why they refuse to buy things from service stations. Mum once said the sandwiches in packets taste weird. As opposed to coffee from a thermos. I hear Heston's using them now to create a sauce with that much-lauded plasticky flavour.

Their early departure gives me an hour and a half to potter round getting ready. I'd planned to doll myself up at the hotel when I got there, but I find myself going through a full grooming routine so I can try and con Amanda that I'm not entirely repulsive. Predictably, I end up watching YouTube videos for the first fifty minutes, telling myself that if I focus my efforts on the right side of my face, I should still cut a fine figure in the passenger seat.

By 8:15 am I'm looking OK from a 180 degree angle and have my tux laid out, so I pop out for a couple of coffees. If Amanda's driving me halfway across southern England, the least I can do is provide refreshments.

I'm back a few minutes before 8:30, and at 8:35 the bell rings. I open the door with the coffees in hand. Amanda's there smiling, with a couple of coffees herself. 'It's going to be a long trip,' she says. 'It's only sensible we double up on the caffeine.'

Slightly Later

We get into Amanda's Mini and head towards the M3.

By the time we hit the motorway, we're both hyped up on espresso shots and rehearsing our pitch at breakneck speed. It actually does feel like a road trip – it reminds me of going down

163

to Devon with my school friends after A-levels. Except I'm guessing the boot is not currently full of Diamond White. Who knows? Maybe Amanda has a thing for low-cost cider.

We stop halfway down, feeling pretty confident about the pitch, which allows the conversation to move onto other stuff.

'So, who's getting married?'

'My cousin, Marcus. It's the first gay wedding in the family. It's quite the hot ticket.'

'Really?'

'You have no idea the status symbol going to a gay wedding is to my parents' friends. They'll be boasting to everyone for the next six months at dinner parties: *And after the vows, they kissed each other and we didn't even flinch…*'

Amanda's laughing. 'Better that than my parents,' she says. 'They'd be standing up shouting "Abomination!" in church.'

'I dunno. Once their kid comes out, they have to shape up pretty quickly or they lose them. It's a pretty good motivation.'

'Do you think you'd ever get married?' Amanda asks. She seems to immediately realise it's slightly too intimate a question, but it just sort of hangs there, waiting for a response.

I hesitate. I don't know why, but I'd sort of convinced myself she knew. That all I was hiding was the fact I had kids. What a great guy. 'I, sort of…' I begin. 'I'm getting divorced at the moment. That time you saw me in the stairwell…'

'Oh, God, I'm sorry – I didn't realise.'

'Don't be. It's for the best,' I say. *Is* it? I hadn't thought that before. But maybe it's true. Look at my life. I'm doing something for the first time in fifteen years. I'm trying out to be a bloody creative. I'm hanging out in a service station with this incredibly beautiful and intelligent woman coming up with ideas for a washing powder commercial?!? It's ridiculous, but it's great. I'm the happiest I've been in years.

164

'What about you?'

'Oh, um… I was engaged. About two years ago. He broke it off a week before the wedding.' She thinks to herself for a second. 'Maybe that's for the best as well.'

'I can't see anyone wanting to break something off with you,' I say, immediately regretting it. Smooth move, Cooper.

'He…' she says, trying to work out how to explain it. 'I can't have kids. I found out about it when I was twenty-five, so he knew about it before, but… I guess when you're committing your life to someone, what you want comes into focus pretty sharply.'

I want to tell her how kids destroy your very existence, your sleep, your social life, your free time, your *hope*. But that's the whinging of someone who's got them. Sure, my life would be better if they weren't about. More fun, more productive. I'd be happier, probably in better shape. But would I change things, if I could? Not in a million years.

'Right,' says Amanda. 'After that depressing conversation, we should probably get back on the road. Don't want to delay the wedding and give anyone chance to change their mind.'

We get to the hotel where the wedding's happening at lunchtime. I see my parents' Skoda estate in the car park and notice the Scrabble trophy's on the dashboard. Mum's name's on it. I have to admit when I see the engraving – that's some fine work for £7.50.

Amanda comes inside to have lunch before heading back. On the way in we bump into Julian, Marcus's intended.

'Hey! Tom! Glad you could make it!'

'Wouldn't have missed it for the world. No second thoughts, I hope?'

'Depends if Marcus wears that cummerbund he's been threatening me with.'

He notices Amanda hovering next to me. 'Who's this?'

'Amanda – but don't worry, she's not staying.'

'Oh. Well, you know – we've actually had a drop out, so we've got a spare seat if you want to?'

There's an awkward pause as Amanda and I look at each other.

'Um… yeah,' I say, at exactly the same time Amanda says, 'No.'

We look at each other. 'Maybe,' says Amanda as I say, 'No.'

'Amanda's from work.'

'I'll try not to hold that against her,' drolls Julian. 'Give us a second.'

We wander off a few feet away.

'Why don't you? You're down here anyway.'

'I don't know anyone.'

'You know me.'

'Yeah, but… I haven't got anything to wear.'

'You look great as you are.'

'Not for a wedding.'

Julian overhears us. 'I can ask my sister, if you want? She came to the dinner last night massively overdressed. You could borrow that. As long as she didn't spill anything on it.'

'I don't know…' She looks resistant, but I convince myself she wants to be persuaded.

'Come on – you've driven all the way down. We can drive back first thing. It'll be fun. It's going to look really bad for my trial period if I'm the only one with a hangover tomorrow.'

'…OK. Let me see if they've got a room.'

She wanders over to the reception. Julian turns to me, conspiratorially. 'She's pretty… Did I do good?'

Yes, Julian, you did good. You did very good.

One Hour Later

Amanda meets me in the lobby before the ceremony. She's wearing a purple satin dress that would've looked tacky as hell on Julian's sister, but on her – my jaw's on the floor. It looks amazing. Even when paired with some Chuck Taylors. Apparently Julian's sister has incredibly small feet.

'I feel really uncomfortable in this.'

'Well, you look… great.' And she does; she really does. A lot better than me in a tuxedo that's now tight enough to stop me doing 99% of yoga poses – including the one at the start where you just stand there with your hands together.

We sneak into the back of the ceremony. It's in the same place as the reception. I point my parents out to Amanda and we watch them when Marcus and Julian kiss. My mum flinches a little and we both burst out laughing. Luckily it's covered up by the round of applause and the intro to Erasure's *A Little Respect* being played over the P.A.. Julian struts in towards Marcus and takes off his new husband's cummerbund with a flourish, and this launches them into a pre-rehearsed dance routine – chucking it in the air after a bunch of finger waggling, while he lip syncs to the '*that you give me no*' bit. It's awesome. And far too much gay for my parents to handle. Mum looks like she's about to collapse and Dad has to escort her from the room. Me and Amanda are in hysterics.

We go up and congratulate them after the routine's over. Amanda talks to Marcus, and I end up with Julian.

'Did you give that cummerbund line to everyone before the wedding?'

'A version of it,' he says, defiantly. 'Can't have a wedding without a few theatrics.'

I give Marcus a big hug. He seems really happy. Then we head towards the waiters and their trays of champagne.

I hear a couple of voices from behind…

'Daddy! Daddy!'

I turn around and there… are Arthur and Carrie.

'Oh my God – what are you doing here?'

I bend down to hug them, confused.

'Well, aren't you going to introduce me?' asks Amanda. Shit. I didn't tell her about them. I should have bloody told her about them.

'Um… this is Arthur and this is Carrie. Guys, this is Amanda – a friend from work.'

'I like your dress,' says Carrie.

'I like yours too,' says Amanda. Carrie pulls up her dress to show Amanda her trainers.

Amanda smiles. She seems remarkably unfazed. Maybe things are going to be all right. And then reality clicks into place. If the kids are here… so is Sally.

Right on cue, she appears.

'What are you doing here?' I ask.

'Marcus is one of my best friends. I wasn't going to miss his wedding.'

I can't believe she didn't mention this. Why has this not come up? 'He's my cousin. You knew I'd be here – you should have said something.'

'I assumed you'd realise. If you've got a problem, you should have told me beforehand.'

'You've hardly talked to me for the last six weeks. How could I have told you?' I blurt out.

I'm starting to get really angry, when I remember Amanda's right next to me. She's just seen me lose it with Sally. You really want to know someone a little better before you start shouting at your ex in front of them.

I try to calm myself down. I turn to Amanda.

'Let's go and have a look at the seating plan.'

As I walk off, Sally shouts after me. 'Aren't you going to introduce us? You were quick enough with the last one?'

'What does she mean?' asks Amanda. I can feel the anger rising inside me, but I need to be my best me.

'Nothing. Ignore her.'

We scan the seating plan and, annoyingly, not only is Amanda on a different table, she's on the same one as Sally. Austin Kimble's name is crossed out. That must be the guy I met in the park. Fuck. Amanda's basically Sally's plus one.

Meanwhile, the champagne's starting to kick in, and I'm just getting increasingly agitated at Sally's presence. I'm trying to hide it in front of Amanda, mainly by keeping my back to Sally and ignoring her, but I know I'm acting weird. I can't tell if Amanda's worried about me or pissed off.

A voice comes from behind, 'Aren't you going to introduce us?'

Unless Sally's voice has gone down a few octaves and developed a mild Brummie accent, it's not her. I turn round to my dad and mum looking far more poised than they did during the ceremony.

'Hi, I'm Roy, Tom's dad; this is Jan, his mother.'

Amanda shakes hands with both of them and introduces herself.

'You didn't say she was coming to the wedding,' says Mum. 'I thought she was just a co-worker.'

'She is…' I say, cursing my mother inside. I try to change the subject. 'What did you think of the dance routine?'

'Oh, very… coordinated,' says Mum. 'We're looking forward to telling people about it at dinner next week.' *I'll bet you are.* 'Pat and Jenny were angling for an invite, but they didn't get one.'

'You'll have more to talk about than that,' I reply. 'Later on, they're going to change into leather-wear and dance to German electronica.'

My mum clearly doesn't know what electronica is, but she seems pretty concerned about finding out.

'He's joking,' says Amanda.

'He's always joking. It's nice to see Tom's working with someone sensible.'

'It's my best quality,' replies Amanda.

'Don't be so negative about yourself. I'm sure you're very good at your job as well,' says my mother reassuringly.

Yeah, and funny and clever and super hot. And able to grasp basic conversational irony.

Amanda and I make a break for it, and I have to admit, I feel like I've perked up a bit from mocking my mother.

Outside the marquee, a few of Marcus's friends are chatting and handing round a spliff. I don't generally touch the stuff, but… when in Rome. Well, Dorset.

I have a couple of drags and realise I probably haven't smoked any pot for about fifteen years, and it seems to have got a lot stronger. Amanda pops to the loo, so I start to head inside when I see Marcus running over.

'Hey, Tom, I want to talk to you. I saw you with Sally. You knew she was coming, right? She said you'd talked about it.'

'No. Must have slipped her mind.'

'I'm so sorry, mate.'

'Don't worry about it – it's your wedding. Just make sure you have a good time.'

'I'm really sorry it didn't work out for you two,' he commiserates. 'I thought you were in it for the long haul.'

'Me too…'

Marcus gives me a bittersweet smile. 'Probably just wishful thinking, anyway. My favourite cousin and one of my best friends – how's that not going to make family meet-ups more fun?' He smiles nostalgically at the promise our relationship used to hold. 'You don't hate me for introducing you?'

I look inside the marquee and see Carrie and Arthur fooling round with some other kids by the children's table.

'No. Some things worked out pretty well.'

And then, the tender moment is interrupted as Marcus is dragged away by a conga line in formal wear. And, suddenly, I'm alone once again.

The Meal

The food's good, but I can't help but notice that the beetroot and white asparagus is suspiciously well-matched to the purple and cream of the table cloths. Marcus must've inherited the family coordination gene as well.

Still, I'm finding it impossible to relax. Not only am I sitting on a table with my parents and their friends, out of the corner of my eye I can see my estranged wife two seats down from Amanda. My mum's stories aren't engaging at the best of times, but this is really putting a wrench in the works of my attention.

'And then I got on the bus… it was the number 24… no, the 28 – which is the one that goes into town, Roy? The 24, that's right…'

Bear in mind, this is a story about not having the receipt at M&S; it has nothing to do with a bus. But Mum's stories are like that. The anecdotal equivalent of giving someone a cake recipe and describing the methods of crop rotation used to grow the wheat.

'Anyway… I normally like to sit at the front, but not if it's busy because then you might have to give up your seat to an old person…' Mum, you're seventy-one, you *are* an old person.

But I'm getting more and more distracted. Sally's now talking to Amanda, her words accompanied by lots of sneering and cynical eyebrow-raising. Amanda's smiling politely, but there's a rage bubbling inside Sally that the alcohol is doing nothing to suppress.

'But that used to be the policy didn't it – like when we took back that scarf of yours, Tom… Tom? TOM! Are you even listening?'

'Oh. Um… The scarf – what was that?'

'Sometimes I don't know why I bother.'

Sally looks like she's building up to something. I've seen the look on her face before. Like a snake sizing up its prey before going for the kill.

'Excuse me.'

I get up from the table, and manage to pull Amanda away mid-lunge.

'Sorry, I need to grab Amanda for a second.' I move her away from the table pretending to show her something on my phone.

'What's going on? Why are you showing me your lock screen?'

'I've got four bars. I wanted to show you how well Three was doing with coverage these days…' Amanda looks confused. 'My ex was about to pounce. I saw her eyeing up your jugular.'

'She did seem angry.'

'I think it might be the vegetables. She's never understood my family's interest in colour coordination.'

Amanda looks at me like 'enough with the jokes'. Mum would be proud.

'I think she's just upset it didn't work out between us,' I explain. 'It's weird when the person you were going to spend the rest of your life with turns out not to be. The wedding's probably reminding her of that.'

'At least you got to have a wedding… I had to do all the planning, and didn't even get to have a party.'

'Did you book in colour-matched vegetables?'

'No, must have been what went wrong.'

'Yeah, ours clashed horribly.' I suddenly have an idea. 'Come on. I want to show you something.'

I lead Amanda through the hotel and out into the gardens. I can see she's freezing so I give her my jacket. Within four seconds, I realise I'm wearing nothing but a shirt in November and may die of hypothermia. That said, I have a bow tie on. Almost a scarf when you think about it. I wonder what the M&S returns policy on these is.

The gardens lead down to the edge of a cliff overlooking the coastline. It's really romantic in the moonlight, the sound of the sea ahead of us. It's almost enough to forget how cold it is.

'We came on holiday here when I was twelve,' I explain. 'Me and Marcus were sitting down by this cliff when he told me he thought he might be gay.' I get myself back on track. 'Anyway, I want to show you this crazy house… it's so close to the edge of the cliff, it's ridiculous.'

It suddenly strikes me this might be read as a metaphor. If people love a house so much they're prepared to risk falling into the sea, surely a relationship's worth risking a potentially awkward time at work for. Fuck.

We approach the edge and I keep talking. 'We saw this whole flower bed just disintegrate while we were sitting here… Marcus thought it was a bad omen. The next day we went down to the beach and picked up the some of the stuff that had fallen. Marcus insisted on replanting it in the hotel garden to lift the curse.' It's too dark to tell, but I wonder if any of it's still here.

'Anyway, look to the right of that sticking out bit… Oh my God…'

'What is it?'

I hesitate, unable to take in what I'm seeing. 'It's gone.'

I stare through the darkness at the space where the little cottage used to be. There's not even a single wall left. I guess it's been twenty-five years since we saw it, but still… This has become a completely different type of metaphor. Nothing lasts; everything is impermanent, that kind of shit. Oh well. There's no better move than escorting someone you like to the edge of some cliffs and confronting them with the hopelessness of existence.

Amanda looks at me like I've just shown her one of the most depressing things ever. 'Well, I don't know what you had in mind with this,' says Amanda. 'But I'm sorry – I'm not going to jump.' She changes the subject, 'We better get back in – it's freezing out here.'

'I'm not so cold.'

'I can see your nipples through your shirt.'

I glance down. They are looking rather perky. It's not the greatest look.

'Well, it's my own fault. I shouldn't have gone without a bra.'

* * *

When we get back to the party, the speeches are in full swing and we manage to nick a couple of desserts and a jug of custard off a waitress so we don't have to go back to our tables. Arthur comes up and stands with us and keeps asking me to explain why people are laughing.

Julian makes a comment about how tonight will be the first time he and Marcus give their bodies to one another.

'What does that mean?' asks Arthur.

'It means that Uncle Julian doesn't know how to act appropriately round children.'

Before long, the band's on. They go by the name of Creedence Queerwater Revival, but aren't exactly a tribute band. That said, the lead singer's called Proud Mary, so they've clearly got at least a passing interest in Southern rock. They're actually pretty good, and romp through a number of wedding classics and gay anthems, and before long, the dance floor's jumping and Carrie's grooving with Amanda while I'm dancing with Arthur. Even my dad's showing off his moves, despite his obvious confusion that there's a stageful of men in dresses and no-one seems to be pointing and laughing.

I see Sally at the side of the dance floor, stewing with a glass of red wine, and I suddenly feel guilty. I don't want her thinking we're stealing her kids. I go over.

'Why don't you dance with Arthur and Carrie?'

'I can't believe you brought someone here,' she snaps.

'She's from work. We had to get ready for a presentation.' She laughs cynically. I have to admit it doesn't sound that convincing. 'You were going to bring Austin.'

'That's different – we're together. It's not like you, bringing one of your sluts to my friend's bloody wedding.' She's really drunk, and looking for a fight, but I'm not going to let her have one.

'First thing, Amanda's not a slut,' I say trying to stay calm, 'and secondly, I didn't know you were going to be here.'

'I suppose that woman from school wasn't a slut either? Do you really think it's a good thing to rub all your fuck buddies in our kids' faces?'

Suddenly I want to explode. She was having sex with people behind my back. I never so much as looked at another woman while we were married.

'Look, Sally, I was never anything but faithful to you while we were together. Sure, I may have been boring, or not driven enough, or whatever the fuck it was that made you do what you did, but I was faithful. Whereas you shagged people, and lied to me, and left. So don't lecture me about my behaviour. If I were you, I'd have a few cups of coffee and try to sober up. I'll see you on Monday evening with the kids.'

'Fuck you, Tom.'

I turn my back on her and head over to the dance floor. The

175

band's finishing up their first set, but I'm fuming – I need to get out of here. I go over to Amanda.

'I think I'm going to go to bed,' I tell her.

'I'll come with you.'

There's a sudden awkwardness at the gap between what she meant and what she actually said. Amanda regains her composure first.

'I mean, I should call it a night too. We'll need to be on the road for 6:30.'

'Yeah.'

I say goodnight to the kids and point out where Sally is. I try to find my parents, but they're currently accosting Proud Mary who's trying to have a cigarette between sets. More ammo for liberal Top Trumps at next week's dinner party.

Amanda and I walk up the stairs together. We're both on the first floor. We say goodnight outside my room.

'Sorry you had to deal with my ex. I think she thought we were… I don't know what she thought.'

'It's fine. It was probably stupid to come.'

'It wasn't. I had fun.'

'Me too.' We kind of hesitate, waiting for something else to say, but all the talking's done. I go into my room, imagining myself running back out onto the landing to tell her *fuck work, fuck rules, come into my room and kiss me like none of the rest of that matters*.

But instead I check Reddit for an hour before drifting off into unconsciousness. And my door stays shut.

Monday

We leave the hotel at 6:45 am and get to the office just before ten. I'm a complete mess. Not only am I hungover, I got woken by Sally storming into my room at 1:30 am to see if I 'had any Calpol'. I tried to see the kids, but she said it was 'no big deal' and went through the front pocket of my suitcase, then left. I'm pretty sure she just wanted to check if Amanda was there, but maybe not. Still, it took me a couple of hours to get back to sleep, so I'm knackered.

The trip back is strange. The whole car journey, it feels like we're together except we're 100% not, so we keep having conversations, but then spontaneously sensing they're too 'couple-y' and stopping abruptly, then sitting in silence.

But we're feeling ready for the pitch. We went through it a few times in the car. Obviously, I've never pitched before, but Amanda's done loads of them and she thinks it's sounding good, so who am I to disagree? Last time I spoke in front of people was at an intercompany accountancy away day, so just standing up there in silence would have been enough to get an ovation (although I pulled out some pretty badass accountancy jokes, including some very well-received digs at QuickBooks users, so kind of a stormer, basically).

By ten, we're all sitting round the meeting room nervously, and at 10:15 JC swans in. 'Sorry guys, forgot we'd arranged a meet. What was it we were pitching again?'

The affected nonchalance is slightly worrying. And we know it's affected, because we all saw him through his office door, rehearsing these exact words. Also, his shirt has shrunk a couple of sizes, suggesting he's done his own washing for the first time in twenty years as research. That's *super* worrying. It's not like JC to do research.

The creative team 'reminds' him what the meeting is about and he nods calmly, reaching for a glass of water, only to be stopped short by his newly tenacious cuff. He rolls up his sleeve and takes a sip.

One by one, the teams present their ideas. We're the penultimate pitchers, so we have to listen to four other ideas. Some of them are pretty good, but JC is looking bored, and, after the fourth one, Amanda looks at me as if to say 'we're in with a shot.' As they come to a conclusion, JC lets out a derisory grunt and turns to us.

'All right. Amanda... Accountant... Give me something interesting...'

'Well, ours is sort of traditional, but also a little bit cheeky,' begins Amanda. The word cheeky doesn't seem to set JC's world on fire, but who's ever had their minds blown by a washing powder advert? Still, he seems slightly interested.

I open the presentation.

'Dennis the Menace, Horrid Henry... the world loves naughty boys.' It suddenly strikes me it would have been good to have some visual aids. My dad would have suggested novelty socks. Annoyingly, he does actually own some Dennis the Menace ones. 'Well, with this campaign we're going to bring you a new little mischief-maker.' We'd planned on calling him Dirty Bertie... but suddenly, as I go to say it in public I realise he sounds like a character from a 1960s porno. I go with our second choice: Messy Jessie.

'So it's a girl?' asks JC.

It wasn't, but he seems to like it. I'm not sure whether to go with it or not.

'That's right,' Amanda jumps in. 'We're turning the whole thing on its head and letting the girls have some fun for a change.'

JC nods approvingly. Amanda's clearly a lot better at reading JC than me. We go through the rest of the pitch as rehearsed, except now it's Jessie causing the trouble rather than Dirty Bertie, the lovable rascal who'll one day grow up to be a sex pest. We end with Jessie flashing a cheeky wink at the camera, and then I come in with the slogan: 'As Clean as your Conscience.'

JC pauses. Then nods. 'Like it. Like it a lot.'

A massive sense of relief come over me. We did it. We really did it.

JC starts to get up. 'Substantially better than the rest of the shit we've heard today anyway. Everybody do some brainstorming on this – we're presenting it to the client on Wednesday.'

'Um, JC,' Doug pipes up. 'I think you might like ours as well.'

'I thought we were done,' says JC, pissed off he's got to listen to another one. 'OK – make it quick.'

Arse. I thought we were done too. I'm slightly reassured however when John gets up to start the pitch.

'Right,' he says, 'so we were thinking about when washing powder adverts go bad.'

'When washing powder adverts go bad…' echoes Doug in the style of a film trailer voice-over.

'It's when they're massively racist.'

'Massively racist… racist… racist…' says Doug letting the word echo out. Annoyingly, it's actually quite funny.

'A black guy comes in with a dirty T-shirt, steps into the machine and suddenly comes out white or Chinese, depending on which racist country has produced it.'

'Has produced it, has produced it, has produced it…' echoes Doug once again.

Amanda leans in to me and whispers. 'He does improv comedy in his spare time.' Great. We're trying to sell an advert and now we're getting it upstaged by fucking *Whose Line is it Anyway*? He'll probably start pitching in the style of a country music song before he's bloody done.

'Anyway,' says John, who annoyingly is managing to somehow pull off being a bit cool, 'we want to play on these, have our say on these, show everyone there's another way on these.' Did he just rap that last line a bit? I think he did. John is rapping in the middle of a meeting and no one's laughing. What is happening? Oh, God. People like John. People don't realise he's embarrassing. The world is ending.

'So the guy goes in white... and comes out black.'

He pauses. There's a tense silence around the room. Do they not know how to react to this? I'm pretty sure there's only one correct response – *don't touch it with a ten-foot barge pole.* I don't dare be the first one who speaks, but it's clearly a terrible idea. Maybe everyone's assuming it's OK because Doug's mixed race. That it deserves considering. I'm pretty sure it doesn't.

JC breaks the stalemate. 'I love it.'

What?!?

'It's subversive, it's edgy, it's what this company needs to stay on top. None of these "cheeky kid" clichés,' he says, looking at us. 'It's disruptive, original. Plus it's a positive message – black is clean, so "fuck you" racists – this is the anti-racist detergent. The detergent that deters... racism. Detergent... insurgents... Something there... Anyway – I love it. Nice work, guys.'

I find myself unintentionally emitting a strange groan. Amanda kicks me under the table, but JC's already heard.

'Something to say, Tombo.' *Tombo?* I don't like that. Really need to make sure that doesn't stick.

'Not really... I just—' The whole office is staring at me. I have no option but to continue. 'I'm just not sure people really *want* their washing powder adverts edgy.'

'In-the-box thinking, Tombo,' patronises JC. 'Don't give them what they want. Give them what they didn't know they wanted. Otherwise, you'll end up with a seven-year-old getting dirty in the garden,' he laughs. This is not fair, he liked it a second ago. 'Don't be a sore loser, Tombo – we're going with Doug and John.'

I keep my mouth shut and everybody slowly files out of the room. I'm frozen to my chair. We worked really hard on this. And we got beaten by a really stupid idea.

'Bad luck,' says John as he walks past. 'But you win some, you lose some,' he continues, patting me on the shoulder. 'No hard feelings... eh, *Tombo?*'

Evening

After the disappointment of the pitch meeting, the rest of the day feels like an anticlimax. I spend the whole time just wanting to get home and wait for the kids to be dropped back. As much as I've felt trapped by my routine, sometimes you just want normal.

But, at seven o'clock, they're still not back. I assume Sally must be just running late – it's going to screw up Carrie and Arthur's bedtime – but by eight there's still no sign, and I start to worry. I text and phone Sally but don't get a response. This is weird. Really weird.

Suddenly, I panic we got our wires crossed and no one picked them up from school. I ring the child minder to see if she did, but she says she spoke to Sally on Friday when she said not to bother. My mind starts running wild. Could something have happened? On the way back from the wedding? I just dismissed the Calpol incident, but maybe... I phone my parents, but they say they saw the kids the next morning and they were fine, so I try Sally again. Every ten minutes for about the next four hours.

I don't know what to do. They're probably fine. Delayed. Calling the police seems too extreme. I don't want to get Sally arrested for child kidnapping or something. Do you have to say 'child' if it's a kid? Is that just kid-napping and using it for an adult is actually wrong? I suppose no one ever 'naps' someone. It doesn't bloody matter.

Then something hits me. Could she have already taken them to Canada? I get so paranoid about this, I actually check the drawer to make sure their passports are there. They are. At least they're still in the country. Thank God.

At about two in the morning, I finally stop calling. Nothing's going to change until the day starts again.

I've got no choice. I just have to wait it out.

Tuesday

I only sleep for two hours and wake up feeling terrible. I go to the school drop off to see if Sally's there with the kids, but she's not and the teachers tell me the kids weren't in yesterday either. Apparently, Sally rang to say they were ill.

A wave of relief crashes over me. I don't think I've ever been so grateful to hear my kids were sick. Not that I believe it. Particularly as they supposedly have norovirus. I mean, come on Sally; if you're going to lie, at least choose a different bloody ailment from last time.

But I'm furious. If this Sally's revenge for me taking Amanda to the wedding, fuck her. I've been worried sick for the last twelve hours. You don't use the kids as a bargaining tool. That's what people normally say, but there's not really been any bargaining. A weapon of war. That's more like it. Well, if you want war, Sally, you've got it. You've bloody got it.

4:00 pm

I get an email from Sally saying she'll drop the kids back at 6:30 pm. No explanation as to why she hasn't phoned or texted. No apology. But still, it's good to know they'll be home tonight. Feeling powerless is horrible.

I've been in a weird mood all day, worrying, so I go to find Amanda. She's heading to New York for a few days this evening, and I don't want her thinking I've got all this semi-ex-wife baggage dragging me down. Thinking Sally's still in my head. She's not.

I'm pretty sure she's not.

I head to Amanda's office, but I can see through the glass partition she's gone, along with the suitcase that's been by her desk all day.

'She had to leave for her flight,' says Hans. 'Anything I can help you with?'

I shake my head, wishing I'd left the whole thing on a more positive note. Fucking Sally.

Evening

Sally drops the kids back at 6:30 pm, all 'I didn't know there was a problem'. I'm fucking livid. The kids are perky as ever – if anything, unusually so. Might be something to do with their spontaneous two-day holiday. I send them inside, so I can spew.

'You have to tell me if you're keeping them. What you did was basically,' – kidnapping or just napping? – '…unacceptable.'

'I know, Tom, but we were having such a good time and I haven't seen them much recently. I think I just got carried away.'

'That's fine. But you have to call me.'

'My phone died.'

'You called the school.'

'I was saving my battery for that. I didn't have my charger with me.'

I don't believe a word of it, but annoyingly it's technically possible. I know I'm stuck in that male mindset of possibilities trumping what you know to be actually true, but I can't help it – the wind's out of my sails and I'm floating towards the coast of forgiveness. 'You should have gone into a phone shop and asked them to charge it for you.'

'Oh God, I should have. I'm so sorry – I just didn't think of it.' Again – could be true. I know it's not, but it *could* be. Fuck. Why do I feel the coast of forgiveness might have a rocky shoreline and I'm heading right into it?

'Well,' I say, 'Next time... you'll know.' I'm really losing momentum here.

'I will. I'm really sorry.'

'And you can't keep taking them out of school.'

'I know, I shouldn't have... I just... ' She breaks off. Is she crying? I think she's crying.

'What is it?' Brace yourself for collision.

'Seeing you at the wedding...' she continues. 'It just got me thinking about... *us*.'

Crash.

I'm completely blindsided. This is not where I was expecting the conversation to go.

'We used to have so much fun, didn't we?' Unless she's got Meryl Streep-level acting chops, it really seems like she means it. 'I just got to thinking... you know, spending time with the kids... remembering what it was like to be a family... Do you remember when we went to Majorca?'

'Course.'

'When Arthur decided he wasn't going to wear clothes for

anything but mealtimes and the concierge told us we had to get some shorts on him or we'd be ejected from the hotel?'

I laugh, but I can't shake the revelation it might have been because of his strange penis. Maybe now's a good time to ask if she knows about a family history…

But this is nice. Reminiscing together. Remembering all the good times we had together. When things were good.

Sally continues. 'What about when… when…' Suddenly, she bursts into tears. She puts her head on my chest. Should I hug her? I feel like I should hug her. I put my arms around her and she looks up at me, vulnerable and human. The person I used to love.

'We had some good times, didn't we?'

'We did.'

She smiles at me. 'I liked seeing you at the wedding. You looked like you did when we got married.'

'Same stupid tux with a rip on the inside of the sleeve.'

'I remember you getting your arm stuck in it after your speech.'

'I was just trying to avoid answering your dad's question about what I thought of his poem. *Love is like a loaf of bread…*'

'*You mix together the ingredients, and one day it will rise,*' Sally responds in a parody of her father's delivery.

'*The flour is the people, sieved by their experience,*' I continue.

'*The water is the conversation… not too warm and not too cold…*'

'*And then you add a bit of yeast…* And he said it with that weird twinkle in his eye, like it was meant to be sexy,' I say, shaking my head. 'I mean, how had he got through life without ever hearing about thrush?'

We both laugh. It's a joke we've shared together a thousand times before. But these are the things that bond us. That hold a relationship together. Like gluten. Maybe Sally's dad should have included that one. And then Sally starts to confide in me.

185

'Things aren't going well with Austin…' Obviously I don't give a crap about her new relationship, she's meant to be married to me, but I think she's trying to tell me something. To tell me she made a mistake.

She leaves a few minutes later. I can see the kids looking at us out of the window. Watching… hoping…

Even though it's not my fault, it makes me feel incredibly guilty.

And it makes me realise how much I miss being a family.

Wednesday

JC is pitching to the client today, so it's pretty tense in the office. I had a look at the company finances this morning as part of my 'Accountancy Fun Hour', and things aren't looking good. If anything, a little more tension would probably be appropriate.

Everyone's distracting themselves with talk of the inter-agency 'Spartacus' race. I think they might have nicked the title from something called the 'Spartan' race. Not that people in advertising would do that…

Anyway, it's happening in two weeks, and as Hans broke his wrist playing handball in Germany the other weekend, they're looking for a replacement. As potentially the least fit person of my generation, I decide to keep my head down. Someone started trying to ask me earlier, but I managed to get away before answering. So, when John walks in, the recruitment team gets his scent. And, as he's cycled into work today, that scent is both figurative and literal.

'Sorry I'm late, Doug – had a puncture on the way,' says John, panting.

He's wearing his usual gear – skin tight Lycra from knee to

shoulder. He's got cyclist's legs so the bottom half looks all right, but the weight he's carrying up top makes him look like a decorative bay tree with two trunks. He's also got a suspiciously un-penis-like lump in the middle of his shorts. I'm pretty sure that wasn't there when I saw him getting off his bike outside the building the other week. Let's just say I won't be asking for a sock loan any time soon.

'Not to worry, not to worry…' says Doug, who seems to have taken over the recruitment drive. 'Hey, John… you're pretty sporty, aren't you?'

'I cycle a bit,' says the man in head to toe cycling gear.

'Then you'd be perfect,' says Doug. 'We need someone for the Spartacus race a week on Saturday.' John seems hesitant, but Doug continues. 'Should seal the deal with JC on this job – the race is pretty important to him…'

A cold shiver runs down my spine. And this time not because I've caught another glimpse of John's cycling shorts. Seal the deal? I knew I was on the back foot after the pitch, but surely Doug is overstating this a little. We've only been on the trial period for a week and a half. I can't have lost it already…

'OK,' says John. 'I'll do it.'

Immediately, I regret keeping my head down earlier. Maybe I should try to show willingness. There's only one space on the team, and now it's full, I can volunteer with impunity. That's got to count for something. What are the chances of actually having to do it?

I try to ignore that, thanks to the Law of Sod, the answer to that question is probably 100%, and volunteer myself.

'Sorry Tom – John's got first dibs,' says Doug.

The fact that I'm interested seems far more attractive to John than the race/job itself, and he suddenly becomes a bubbling pot of enthusiasm.

187

'Yeah, and I'm totally into it. It sounds wicked. Who wouldn't want to do the Spartan race?'

'Spartacus race,' I reply.

'Doesn't matter what it's called – I'm doing it, and you're not,' he snaps. 'Not like you're exactly sporty anyway, is it Tom?'

True, but I look slightly less terrible than you in Lycra. I mean not much, but, Jesus, it's like I'm talking to a melon stabbed with a couple of knitting needles.

'Well, tell you what,' says Doug. 'We'll put you down as official reserve.'

Official reserve. Probably the most glamorous of all roles that involves not actually being involved.

It's less than ten minutes later when Marina, our leading athlete, falls down the stairs and sprains her ankle.

I almost feel responsible.

Thursday

With Amanda away, work's just… work.

When I moved upstairs after my hour of accountancy today, I didn't massively notice a difference. The whole floor's just waiting to hear the outcome of JC's pitch, so we're basically doing admin while we stew. JC said the meeting went well, but when it comes to his own achievements, JC makes Pollyanna look like a bit of a downer.

But when it comes to us getting the pitch, I'm conflicted. Obviously, the company needs this to work or we're fucked, but it's definitely another nail in the coffin of me getting the job.

Meanwhile, everyone's talking about the Spartacus race. Maybe if I can prove myself in that, it might help me. I should probably do some training…

Damn it, I'm missing Amanda.

Friday

'We've got it!' JC exclaims as he bursts into the conference room. Acting cool about the washing powder ad has gone the way of a stubborn stain. 'We've fucking got, it idiots.'

'Thanks to my new ad idea,' JC brags, 'we just won ourselves a new client. Of course some credit must go to the dream team.' He points to Doug and John. Some? I mean, I think it's a terrible idea, but surely *all*. Doug must be used to this though, because he does a little fist pump – must be as good at it gets here. John looks smugly around the room. I see him checking if Gemma, one of the interns, is looking over. Annoyingly, she is and smiles. John appears to have successfully raised himself in the dominance hierarchy and is now getting smiled at by interns. Where's Charlie Brown to say 'Oh, brother' when you need him?

'Anyway, we're shooting next Wednesday, so we need everyone to be on call this weekend. Course, the production company's going to be doing the heavy lifting from now on, but we need to be available in case they have any questions about anything that doesn't involve picking up a camera and pressing "Record".' He laughs, smugly, and everyone else joins in. Everyone but me. I have some integrity.

JC looks over. I laugh too.

'Anyway – well done,' says JC, exiting the room with a flourish.

Everyone's pretty buzzed. Apparently the turnaround is never like this. It's normally months before things actually happen, but the shoot's already set up so it's happening immediately.

Later, I get an email from Amanda asking how things are going – it's really friendly and positive, only she keeps mentioning some guy called Vin. I'm assuming it's a guy. No women are called Vin. Well, outside of a Brandon Sanderson novel. Wow, my head is full of the kind of highbrow references that make women swoon.

But who cares either way? I'm just being jealous. I'm sure it's nothing. I'm pretty sure it's nothing.

Saturday

Mark's agreed to do some training with me today to prepare for the Spartan/Spartacus race. He's suggested we start off with a 5K run. It got my back up immediately. I mean, how's that something to 'start off' with? It's basically the equivalent of ordering a full steak dinner as an hors d'oeuvre. Only less fun. And more likely to give you a heart attack.

To be honest, I'm pretty unhappy to be exercising at all. Exercise is overrated. I mean, look at recent events. Hans sprained his wrist playing handball, two other people in the office have a pulled hamstring and a twisted ankle. I haven't twisted or sprained anything since I was fourteen. My last injury was in a school rugby match, in which I was a less-than-willing participant. That was the last time I was incapacitated. Since then, I've been pretty fucking capacitated. You know why? *Because I haven't exercised.* Says the uninjured soon-to-be-fat man with a low life expectancy.

The kids walk round with me to Mark and Karen's. Karen's agreed to take them for a play date while Mark and I 'push our bodies to the limits'. Well, *my* body to the limits.

Mark answers the door in activewear. It's pretty obvious he knows what he's doing. Either that or he's a mum in any coffee shop in south-west London on a weekday, but that's beside the point. I'm wearing beach shorts, a far-too-smart T-shirt, and a wool jumper that's as inappropriate for exercise as it is for a 60-degree wash cycle. Based on the outfit I'm rocking, my pre-work-out warm up should probably involve writing a will.

We head down to the river, ready for the torture session.

190

'OK – I've got a point I run to and back. It's just under 5K. Should take about half an hour.' Half an hour? We're running for half an hour?

Mark shoots off in what looks like a sprint, but is apparently a jog. He shouts at me to get started. In under three minutes my whole body is hurting. I've heard people say they had muscles aching they didn't know existed, but I've got things aching that aren't even muscles. My *ears* are hurting. I'm pretty sure they're not involved in jogging, but maybe I have a particularly weird gait. Like I'm somehow harnessing the weight of the lobes as an aid to propulsion. I also have pain in my left ball, which is freaking me out. Am I harnessing ball power as well? Maybe that's good. If I eat a bit of protein after this I could end up with a spectacularly well-built left testicle.

What makes it worse is Mark is actually trying to have a conversation with me.

'So what happened with you and that girl from the bar the other night?'

'A... man... da...'

'Yeah.'

'Job... fell... through... work... together... now.'

'So what?'

'Never... happen... think... going to be...'

'Sexually frustrated forever?'

'...sick.'

I double over on the floor, impressed with myself that I manage not to vomit.

'Come on,' says Mark, 'we're only halfway.'

'So we can turn back?'

'Halfway to *where* we turn back.'

Part of me dies inside. The only good news is I've now got pain in my right ball too, so hopefully they should develop symmetrically.

An hour later and we're finally back to the beginning. When Mark understood quite how unfit I was, he suggested I do the remainder of the distance as a speed walk. Apparently it's a very good form of exercise, rather than just an incredibly embarrassing way to go round the park.

Then we move on to stretches. Which I'm pretty sure you're actually meant to start with.

'No, they found out they're more effective if you warm up first,' explains Mark.

In what sense is a bloody half marathon a warm up? Maybe we can cool down by swimming the Channel.

We finish off by going to this outdoor gym bit by a playground and doing pull ups (Mark: three sets of twenty; me: one set of one), dips (Mark: three sets of twenty; me: two sets of half a one) and push-ups (Mark: fifty; me: ten.) Still ten's not *terrible*. Maybe that floor-thrust-a-thon I did a month or so ago is starting to pay off.

After that, I plead mercy and limp back to Mark's house. You know you're doing something un-fun, when you're desperate to stop spending time with your friend and get back to childcare.

Mark cooks us all lunch and I lie on their sofa unable to move. At four, in my most extravagant gesture since my children's birth, I order a taxi to take us the five-minute walk to our flat.

It's official. I am not Spartacus.

Sunday

Bed/sofa/mealtimes/sofa/bed. Haven't got as far as the living room. Kids may have remodelled.

Monday

Make it into work. Counting that as a result.

Tuesday

I wake up to another email from Amanda. It's all fairly standard stuff – there's a kiss at the end, but we're in advertising, so that doesn't really mean anything. Annoyingly there's also more Vin talk. I try to put it out of my mind and do a fifteen minute speed walk before heading into the office. Look at me go. Olympic athletes probably don't train this hard.

At 10:30 am, JC asks me to sit in on a meeting with the production company. I'm not meant to say anything – it's just a case of one-upping the client and the production company on numbers so we look like we care. Who those numbers are seems pretty irrelevant – I think I may have seen JC dressing the cleaner up in a suit. Well, a denim shirt and Palestinian desert scarf, but you get the idea.

The meeting room is full when we get there. There're four of the client, who look like vaguely normal people, five of the production company, who look somewhere between cool and normal, and ten of us, who look like arseholes.

There's also the director, who's Spanish but lives in Istanbul and is potentially the most pretentious man I've ever met. His presence is the only thing that stops me from wanting to kill myself for being part of the agency. He's currently holding court about the meaning of washing our clothes – how it represents a return to innocence and a cleansing of sins. I thought it was because people wouldn't be friends with us if we were covered in stains and smelt weird. Ironically, the director looks like he doesn't

193

wash much, so maybe the whole meaning thing *is* more central to him.

We start talking about the colours of the set. This is exciting. I can only imagine the subtle psychological manipulation that goes into this. Do we go with red to excite the viewer, or green to create a feeling of tranquillity which encourages trust in the brand…?

'I like purple,' JC shoots out as an initial bid. Everyone nods. They all like purple. But why? JC's probably about to drop some psychological bombshell. I'm waiting; here it comes… any second…

No. It appears he just likes purple.

'I like purple too,' says Poonam, who seems to be the most important person from the client. 'But I also like blue.'

JC nods, like she's just said something profound. 'Blue's good. Blue's very good…' He pauses and then the thunderbolt hits him. 'But have you thought about green?'

Poonam's reality explodes. 'I *haven't* thought about green,' she says, like JC has just invented it. 'But I like it.'

A few more 'ideas' are thrown around accompanied by nods, and low-level noises that would be more appropriate at a fireworks display. I really feel like I'm missing something here, something unspoken that everybody knows about apart from me. But it really does seem like people are just listing names of colours.

I think about joining in just to see what happens. No one's done orange yet, surely that's going to knock people sideways. I'm just about to say it when John pipes up, 'What about orange?' Fucking idea-nicker strikes again. Suddenly the mood in the room changes. A chorus of, 'No, not orange,' fills the room. John looks suitably chastened. Glad I didn't come out with that. Phew. What an idiot.

The list starts to broaden to less 'Route One' colours – magenta, cobalt… I'm half expecting someone to pull out a cyan.

Suddenly the director stands up, and spits on the ground. I think it might have been prompted by the production manager mentioning turquoise. 'Brown. And then… white. No, not white – grey.'

Suddenly there is silence. The messiah has come down from the mountain with his weird white-person afro, and has told us in a strange Catalonian/Turkish accent: 'Brown and white. No – grey.'

After that, we move on. Point after point is decided in the same way… a bunch of random motiveless ideas, trumped by the director coming in with another random motiveless idea delivered with a bit more confidence. I always thought advertisers were master manipulators: inserting the instruction of 'add an egg' to a packet of instant cake mix, to create a feeling of agency and harnessing a Freudian symbol of motherhood to access the cook's subconscious need to nurture. But no; they just quite like purple.

Post-meeting, JC takes me to one side.

'Like the way you kept your mouth shut today.' Really? Maybe I've got what it takes to move forward with this advertising thing.

'You should pop along to the shoot Wednesday,' he continues. 'Doug's going to have his hands full, so keep an eye on John, make sure he doesn't pipe up with any more of that 'orange' shit.'

Will do, JC, will do.

Score one for Tom Cooper.

Wednesday

I get to the shoot at 8:00 am. The unit base is basically a car park with a few buses parked round. I don't know what I'm meant to be doing, so I head over to the other agency people and say hi. John looks down his nose at me with a bit of a sneer.

'Decided to come and watch a successful idea become a reality, have you?'

'No, I was told to be here,' I state. *To make sure you didn't suggest 'orange' again, if you must know, idiot.*

Breakfast is amazing. You can literally have anything – there are all these trestle tables with every cold breakfasting delicacy you can imagine. But I hesitate – I don't want to look like I'm just here for the free food, and besides, I'm meant to be training. Luckily, John leads the way, and tucks in like he's training for an eating competition, stuffing his face with anything and everything the buffet has to offer. It's basically a repeat of the orange scenario from the other day. Seeing other people's reactions is the only thing that stops me from doing it myself. Instead, I take a small glass of buttermilk and avocado smoothie, which doesn't make any sense but is delicious, and drink it with my pinkie raised, like a debutante at their first ball.

I'm less controlled when the catering truck opens up. I ascend the little wooden steps to the far-too-high serving hatch, feeling like a child at a hot dog stand. I'm behind someone who has everything, so I follow suit. Then I realise he's in the crew, and might actually have a bit more to do than me. But I con myself – a plate of bacon, sausages and eggs is good for my new regime. If it wasn't for the toast and multiple hash browns, it's basically Atkins.

After gorging myself out of sight on the top floor of the dining bus, I head to set. We're sitting in what everyone calls 'video village', although it definitely lacks the idyllic qualities that might imply. 'Video industrial estate' maybe. It consists of three video monitors surrounded by plastic chairs and a sofa for the client, in the middle of a warehouse. There's also another food table, stacked with pastries and biscuits. Maybe the aim is to put the client into a carb coma, so they'll sign off on anything. Well, if John doesn't clear the table before they get a look in.

But I'm excited. I'm on a film shoot. This must be what it was like for Scorsese and Spielberg… if they'd been shooting potentially offensive adverts about washing powder. But who cares? It's *similar*. Tom Cooper has got his buzz on.

* * *

It's ten o'clock before the camera rolls. I'm bored out of my mind. Nothing's happening apart from people talking about lighting and working out what they want in the background. It seems irrelevant. When has anyone ever watched an ad and said – *well, that looks good, and the kids seem happy, but I'm not going to buy something owned by a family with that vase on the kitchen counter.*

I'm starting to understand the constant presence of nibbles. It's the only thing that gets you through the day. Even when we start filming, it's just a random shot of a guy walking into a flat. But everyone's got an *opinion* on it. I keep my mouth shut, just saying, 'I see your point,' and, 'interesting thought,' whenever someone talks to me. It seems to work and John's keeping schtum, mainly because he's had a mouth full of food since the start of day, but *technically* I'm still doing my job.

It's just before lunch when they start to film something I do have an opinion on. The guy puts his T-shirt in the wash, and then *gets in with it.* I'm not sure if this was in the original pitch, but the director suggested it, and everyone seems to like it – apparently it was what happened in the ads they're spoofing, but I'm pretty sure it's a terrible idea. Especially when the guy comes out with his clean T-shirt and is black. I get that they're trying to subvert the idea, but couldn't another interpretation be that the dirt had come off the t-shirt and *turned the guy brown.* Which would make this advert *incredibly offensive.*

No one else seems concerned. And I've been told to keep my

mouth shut so I do. But this seems like a spectacularly bad idea. They really should have gone with our idea. Even the Dirty Bertie version would have been better. Maybe I should mention it to someone – perhaps if he just doesn't get *into* the washing machine... I'm next to John, so I test the waters.

'John – don't you think there's a chance people might think this is a bit... racist?'

John finishes off his mouthful of flapjack and shakes his head. 'You just don't get it.'

'Oh, no. I get it – I'm just worried he shouldn't be getting *in* the washing machine.'

'Look Tom, I won. You lost. Don't be a bad loser. I don't even know why you're here.' He's got a point. Now he's keeping his mouth shut, I don't know either.

I nod and wander off into the darkness of the studio. There's a guy sitting in front of a few computer screens on his own, far away from the clients and agency – a little oasis of non-political conversation.

'What do you do?'

'D.I.' Well, that's a pair of initials that could literally stand for anything. Drug Informant... Duplicitous Interloper...

'What's that?'

'Digital Intermediate – I convert everything into files for editing.'

I take this in for a second, then ask him what's on my mind. 'What do you *think* of this?'

He looks at me properly for the first time, trying to make sure it's not a trap. 'Honestly?'

'Yeah.'

'Massively offensive. Like the dirt's come off the shirt and gone onto his skin. I'm going to make sure my name's taken off any paperwork.'

'That's what I think too. I should mention it to someone.'

'What do you do?'

'I'm in a trial position at the ad agency.'

'And is the client happy?'

'At the moment.'

'Then my advice to you is: keep your fucking mouth shut.'

Evening

Amanda's back tomorrow. A day of keeping quiet on set has given me time to think. Maybe what Mark said was right. So what if we work together? So what if she's my boss? Maybe it's just everything in the news – so many bloody men seem to be sexual predators, you start worrying if *you're* one. But she's *my* boss. If it was the other way round, I'd have to tread carefully, but as it is, I'd hardly be Harvey Weinsteining my way into her pants. '*You'd better go out with me, or before you know it you might lose a creative assistant on a trial period.*'

I should think about this from her point of view. Maybe she's worried about asking *me* out. Yeah. That's probably the only reason she hasn't done it. I'm… reasonably attractive. Isn't that what everyone wants? A reasonably attractive creative assistant on a trial period? The moniker itself just basically says 'sexy', the office equivalent of 'surgeon' or 'fireman'.

I should do it. I should ask Amanda out. It might end up awkward, but that's OK. Awkwardness is the stuff of life. Men have crashed and burned throughout the ages, and who am I to scoff in the face of tradition? I'll do it. I'm going to bloody do it.

Friday

Everyone's feeling pretty pumped about the shoot yesterday. That's probably a good sign. JC actually popped open a bottle of bubbly at eleven to celebrate. No one touched it, so I didn't either. Maybe it's a test. There aren't any laws against entrapment in the advertising industry.

I manage to do my second 'run' of the week at lunchtime. Probably a bad idea as it means tomorrow's race will be smack bang in the middle of my recovery period. There goes that extra inch on my calves by Monday.

Amanda gets in at four. She wheels her suitcase across the office floor to comments of, 'Did you get me a present?' and, 'Sorry you have to slum it with us again,' but she doesn't stop until she gets to me. I think that's a good sign.

'Hey…' she says tentatively.

'Hey,' I return.

There's a slight pause that says everything unspoken between us. And then Amanda moves onto what we *can* talk about.

'How did the shoot go?'

'OK… I think. Well… everyone else seems to think. I actually thought it was massively racist.'

'Yeah,' she muses. 'The New York guys were a bit worried when I told them the idea. Vin thought it was hilarious. Until he realised it was actually happening.'

'Oh right, Vin. I think you mentioned him in your email.'

'You'd like him. He's really funny.' That's annoying – I was really hoping he wasn't. I mean he's already more successful and handsome than me. Not that I looked him up on LinkedIn or anything.

'Um…' Amanda continues. She's hesitating for some reason. Like it's bad news. 'There's something I need to talk to you about.' I knew it. I fucking knew it.

'Oh right,' I say, trying to pretend my world isn't falling down around me. I hardly know her – she's just someone from work – It doesn't matter, I tell myself. It doesn't matter at all.

'What is it?' I ask.

'When I was in New York… I…'

'Amanda!' comes a cry from across the floor. JC has stepped out from his office. 'The prodigal daughter returns. Come on. I need you to fill me in on what's been happening.'

'Um, sure… I just need to put my bag in my office.'

'Tombo'll do that for you. I'm like a Windows operating system. I need to be up to date.' He raises his arm in a gesture that suggests it's about to be around Amanda's shoulder, so she'd better get a move on.

'I'll talk to you later,' Amanda whispers to me, as she heads into JC's office/grasp.

She's in there for the rest of the afternoon. At one point Doug and John get called in for a few minutes. They too get arms round the shoulders, so at least he's not sexist with his inappropriate physical contact.

I want to hang round until she gets out, but I've got to pick the kids up from the childminder. I love my children, but when it comes to messing up your life, they're bloody annoying. As I'm putting my coat on, John comes over and hangs round my desk.

'Nice to see Amanda again, is it?'

It stops me like a rabbit who's got a crush on some headlights. Fuck – he's picked up a vibe from me. That's not cool. That's not cool at all. If Mr No Social Skills has worked out I fancy her, everybody in the office must bloody know.

'Um, I guess,' I say, trying to act all cool. 'What is a trainee without a mentor?' I joke in a mock-serious voice, but John is having none of it.

'Well, sounds like she had a good time.' He says, attempting to load it with meaning, but overemphasizing the words like one of the child actors in the first *Harry Potter*. 'Seems to be talking about that "Vin" guy a lot.' He winks, then wanders off, job done.

I wrap myself up in my coat and head out, walking home engulfed in multiple layers of clothing, like a present that nobody wants to open.

Evening

I have a depressing drink with Mark in the pub. I would have cancelled, but didn't dare due to potential babysitter reaction. Should probably find someone less aggressive to watch my children.

We talk about the whole Vin thing. Mark thinks it's not necessarily bad and suggests I see if she's free to come to their Christmas party on Sunday. I'd actually forgotten it was happening, so it's lucky he mentioned it.

And why not? It's daytime, it's casual, it's also their kid's birthday, which does make it kind of weird, but still… why not? I'll ask her tomorrow. After the race. Maybe tonight wasn't a total loss after all.

Saturday

It's the day of the Spartacus race and I'm feeling ready. I'm trying not to think about the whole Vin thing, and strangely, the few bits of training I've done this week actually seem to have had some effect. The regular exercise everyone else is doing is the equivalent of wearing a coat indoors. They'd do a week of three speed walks and simply wouldn't feel the benefit. Whereas me… I'm a new man. Plus they've got far too little body fat, so probably *do* need to wear a coat indoors.

I've also been to the shops and got a better outfit. I look like someone who actually does sports. Sure, it's all cheap Nike knock-offs, but if I maintain my distance, I look good. And just because 'all the gear and no idea' rhymes, it doesn't mean it's true. I'm sure there're plenty of very positive things that rhyme too… 'All the clothes, one of the pros' … 'Full sportswear, a certain flair' … 'Slick attire, the man's on fire' – I could go on. Actually, those took quite a long time to think of so I probably couldn't, but three's enough to prove a point.

The course is basically a loop we run round before relaying to the next member of our team. Annoyingly I'm last, as the order is alphabetical (based on first names to keep it 'informal'). It's far more pressure than I wanted. Where are all the Zachs and Umbertos when you need them? Even a Vicki would have done. If I'm ever in a position to hire people, don't blame me if I have an irrational bias in favour of people with late first name initials. *Well, Winthrop, I see there's a ten-year gap on your CV and you have a conviction for assault, but the moment I read your forename, I knew you were the guy for us.*

What makes the Spartacus race different is that there's basically an obstacle course in the way. We have to climb netting, jump through hoops and lift buckets – you know, like Spartacus would have done. But maybe it's a good thing. I'm clearly not the best runner, but obstacles might even the playing field. Besides, I was pretty convinced I had exceptional agility as a child. I'm not even sure I know what agility is, now or then, but I was pretty sure I had it… In my head, it's a combination of balance and bendiness. I think my reasoning was that I was basically Spider-Man. Spider-Man had good strength, speed and agility, and, as my strength and speed were decidedly middling, by a process of elimination, agility was probably my thing. Not that that idea has stayed in my brain for the last thirty years or anything.

Anyway, as there's no reason to think I have exceptionally low agility, it's possible I might be able to keep up with enemy agency employees with late alphabet first names. The downside is the last person from each team (i.e. me), after running the regular circuit, has to leave the course, jump over what looks like a pile of logs, then go to the finishing line. Seems fine. I just have to hope I don't trip up.

Amanda is first for our team. There's another woman and two guys up against her. The woman looks ridiculously fit – like she can bench press a cow and crack nuts with her buttocks. Not that anyone should do that.

The gun goes off, and Nutcracker shoots off into the lead alongside one of the guys, but Amanda's not far behind. She goes down under the crawl obstacle at a semi-decent speed and makes it out of the other end reasonably close to the others. Nice. She's actually pretty good and holds her own most of the way round. Still, I'm dreading my turn. That is, until I see the fourth obstacle: a spear. You actually get to *throw a spear*. Suddenly, I'm interested. If someone had told me I could've spent the last week doing spear-throwing practice, it would have totally changed my attitude to getting ready for this race.

By the time it gets to John, our team and Creative X are neck and neck, with the others behind us. We're actually in with a chance. John goes out of the gate full throttle. He may not be cycling, but he's actually got some speed on him. Probably pretty rubbish agility though. He goes under the crawl space and gets stuck. Even though it's probably going to lose us the race, I can't help but cheer inside. That'll teach you to nick my idea. He edges out backwards and does a ten burpee penalty. Still, it's not much of a hindrance, so he's not far behind afterwards. The rest of the course he kicks ass, actually managing to take the lead. By the time he hands over to Sarah from HR he's substantially ahead, and everyone's high-fiving him as she takes off round the track. Fucking John.

I move onto the start line, ready for Sarah to tag me. A woman who looks like Theresa May comes and joins me. She's from Creative X, who are still our only real rivals. I'm rubbish, but I'm feeling confident. I must be able to outrun Theresa bloody May. But then, some bloke from Ogglebox comes and joins us. They're third. And he's massive. And probably really fit. If this was a fight I'd be dead. But it's not. It's a weird adult obstacle course that may favour people with imaginary agility. I look him in the eye and give him a nod. He nods back at me. *All right, person in far better physical shape than me. It's on.*

Sarah's still just about in the lead when she reaches me. I'm slightly annoyed that it's probably mainly due to John, but I can't think about that now. This gives me the opportunity to do averagely well and take it home for the team. That, or massively fuck it up.

She tags me and I leave the line as fast as I can. I'm already out of breath by the time I reach the crawl obstacle, and Theresa has caught up with me, but I figure I can get the lead back while crawling. However, as I approach the obstacle my confidence fades rapidly. For the first time I see what we're crawling under: barbed wire. *Barbed fucking wire.* Who the hell thought that was a good idea? This is the material used by sheep farmers and concentration camps. It's not meant to be a part of leisure activities. Still, I'm a lot thinner than John; maybe I can make it.

I get under and I'm actually pretty good. All those times rescuing Carrie when she was stuck at the soft play are paying off. I see the built guy behind me, struggling to fit. Those muscles aren't so useful now, are they? Except he's moving pretty fast. He's clearly got some Jocko Willink win-at-any-cost mentality though, and is just cutting up his back as he crawls. What is wrong with people? Isn't this meant to be fun?

I get out just after the Maybot, and we run together to the next obstacle. It's clear that she's actually quite a lot fitter than me. I see the guy coming out of the crawl obstacle, his shirt completely shredded. A shiver goes down my spine. I'm not sure I've got what it takes to win this. Sure, I'll give it my best, but *bleeding*? I'm not even sure I'm up-to-date on my tetanus shot.

Then we get to the bucket hoist. I start pulling on the rope and it's surprisingly doable.

I feel powerful. I feel strong. I feel manly.

'You're doing the woman's one,' shouts the steward. I look to the left and see a far bigger bucket waiting for me. Shit. I move to the new bucket. It is FUCKING heavy. I can pull it up, but only just. Theresa's absolutely nailing it. My hands and arms are killing. I even feel the ear pain coming back. And I'm sure it's only a matter of time before the pain moves ball-wards.

I feel weak. I fell powerless. I feel completely and utterly emasculated.

Built guy comes over and lifts it hand over hand at rapid speed. He must have accidentally got the woman's one as well. I check. Nope – he's just twenty times stronger than me. I look over and see Amanda shouting 'come on', not seeming to notice I'm massively embarrassing myself. The bucket reaches the top and I start to lower it. It has to hit the ground gently, otherwise you get fined burpees. Unfortunately, I let go of the rope halfway down and it starts burning through my hands. Just in time, I grab it and the momentum pulls me about six feet into the air. My trajectory slows as the bucket reaches the ground with a genteel plop. I look over at the steward; she gives me the thumbs up. I did it. I bloody did it. I drop from the rope and run on. The guy is a few seconds behind me. And not showing any signs of tiring.

Next up is traversing a rope over water. Given the presence of barbed wire, it goes through my head that maybe they've introduced a shoal of piranhas into it to up the stakes. I straddle the rope and start to slide myself across. Within seconds I'm getting major crotch burn, whereas Theresa isn't batting an eye. It's completely unfair that they have a different weight bucket for women, and absolutely no consideration for the fact that men have far more inconvenient genitals for this kind of activity. Not that it'll bother the guy behind me. In a few minutes, he'll be holding the trophy above his head, smiling like a madman, a single remaining testicle hanging from his decimated scrotum.

I flip underneath the rope and it's a lot easier. As long as you don't touch the water, it's allowed, and I start catching up to Theresa. By the time I ring the bell, we're neck and neck. We drop off together and she sprints towards the next task with me speed walking close behind. The rest of our agency cheer, thinking I'm being cocky, but it really is the fastest way for me to move right now.

Theresa manages to maintain her lead over the next few obstacles, but I'm not far behind.

And then we get to the spear. It's the only one I've been looking forward to. As I reach the obstacle, Theresa's already got hers and chucks it at the target as I pick mine up. Her spear goes flying through the air and I throw mine, desperately hoping I hit the target. Then suddenly I hear a scream. I look over at Theresa and she's got her hands over her mouth. Then I look back to the course. There, in the middle of the range, is a steward with Theresa's spear through his shoulder. Oh my GOD. I guess that's why you should get these things professionally organised. Theresa runs towards the guy shouting, 'I know first aid!' I start to go over too, only to be nearly impaled myself by the built guy's javelin. He's still bloody competing!?!

He runs off towards the next obstacle. I'm completely lost as to what to do, when JC screams from over by the impaled steward, 'He's fine. Run! Bloody RUN!'

I hesitate, but JC's having none of it. 'If you want to keep your bloody job, fucking MOVE!'

I start running despite myself. I couldn't deal with a spear wound anyway. I may as well try to stay employed.

The penultimate obstacle is a wall with holes where you have to go over one, under the next and then through the third one about three times. The guy is way ahead of me, but he's being slow. I realise this is my chance. The type of obstacle that might favour someone with *agility*.

I run and jump over the wall, then go under the next and through the third. I'm actually good at this. I'm gaining on him. The next one and we're neck and neck. By the third I'm ahead. I did it. I do have agility. I knew it. I'm Spider-Man. I'm fucking Spider-Man. I run with renewed enthusiasm to the final obstacle – I've still got a stitch, but it doesn't matter anymore. I'm DOING THIS. This must be what people mean when they talk about breaking through the pain. You just have to be strong. Or fucking SPIDER-MAN!!!

Then I get to the last obstacle, and I realise what it is. I'm fucked. There're these massive boulders you have to carry for twenty-five metres. There're big ones and small ones. I'm tempted to go for the small one, but I know it'll just be another sexist conspiracy against slightly weak men. I pick up the big one. I think it's the heaviest thing I've ever picked up in my life. Like two week's worth of shopping plus the car you'd put it into. There's no way I can carry this twenty-five metres. I take a step forward and then have to rest for a second before the next one. Meanwhile, my competitor's just caught up and picks the boulder up with ease and starts to move forward at a slow steady pace.

He's not exactly fast, but it's enough to leave me in the dust. Fuck. I've failed. I've bloody failed.

But then I have an idea. I shout at the steward, who's understandably distracted by her colleague having a gigantic spike through his shoulder.

'What's the penalty?'

'Sorry, what?'

'What's the penalty for failing this?'

'Um… burpees?'

'How many?

'Twenty-five.'

I look at the built guy. He's about five metres in and covering a metre every three to four seconds. I use the power of accountancy (also known as 'maths') and realise: I might be able to do this.

I start to burpee. They're knackering, but no one seems too concerned about form. I feel like a complete idiot doing them while Hercules ahead of me is carrying a giant boulder – if he's Spartacus, I'm the Colosseum's head cheerleader – but I push through. This is my best shot. Besides, it takes a real man to perform a truly unmanly act.

I finish my twenty-five, and see the muscle-head resting about three metres from the end. I run as fast as I can and before I know it, I'm in the lead. I'm going to win this. I'm going to be the company hero. Fifty metres ahead is the pile of logs that I've got to jump over. So what? Who can't jump over a pile of logs? *Way to end on a low point, organisers.* But I don't care. I've won. I've bloody won!

And then I see the flaming torch. A man's carrying it over to the logs… The logs which he then proceeds to set on *fire*. I find myself slowing down. We're meant to jump through a wall of fire? Why did no one tell me about this? This really should have been the first thing they led with.

I reach the wall of flames and come to a stop. I look behind me. I could probably get a few burpees in before he catches up. I just need to ask the steward.

'How many burpees for this one?'

The steward looks confused, then suddenly twigs my meaning.

'Oh, no,' she says. 'You can't burpee on this one. You have to do it. '

Damn you, Spartacus race. DAMN YOU.

I look round at my workmates screaming at me. I take a few steps back, ready to take on the wall of flames. And I GO.

I jump through the fire and suddenly… I'm out the other side… and I'm OK. I'm OK! I sprint towards the finish line. No one else has even reached the flames yet. I'm home free. I can hear Amanda shouting encouragement behind me, and suddenly everything feels right in the world again.

I'm nearly at the finish line when I smell it. Burning. It must be the wall of fire, but, strangely, it doesn't seem to be getting any fainter. If anything, it's getting more intense. And then I feel the heat on my back. And I realise Amanda's shouts of, 'You're on fire!' were not a compliment. I'm on fire. I'm on actual fire.

I look over my shoulder and see the flames coming up my back. It must be the knock off Nike fabric. Damn it. Never buy cheap polyester sports clothes. Especially if you might have to jump through fire.

The finish line's five metres ahead. There lies victory. But, for God's sake, I'm on fire. I see JC shouting, 'Keep going, I'll put you out,' as he runs towards me with a small water bottle. It's a quarter full. That's not going to be enough. I make an executive decision and start sprinting away from the finish line and back towards the first water obstacle. I can smell my hair singeing and I run faster than I ever have in my life. Behind me I hear the big guy celebrating as he reaches the finish line. If he didn't stop for someone getting impaled, he's hardly going to for second degree burns.

Seconds later, I jump into the muddy lake before me. As the sound of hissing subsides, I lie there in relief. Twenty seconds later, JC appears above me looking very angry. He pours his quarter bottle of water over my face.

The fact that I'm surrounded by water on all sides makes it difficult to interpret as a positive gesture.

Job prospects not looking good.

After the Race

'I feel like such an idiot,' I say. 'I should have just finished.'

'You were on fire,' replies Amanda. 'It's a good excuse.'

My back's feeling sore, but the paramedic said it was nothing serious. And it *is* a good excuse. Definitely better than norovirus. Maybe Sally should jot 'being on fire' down for next time the kids are ill.

'I'm not sure JC'll see it that way.'

'Well, he's an idiot. Everyone in New York's feeling pretty uncomfortable about how he's running things. Between you and me, I don't know how much longer he'll be in charge.'

'Probably at least till the end of my trial period.'

She starts to contradict me, then stops. 'Probably, yeah.'

She smiles at me. And it feels like a genuine smile. Now's the time – I should ask her to the party tomorrow. That whole Vin thing was just me being paranoid. *What are you doing tomorrow?* It's as simple as that. *What are you doing tomorrow?*

'What are you doing tomorrow?' I try to sound casual, but it ends up *too* casual. Like I'm just interested in what she's doing tomorrow, rather than asking her to spend it with me.

'Meeting my new niece in the morning,' she explains, getting out her phone to show me a picture. It's not a problem. It's the morning. No one wants people hanging round all day when they've got a new baby. I just need to be more specific in the follow up.

Amanda suddenly notices the time on her phone. 'Shit. I've got to go.'

'Everything OK?'

'I've got to get back for a Skype call – sorry.'

'Oh. Important?'

'Just…' she hesitates, 'Vin.'

And there it is… Vin. She's already getting up and leaving.

'Sorry – look we really need to talk. Let's try to make some time on Monday.'

As I watch her walking off, I can't fool myself any longer – something definitely happened in New York. I guess in-company romance isn't such a big deal when the person you're doing it with lives an ocean away.

Fuck. Fucking Vin.

Oh crap. She's fucking Vin.

Sunday

I'm in no mood for Mark and Karen's Christmas bash, but it's also Amelie's birthday, so Arthur and Carrie won't let me skip it. It's become an annual event. What started off as Amelie's party has morphed into something else completely. At least I think so. Pretty sure Amelie wasn't pushing to have Mark's friend Ranj on the guest list. Maybe she's hoping to learn how to 'neg' the kids' entertainer.

I'm in the kitchen when, for once in my life, Ranj actually comes over to *me*. 'I know you, don't I?'

'Yeah – Tom. We hung out in a bar a few weeks ago.'

He tries to place me. 'Nah – think it was something else.' For God's sake.

I try to jog his memory. 'You went home with some girl who ran an art gallery...'

'Luciana...' His words trail off into a kind of dreamy reverie.

'How did that go? Successful bit of 'negging'?' I joke. Sarcastically.

He stops me dead. 'She broke my heart.'

'Oh, right.' Maybe she was just using him to soften up his better-looking friend... actually, he was there with me. Luciana *really* hated me.

I try to engage him in something else, but the conversation is over. Ranj is deep in his heartache. He just wants to be alone.

'Excuse me,' he stutters. 'I think I'm going to go and watch Smartie Artie.'

Ranj heads off to the kids' entertainer and I notice Gary's over the other side of the room. I haven't spoken to him since I broke up his marriage, but I can see him looking over. Talking to people at kids' parties is always awkward, but this is really taking the biscuit. Oo. Biscuit. I might nick a Party Ring from the kids' table.

Gary taps me on the shoulder.

'Tom – could I have a quick chat?'

'Do you think that's a good idea?'

'I just wanted to say sorry. About what happened with Sally.' Does he expect me to *forgive* him?

'Well, actually...' he continues, 'nothing happened. She was just being a bit flirty. Things weren't going well with Samantha, and I leant in and kissed her... but she just pushed me away.'

'Oh. Right,' I reply. It was almost like... she was being faithful. Did the kids just have completely the wrong idea about what happened? Do I?

213

'Anyway, Sammy and I are back together now, so I hope we can move on from it and everything?'

'Um, yeah… sure,' man-my-wife-rejected. He's clearly looking for something else though.

'Anyway, you said something before – and I'm sure you were just angry – something about me being a… pre-pubescent Muppet… I think? Can't remember exactly. But something like that. Exactly that. Just a bit hurtful, that's all.'

I think he's expecting me to say sorry. To let bygones be bygones. I think about being magnanimous. About putting it all in the past… But… nah; that'll teach you to try and get off with my wife.

'That's a shame,' I reply. 'Anyway – excuse me. I'm going to go and watch Smartie Artie. Apparently he has this hilarious new high-voiced puppet…'

Monday – The Shit Hits the Fan

The news comes in at 10:00 am. Someone's leaked a rough edit of the ad on YouTube and it's gone viral. Apparently my instinct that it was massively racist was shared by… the *world*.

We watch as the ad spreads across social media, into news outlets, and eventually to our clients, who start calling and cancelling their accounts. At 11:15, JC summons the sales guys and the whole of the creative team into the conference room. We've got some business-saving to do.

'Right. Major problemo. You've probably heard. Turns out the general public… and the press… and the Equality and Human Rights Commission… haven't quite *got* the ad. Satire's lost on these people. You want to bring them up to your level, but they keep dragging you down to theirs.' He turns to Jake, the head of client accounts. 'OK – what's the sit?' His abbreviation doesn't quite land. '…u…' still nothing '…ation?'

Jake gives us the lowdown. 'Well, so far we've lost eight smaller clients… plus Tesco, Virgin Mobile…' – he looks down at his beeping phone – '…and Whole Foods – we just lost Whole Foods.'

All the colour has drained from JC's face. I'm not sure being more white is what this company needs right now. But JC's not going to be beaten. He gathers himself, ready to rally the troops, only to be interrupted again by Jake's phone beeping.

'Oh and chocolate,' Jake pipes up, '…we just lost chocolate.' Makes sense – probably worried we'd channel all our resources into Milky Bar.

JC gathers himself again. 'Well… looks like we're bleeding clients like a medieval doctor,' he jokes. No one laughs. 'We need to think damage limitation. Jake – you need to call everyone ASAP; tell them we're dealing with this.'

'On it.' Jake's phone beeps again.

'Don't tell me we've lost another one.'

'No,' says Jake, 'just a potential one. Our negotiations with The White Company just fell through.' That stands to reason. They were treading on thin ice with that name at the best of times.

'OK – get on it.' Jake runs from the room followed by his team and we see them through the glass divide, spreading across the office making calls on their mobiles, like an army battalion on a charm offensive.

JC turns to the remains of the meeting. 'Right – any ideas?'

'I think we just explain what we were trying for,' explains Doug. 'Subverting racism rather than… doing it.'

'Good thinking. And if you're ever caught in a stampede, maybe hand the lead bison a handwritten letter to explain why you shouldn't be crushed underfoot. Fucking moron.'

Annoyingly, JC's right. Now is not the time for reason. And Doug seems suitably chastened. But JC hasn't finished yet.

'I can't believe we went with your bloody idea. I knew it was dodgy.' Rather predictably, the creative credit has been returned to its original owner. Doug looks like he's just come out of three rounds with Conor McGregor. John seems like he's actually shrunk to half his normal size, i.e. his legs and head look small, but his weird body is kind of average.

It strikes me there might be an upside to this – I'm back in the running for the job. Well, if there's still a company in two weeks' time, that is...

'People who aren't responsible for this monumental fuck up – ideas?'

Amanda puts up her hand hesitantly. 'Obviously, we need to put it by New York, but my feeling is we should probably just... apologise.'

'Fuck New York. They don't get our culture and they won't be up for another two hours anyway.' He says it like it's evidence of laziness, rather than a consequence of the time difference. 'I'm taking the lead on this. This company has flourished under me for twenty years. We don't need New York to come and bail us out.'

By the end of the day, we've lost 60% of our clients.

New York coming to bail us out might not actually have been so bad.

Tuesday

I go up to the office at ten like normal, only to find the whole place buzzing with activity. Everybody looks like they've been in for ages, and at the centre of it all is this incredibly handsome guy, going round the office giving people things to do. JC's skulking next to his assistant, trying to look like he's busy, but it's pretty clear he's been outranked and is trying to pretend otherwise. The handsome guy looks weirdly familiar. It could be just that he's reminiscent of every billboard I've seen in the last six months. Then, I suddenly recognize him from his LinkedIn page. It's Vin. It's bloody Vin. He's not in New York. He's here. And he's even more handsome than his bloody photo.

He turns to me.

'You?' he says in a full-on American accent. 'Who are you?'

'Tom.'

'Oh, yeah. Where've you been?'

'Um… downstairs – JC likes me to do an hour in Accounting before I come up here.' Why do I feel like I'm not the alpha male in this situation?

Vin rolls his eyes in disgust. I'm pretty sure it's at JC's management rather than me, but I'm not 100% sure.

'OK – Amanda's got the briefs – I've managed to persuade about twenty clients to delay their decisions to leave, but we need to wow them with new stuff, so no more accounting till this is over, OK?'

I nod and head to Amanda's office, stealing another glance at Vin. He's so handsome. Like a bloody Scandinavian model or something. Of course Amanda prefers him to me. He's like a Greek god – the nearest I get to that is having white bits in my beard. And a dad with a temper. I'm more like the Greek bloody economy.

Vin notices me looking and gives me a smile, as if to say – 'Yes, I am better than you'. I smile back to try and avoid the implication, but feel like a complete beta loser. It's strange; I never really cared about being 'manly', but now that I seem to have been massively out-manlied by a sexual competitor, I feel awful. Like I've just been bullwhipped with his penis.

That came across as far more homoerotic than I was hoping. That said – he is very handsome.

Wednesday

The office has calmed down a bit, although everyone seems to have developed a new American-style work ethic under Vin's rule. As much as I resent him for coming here and wrecking any hopes I had with Amanda, he's actually pretty decent as a boss. Maybe he doesn't realise I'm on a trial period, but he seems to be treating me more like an equal member of the team than JC ever did. Maybe it's because now, the whole company's on a trial period.

What's worse is Vin's stolen Amanda to help him spearhead the comeback, so I'm working exclusively with Hans. Hans is a nice guy and all, but, from the few weeks we've worked together, it's clear he's possibly the least creative person I've ever met. I mean he looks creative, he dresses creative, but by the time he gets to the office he's got nothing. It's like he just spunks it all out at the wardrobe every morning. Maybe one day he'll come in wearing a shirt and V-neck jumper and spend the rest of the day blowing our tiny minds. But until then, he's useless. We did some word association the other week when we were first talking about washing powder. His contribution went, 'Detergent, white, powder, cleans, clothes.' I'm pretty sure that's just a sentence describing what washing powder does that's been over-punctuated with commas.

Anyway, we've got a pitch for a custard ad to sort out and, unless it's going to consist of the words, 'Yellow, sauce, for, puddings,' it's sort of my responsibility. That said, it's the biggest client the company's got left, so there're four other teams on it as well. But it'd be nice if we were the ones that cracked it.

Cracked... Real custard isn't all it's cracked up to be. Nah, rubbish. Agggh.

I can see Vin and Amanda in their office. I try not to look, but I can't help it occasionally. They're super touchy feely. Kind of like JC and Amanda, but OK because both people are doing it. God, I wish I was really handsome. How great would life be if you looked like that? David Gandy-level great, that's how.

But I'm starting to accept the fact that Amanda and I aren't going to end up together. I wish I wasn't such a dreamer – imagining what it'd be like to grow old with someone before the end of a first date. I was the same way at school. Staring at some girl across the classroom, completely unable to ask her out. Feeling that pain in your stomach that's sort of like a sickness that won't go away until you fall asleep. But I've never had that before as an adult. Not that I've never fancied anyone – but if someone rejects you, you just don't see them any more...

I need to get out of here. I'll finish the trial period, so I'll know if I can get the job, but then I'll leave. Whether that be to the Accounts department or somewhere else, I don't know. But I can't feel like this any more.

So I have to go.

Thursday

I've got the day off to go to the nursery/school nativity plays. The ones my kids are in – I'm not a weirdo. And by 'weirdo', I don't mean paedophile. Seeing a children's Christmas show that doesn't include your own flesh and blood would be a whole other level of deviancy. But for a parent, they're... interesting. A combination of theatre and an insight into the level of childcare your kids experience on a daily basis.

A non-parent might think these are simple affairs – a basic retelling of the nativity story, cute children struggling to remember their lines – nothing could be further from the truth. The modern nativity is an extravaganza – pre-recorded songs, dance routines, and a mash up of the Christmas story with something random to give the show a 'twist'. Whether that's a lamb with a dicky leg, or a Pynchon-esque narrative telling the whole thing from the point of view of the manger doesn't matter. It's what keeps the audiences coming back. Well, that and parental obligation.

I bed myself in at a Starbucks five minutes from Carrie's nursery and order a flat white, ready for a few hours of thinking about custard.

Right: Custard… Custardy… Cus-tardy. Tardy. Never too late for custard. Something about non-instant custard taking a long time… Ugh. Cus*turdy* more like. I've got nothing. Why is it that everyone wants to be creative, but when it comes to doing it, it's like pulling teeth? Except someone who's pulls teeth actually *does* what they get paid for.

At 11:00 am, I head down to Nursery. The door doesn't open till half past and there's already a massive queue. Fuck.

I join the back, depressed. I'll still be able to see, but that's not the point. The kids need to see *you*. Anything except front row and you're in unchartered territory. Sure, you're only a few metres away, but when you're talking about creatures who can't spot a pair of slippers three feet in front of them, normal rules of perception don't apply.

I get a third row seat in the end. Well, fourth but the front row are on baby chairs, so they won't block Carrie's view *and* they look stupid. There was a lone chair, which I guess is one of the upsides of being a single parent. Society is so quick to condemn us, but they really do downplay the advantages.

The play starts a few minutes later, and the whole thing is

fucking chaos. At one point, Joseph steals the baby (which technically hasn't been born yet), and makes a break for the bathroom. Luckily, Mary is faster than him and grabs unborn Jesus's leg, pulling repeatedly until Joseph lets go. Joseph responds by hitting her, at one point *with* the baby, all to the tune of *Hark the Herald Angels Sing*. Ah! Christmas!

Carrie spots me while they're singing the third song. Well, not *singing* exactly; more opening and closing their mouths while the teachers carry the tune, like some weird piece of performance art. She seems happy to have spotted me, and keeps waving for the rest of the show. You know, like an angel would in real life. I have to plaster on a grin for the rest of the play, like I'm watching the world's most insecure stand-up, but it pays off – after the show, Carrie seems really proud.

'Did you see me?'

'Of course I saw you. You were great.'

'Thanks, Daddy,' she beams, super-cute in her makeshift angel outfit. We hug and she goes back in for a full Christmas lunch and an afternoon's schooling. I feel like a great father, trudging off up the road for a limp sandwich accompanied by more custard, as I wait for round two at Arthur's school.

Luckily, Arthur's play is a lot better – perhaps something to do with its cast being able to pronounce words properly etc, and watching it is almost… enjoyable. The play's called *The Nativi-tea*, and involves a shepherd who runs out of tea and travels from supermarket to supermarket only to find there's no stock except in the Bethlehem Lidl. In the hot drinks aisle, he bumps into two of his colleagues who are equally uncaffeinated and they decide to pop in on Jesus. Maybe the supermarket was out of milk, and the stable was the nearest place with cows.

As much as I want to be sarcastic about the whole scenario, it's actually pretty fun. And quite close to one of JC's advertising ideas. I can actually see him banking it as 'potential idea if Twinings want a Christmas ad'.

We're halfway through the show when I spot Claire standing at the back on the other side of the room. I get the sense that she's already seen me and is looking away. I catch her eye and try to give her an apologetic smile, but she looks away and chews her lip. Does she hate me? Was I an arsehole? Maybe I need to explain what happened. God, being married was great. None of this awkwardness and regret to deal with. But I guess that's over now. Strap in for the rest of your life, single boy.

At the end of the play, the kids come and join their parents for an early home time. A little thank you from St Mary's Primary School – *for Christmas we give you the gift of extra childcare.* I guess the custard ideas will have to wait till tomorrow.

On the way out, I end up in the crush next to Claire.

'Hey,' I say, cautious.

'Hey,' she replies.

'All ready for Christmas?' I say. Small talk seems like the best option here.

'Not really. How's the divorce going?'

So much for small talk.

'Um… I've got to fill in the forms this weekend. My parents are going to take the kids so I can get my head round it. Should get me in a festive mood. Nothing says "Christmas" like divorce bureaucracy.'

She smiles a little bit. Then decides to tell me what's on her mind. 'What happened between us… it just went wrong because of the kids, didn't it? I wasn't too full-on?'

I suddenly realise how vulnerable she is. I'd always assumed she was this confident single person a few years ahead of me in the wasteland, but underneath it all, she's still just as damaged as me.

'No, I just…' *don't know what to say.*

I see Oliver making a nasty face at Arthur, but I decide it's better to lie. I don't want her feeling her dick kid is going to stop her ever having a relationship again.

'I just wasn't ready for anything serious.'

She nods. Placated. *Relieved,* maybe. I don't know if she believes it or not. But I think she appreciates it that I've taken the blame away from Oliver. It's not her fault he's the spawn of Satan. I'm pretty sure those genes came from his father.

I feel good. Sometimes it's better not to tell the truth. But what *was* the truth? That Oliver got in the way? Or that I was just falling for someone else?

Friday

Another day of pain at work; constant longing for Amanda interspersed with attempts at creativity that feel like trying to use the bathroom on your first three days in France (do they actually have a word for 'fibre'?).

We have a meeting where the custard teams pitch to Vin. Amanda sits next to him and they both give feedback. The reassuring thing is everyone else's ideas are as bad as mine. I say mine, but Hans does contribute at one point ('maybe something about yellow?' Maybe, Hans... May*be*...) But the overall outcome is that no one's got anything we can present. We've still got another week. Vin gives us some smaller accounts to work on at the same time in an attempt to loosen us up.

At the end of the meeting Amanda grabs me and takes me to one side.

'Can we talk? You've been totally ignoring me for the last few days.' Huh?!? Apparently, I'm better at looking away before people catch me staring than I thought.

223

'Um, I dunno… I really need to get on with things.'

'It's just a couple of minutes. There's something I need to talk to you about.'

'It's OK. I kind of worked it out. Seeing you and Vin, I kind of put two and two together.'

She seems a bit surprised. 'Oh. Right.' I think part of me is hoping she's going to say I've got the wrong idea, that she's not interested in Vin – that for some fucked-up reason she prefers me. But no. She just nods and takes in the fact that I got everything exactly right.

'Is that why you've been ignoring me?' she asks.

'I dunno. Look – I just don't want to talk about it, OK?'

I walk back to my desk and do some brainstorming with Hans. Well, braindrizzling. I can sense Amanda behind me. This incredible bloody woman who 'just wants to be friends'. But I can't take that at the moment. Sure, we get on amazingly. But that twisting in my gut. I can't live like that. I wouldn't be friends with Mark if hanging out was always accompanied by the symptoms of E. coli poisoning. I need to move on. I really need to move on.

Evening

I come home to an empty flat. My parents picked up the kids from school to give me some space. A romantic weekend of just me and some divorce forms.

I pull a beer out of the fridge and look through the pages. They're not that long, and most of the questions are pretty straightforward, but it just feels so… final. Like turning off the life-support. When this is over, I won't just be moonlighting as a single dad. I'll be one for real.

And I'm not even really thinking about Sally. I'm doing the

paperwork for the dissolution of my marriage, and what I'm actually trying to accept is the end of me and Amanda. Something that never even happened in the first place. I need to get my head together. This Sally thing is real and we've got mediation next week, so I have to get these finished.

Two hours later, and I've filled in my personal details, and ticked the box saying 'adultery'. I've also drunk four more beers, eaten a Chinese takeaway and watched the first episode of *Ozark*, so the evening wasn't a total loss. But I'm depressed. The world feels so empty. With the kids here, at least I would have had something to take my mind off things. But, without them, I'm in a vacuum again.

At ten o'clock the doorbell rings. Must be someone for the other flat pressing the wrong buzzer. It doesn't stop, so I hit the intercom and declaim a sort of, 'Leave me alone,' before I remember it's broken. I head downstairs – angry, but with some mild booze munchies – hoping that someone else has ordered takeaway and I can intercept it and have a second one.

Buzz. 'I'm coming, I'm coming,' I say, switching on the light and stumbling down the corridor to the front door.

I open the door, hoping it's an Indian rather than a Chinese. I mean having a second Chinese would seem greedy, but a curry… that's not so bad. Should probably check it hasn't been paid for. Intercepting someone's takeout is one thing, but expecting my neighbour to foot the bill, well… I'm not an animal.

But it's neither an Indian or a Chinese.

It's Claire.

I instantly sober up. Well, about ten percent. Enough not to lead with my planned, 'Have I already paid for this?'

'Oh… hey…' I stammer.

'Can I come in?'

I'm drunk, lonely and not thinking straight.

So I tell her yes.

There's a voice in the back of my head saying something, but it's got all slurry and is also asking, 'Where's my bloody curry?', so I ignore it, and two minutes later we're sitting on my sofa with glasses of wine. Claire's telling me about how she always feels really lonely this time of year, trying to give Oliver a proper Christmas, and she's got her hand on my leg and is snuggling in. The voice is shouting now. And not about samosas. But I'm not backing away. It just feels so nice and cosy and sexy, and the world that had seemed so empty twenty minutes ago seems full again.

She looks up at me and starts to speak.

'You said you weren't ready for anything serious. What about something not serious?' and with that her hand slides up my leg and the voice in my head could be speaking in a different bloody language for all the attention I'm giving it. I'm weak. I'm so bloody weak. I hate being a man. God I hate being a man.

I lean in and kiss her and suddenly, it's like every bit of me is switched on, and I'm lost to rational thought.

And it's fucking amazing.

Saturday Morning

I wake up with a foot touching mine, and for a second it feels like I'm still with Sally and the last few months have been a dream. The moment I realise it's Claire, I go into a massive panic that the kids are here, before remembering they're with my parents and then totally relaxing. The whole rollercoaster takes less than a second.

My mind starts to turn over – was this a good idea? Now there's no chance with Amanda there's no reason not to, and Claire said she didn't want anything serious, but before I can come to any conclusions, it's Claire that's turning over. She rolls her naked body onto mine, and instantly I'm back in the zone. But I'm sober now and I realise before anything happens, we need to be clear on some ground rules.

Twenty minutes later, we've finished having sex. Seems the ground rules have taken a rain check.

We go out and get a coffee, Claire reads the paper while I put crosses in boxes and write out the name of the person my spouse has committed adultery with. There's only room for one. Obviously, they're not expecting a comprehensive list. I put 'Austin' and text Sally for his surname. How fucking weird is that? *Sorry would you be able to give me some deets on the person you're banging? Also, what are his hobbies? I'd like to get him something for Christmas.* For all I know, it might have just been Austin anyway. The kids don't know what's going on. They still think their Christmas presents come down our non-existent chimney.

The forms are a lot more approachable now I'm with someone. We have lunch together, then head back to my flat to 'Netflix and Chill.' I'm a bit annoyed when it turns out to be a euphemism, as I'm quite keen to watch the second episode of *Ozark*. My stamina's not what it was and I really want to find out what happens to Marty. They should really only have euphemisms for sex that describe things that are actually worse than sex. Like rolling in the hay. That was a good one. I mean, I have allergies. Whereas relaxing while watching Netflix… well… they have some really good series on at the moment.

At five, Claire has to go and pick Ollie up. Ugh. I can't believe I'm calling him 'Ollie'. It's like calling Stalin 'Stalie'. But, the forms finished, I spend the evening watching *Ozark* and feel strangely content. Relaxing, watching telly. Such a relief after all that sex nonsense.

Sunday

The kids are meant to be back at lunchtime, but weirdly it snows and my parents get stuck on the motorway for most of the day. I work on ideas for the non-custard accounts between episodes of TV. At one, point, I see the neighbours' kids out of the window, making a one-foot-high snowman with the thin dustings of white on car bonnets, leaving little trails on the metal. I can't help but feel that's what I should be doing. Playing out there with Arthur and Carrie. Watching them just makes me really sad.

Because that's what I am now. A dad. Sure, I spent the whole of yesterday being a stud with an exceptionally low level of stamina. But that's not the real me. I'm a parent. I'm not sure how having sex with Claire fits into that. But that's a question for later. As my parents' car pulls up outside the door, I close my laptop and head to the front door. And as the kids rush past me, the cold air streaming into the corridor, it feels like the central heating's been turned on.

Monday

Vin seems really pleased with the ideas I came up with over the weekend, and says he's going to pitch them to the clients later in the day. He's so friendly and supportive it just makes me feel terrible that I kind of hate him.

I spend the rest of the day trying to think of ideas for custard ads. Again. This is what hell would have looked like for Sisyphus if he'd had a dairy intolerance. Seeing Amanda makes me really hate myself for what happened over the weekend. Like I've been unfaithful to her. But you can't be unfaithful to someone you were never with. That's ridiculous. I'm being ridiculous.

Claire texts me at eleven. 'I had fun. Same thing next weekend?'

228

I decide to text back all positive – I need to move on from Amanda. Being with Claire like this is healthy.

'Me too. Good times!' I type in. I erase 'good times' – that sounds like I went on a weekend away with friends. I try, 'Really sexy time!' but realise I sound like bloody Borat. Eventually I go with 'Me too. Will text about next weekend xx.' I feel wrong when I do it, but we're two consenting adults. There's nothing bad about it. If anything, I should probably follow up with something a bit more flirty—

'Hey,' says Amanda and I launch my phone about four feet into the air. She goes to pick it up and I scramble ahead of her like a hobbit grasping for the Ring.

I lock the phone and put it on the desk. Amanda looks at me like I'm acting weird, but carries on.

'I just wanted to say I hope we can still be friends.'

I hesitate, so she continues.

'It's just we get on so well – I'd be really sad to lose you like that.'

I try to think of how to respond, only for my phone to beep and the message, 'I loved having you inside of me,' come up on my lock screen. Who the fuck thought putting messages on the lock screen was a good idea? Someone people didn't love having inside of them, that's who. I think I manage to turn the phone over before Amanda sees, but I'm not sure.

As she's still looking at me, waiting for an answer, rather than incredibly embarrassed/horrified, I assume she hasn't. 'I don't know. I need to think about it.'

She seems to take that as a bit of progress, nods, and goes back into her office where Vin is waiting for her.

I look at her and then I look at Vin. She'll be happy with him. He's the kind of guy she deserves. I understand. I just don't know if I can be friends with someone who I love. Who doesn't love me back.

Oh God. Do I love her?

I'm fucked. I'm completely fucked.

Tuesday

No ideas. Stare at Amanda, stare at Vin, feel like shit. Maybe I'll drink heavily tonight so tomorrow I can pretend it's due to a hangover.

Wednesday

Still no ideas, still trying not to stare at Amanda. Vin catches me looking at him a few times though. Feel even more like shit. Hangover practically non-existent – should have bought a cheaper bottle of wine.

Evening

Mediation was predictably horrible. Sally spent the whole time claiming that I couldn't provide the children with the life they were accustomed to, so she should take them to Canada.

The good news is the mediator basically said she hasn't got a hope in hell and, while it's exactly what I was praying for, it sounds like joint custody is going to involve the kids travelling halfway across the world every time school breaks up.

No more summers, no more Easter… no more *Christmas*. Nothing but school drop-offs and weekends till they turn eighteen.

Jesus. No more *Christmas*.

At least I might get to keep them for this one…

Thursday

My life is in pieces. I'm single, the kids will only have a mother for a few months a year and the company's dissolving, which is basically my fault as well. (Me applying for job à John applying for job à racially insensitive advert à company collapsing à me and everyone I know being unemployed). What's worse – tomorrow is the company Christmas party, which will either be the most depressing party ever, or an orgiastic fin de siècle blow-out climaxing with Amanda and Vin acting out some kind of pagan sex ritual on the dance floor while the Accounts department watch on, chanting their allegiance to Pan. Either way, I'm not exactly looking forward to it.

It strikes me my best hope of not having to see some Amanda-Vin action is some kind of 'no relationships/sex on the dance floor' policy at the company. I head down to Accounts to pick Carol's brain. She must have some office-manager-style inside info on this I can reassure myself with.

'Hello, stranger. Decided to grace us with your presence again, have you?' asks Carol. 'Haven't seen you down here for a while.'

'Vin's got everyone working 24/7 on this new account, so I don't get my little accountancy treat in the morning.'

'I heard,' she says smiling. She's a nice woman. She really is a nice woman. 'Saved the company yet?'

'Not yet.' I smile back, slightly sheepish at the fact that all of our livings are hanging in the balance and I still can't think of a bloody advert, but I get back on track. 'Look – Carol – I was just wondering… what with the company party tomorrow night; are there any rules about… how should I put this… inter-office romance? Intra-office? You know what I mean.'

Carol smiles like she totally gets it. 'If you're asking because you want to take me up on my offer, you have nothing to worry about. I'm very discreet.'

I suddenly remember what Carol's offer was. I'm pretty sure I don't want to take her up on it. That seems worse than a having a fuck buddy. That said, having an elderly woman visiting occasionally might be easier to explain away to the kids. '*Daddy, why are you locked in the bathroom with Carol?*'

'*When people get to this age, sometimes they need help.*'

'Thanks Carol, but I've kind of… met someone.'

'Amanda?'

Oh God, even bloody Carol knows.

'How did you…?'

'I saw you together once upstairs. I think she likes you too.' I try to hide my cynicism. Carol squeezes my hand reassuringly. 'Anyway, the good news is – there are no rules. The path to true love is clear.'

I plaster on a fake smile, and head back upstairs. Arse.

Afternoon

Claire texts again later that afternoon: 'How's the weekend looking? I've got a present for you.' A photograph comes through of Claire wearing what can only be described as… a piece of tinsel. Because it's a piece of tinsel.

I text back: 'Things a bit messed up at work. Can I let you know?'

'Sure.' Another photo. This time, a hand holding out some tinsel.

I know I'm probably meant to send back a shot of my penis covered in wrapping paper or something, but I leave it hanging. Jesus, all this sex about and I don't want any of it. Six months ago this would have been my ultimate fantasy.

Maybe it means I'm finally becoming a grown-up.

Friday

Looks like we're losing custard. They've given us an ultimatum. We've got until next Wednesday to wow them, or they're signing with another agency. Happy Holidays! No one's come up with anything worthwhile. A lumpy, curdled excuse for creativity that no amount of whizzing with the hand blender of inspirational leadership will save.

After work, everyone heads down to the party. We're all pretty subdued. I want to skip it, but my new babysitter's booked and attendance definitely seems obligatory – more like a wake than a party. We don't want to disrespect the dead. Or the almost bankrupt.

JC seems to be the only one who's unfazed by the current state of affairs. He's waiting for us all at the venue, rocking an ironic sparkly jacket, and trying to get people dancing.

He comes over and pats me on the shoulder. 'Not going to join me on the dance floor, Tombo?'

Standing there in front of the glittery curtain I feel like I'm on some weird 1970s game show: *Welcome to "How Not to Lose Your Job"! If you can guess the correct answer to your boss's questions and avoid going into an aggressive downward spiral after three mojitos, you could… not lose your job!*

That said, I don't really give a fuck any more. 'Maybe when I've had a bit more to drink, thanks.' *And not even then, thanks.* I think everyone feels the same as me, but alcohol has a way of working its magic, and after – yeah, on average three mojitos – people are actually starting to have fun. The Accounts department have pretty much demolished the buffet, and are already grooving to Christmas classics. I guess that's one of the benefits of being completely uncool. Nothing gets in the way of having fun. I kind of miss Accounts. All this detachment and being cool is too much for me. Right now, I should be wearing a Christmas jumper non-ironically and bopping to *Jingle Bell Rock* like the rest of them. I might aspire to creativity, but my soul is definitely a bookkeeper with a low tolerance for alcohol.

Over the other side of the dance floor, John's trying to chat up Gemma, the intern, who's a lot less responsive now he's the office pariah.

But I'm not paying much attention to him. Vin's with Amanda, again. The best of friends. There are a few others around them but they always seem to be together.

Vin notices me looking over. I feel like I should roll my eyes or something, but instead I just do a kind of alcoholic wobble. He smiles. *Stop being nice, dickhead. Stop being so nice.*

10:00 pm, I go outside for a cigarette. I don't smoke, but once or twice a year when I get really drunk, scabbing a cigarette off someone and standing outside in the cold seems like a good idea. No one's got anything other than roll-ups, so I head back in. Probably for the best, anyway. I don't think the kids would appreciate their father getting lung cancer. Even if it meant they got to live in one country for the rest of their childhood.

On the way back I bump into Vin.

'Hey Tom – can we talk?'

'You're my boss. If you say we talk, we talk,' I slur. I have literally no idea if that sounded as sarcastic as I meant it to or not. I'm aware I also have a weird drunken smile on my face, so subtlety of tone probably isn't one of my strong points right now.

'It's not really a work thing,' Vin replies. 'It's more personal.'

Just what I need. Some patronising *I'm really sorry I stole her from you and she thinks you're really great* shit. Then he'll start telling me *she's really upset* and *can I make an effort to be friends with her?* Well, fuck you, Vin. As far as I'm concerned you can stick it up your ass. How'd you like that?!?

234

'Fine,' I say, dismissive, but I'm aware that, for all I know, it might have come out as 'flirty'. 'Go ahead.'

'I've noticed you looking at me.' *Tactful, mentioning that.* Bloody Americans and their lack of social skills.

'Yeah, yeah, yeah…' I reel off, 'it's inappropriate for the office, I get it.'

'Maybe, but… I understand.'

I think I'm going to vomit. And not from the three mojitos. Even us accountants can cope with that. Nice people make me sick. What is wrong with this guy that he needs to be sympathetic to my plight as well? Just go and grab Amanda, do your dance floor sex show, and let's be done with it.

'Because…' Vin seems to be searching for the word. He's hesitating. What's it going to be – *because I've been hurt too? Because I have inhuman levels of empathy?*

And then he kisses me. Straight on the mouth. I'm so drunk he gets as far as putting a bit of tongue in before I pull away.

'It's all right,' he says. 'They're cool with relationships at work, and hey; if no one makes out at the Christmas party, what's the company coming to?'

I start to laugh. I shouldn't, but I do. I've never been so happy to be kissed by a man before. Well, I've never actually kissed a man before, but, if I had, I wouldn't have been.

'You're gay?'

'Yeah… Aren't you?'

'No, I… I didn't know. I thought you were getting it on with Amanda.'

'Amanda – no, we're just friends. Is that why you were staring?'

'Yeah, because I'm totally in love with her.'

'In love?'

I pause.

'Don't repeat that. Don't ever repeat that.'

Vin is taking this in. 'I'm sorry, dude. I was getting really strong vibes from you. I'm so embarrassed right now.'

'Don't be. That kiss made my bloody night. You're awesome. You're totally awesome. Out of all the men I've ever met, you're definitely the one I would have most liked to have been snogged by. Hell, I probably would have banged you in exchange for news this good.'

'Don't make any promises.'

'Sorry – I have to go.'

I dash round the party looking for Amanda. I can't see her anywhere. Eventually I notice her by the side of the dance floor, trying to brush off the stranger-come-hither moves JC is pulling.

'JC – sorry; I need to steal Amanda.' He looks like he's not that happy. 'I had a great idea for the custard campaign.'

'Well, tell me too.'

'I need to talk it over first. Telling you… It'd be like whistling a tune I'd just thought of to Beethoven.' Yuk, I never do obsequious flattery like that. I feel dirty. He'll see through me in an instant.

'Fair enough.' No, it worked. Wow. Note to self – try to be more of a sycophant in future. People really have no radar for it.

I lead Amanda into a little corridor off the main room. She seems confused that I've stopped ignoring her, but also intrigued about what the hell I want. We get away from prying eyes and I start to say my piece.

'Vin's gay.'

'Yeah,' she replies, 'so what?'

'So you're not together.'

'Together?' Amanda gradually takes in my meaning. 'Oh my God – you thought me and Vin were together?'

'I thought that's what you were trying to tell me.'

'No – I've been offered a job in New York. They want me to move over there. I thought that's why you were being a dick.'

236

But the whole New York thing washes over me like water off the proverbial.

She's not with Vin. She's not with Vin!

I don't know if it's the alcohol, the sheer relief, or the fact that I've already warmed up with a bit of snogging – but I suddenly find a reserve of confidence deep inside me. I move closer. And kiss her. And she kisses me back. Hard, sexy, and reassuringly stubbleless.

'Do you want to get out of here?' I ask.

She nods.

We jump in a cab outside – I was planning to get the Tube to save money, but if this isn't a special occasion what the hell is? We get inside and within seconds, we're intertwined with one another. Kissing Claire was great, but this is a totally different thing. Because I love her. Something I'm never going to bloody mention, but it's true. I love her.

The taxi drops us off outside my flat, and we run to the door hand in hand. As I open it, I check the time on my phone to work out how much I have to give the babysitter, but then I notice something.

I've got eight missed calls. Shit.

Suddenly, my loved-up bliss is replaced by a massive panic about the kids. Has something happened to them? Oh Christ. Something's happened to the kids. I rush up the stairs, where Marta, the new sitter, is squatting outside the door to my flat.

'What are you doing? What's happened?'

'A woman,' she tells me in broken English. 'I open the door and she force her way in, tell me to go. Say she watch the kids till you come back. I try to call but you not answer.'

Claire. Oh no. I said I'd text her back. She must have decided to surprise me. This is a disaster. The woman I love is about to see I have a… fuck buddy. It suddenly seems so dirty. And I wanted this to be perfect. No-one else muddying the water. Just two people. Two people who actually like each other. The start of a relationship.

But instead, I'm a dirty ape with a fuck buddy. I knew it was a mistake. Damn it. Stupid being-a-man stupidity.

I think of telling Amanda to wait downstairs, but I don't want our relationship to start like that. We've got to be honest with each other. About who we are. About whether we're seeing gay work colleagues. About whether we previously had… ugh… fuck-buddies.

'I'll deal with it.'

'Should I go?'

'No,' I say, acting a lot more confident than I feel. 'It'll be fine.'

I hand Marta a few notes (not that she deserves it – she basically got my kids… napped), open the door and start to rehearse the speech in my head. *I'm sorry Claire, but I've met someone. I didn't think it was going to happen, but it has, so I'm afraid you'll have to leave the flat.* Good: Polite, civil, to the point. *Shit.*

I walk into the flat, and head to the living room where the light's on. She shouldn't have done this. It's not OK. God, I hope she's not just wearing tinsel. If I'd thought of that as a possibility I wouldn't have Amanda three feet behind me right now.

But as I turn into the room, suddenly everything gets a hundred times worse.

It's not Claire.

It's Sally.

Well, at least she's not naked apart from Christmas tree decorations.

She stands up from the sofa and looks me straight in the eye.

'I've been thinking,' she tells me. 'I want to come home.'

* * *

It's half a second later when Amanda comes into the room. It's clear she heard every word.

'I think I should go.'

'No, Sally shouldn't be here. She shouldn't have come in like this. Give me a second.' I turn to Sally, trying to pretend that my world isn't collapsing around me. 'Now's not a good time.'

'I want to come *home*. Any time should be a good time.'

'I... can we talk about this tomorrow?' I stumble.

'Tomorrow?!?' Sally exclaims. 'I can't believe you're being like this. Isn't this what you wanted?'

Is it? I want to tell her to fuck off, to get out and never come back. But then I think of our kids ... our innocent, hope-filled kids...

I look over at Amanda, whose eyes are asking the same question. She takes my lack of response as an answer. 'I'm going to go.'

'No... please... don't.'

'I'll see you at work on Monday.' She leaves the room. A moment of hesitation and everything I've been dreaming about has just gone to shit. A few seconds later I hear the front door close. And she's gone.

For Sally, the moment's nothing. Amanda's nothing. Just an annoying inconvenience that's been brushed out of the room. Another fuck buddy. But for me, it's everything. It's love. But now it's gone.

I turn to Sally.

'OK,' I say, 'let's talk.'

Saturday

We stay up most of the night chatting. Sally thinks she made a mistake leaving. It looks like the whole 'only having the kids for half the year' thing is getting to her as much as me. And it's not going well with Austin. Apparently nothing happened with any of the other guys the kids talked about – they were just people from work. What did I say before? Never listen to what your children tell you. They have literally no idea about anything.

She's still there when they get up.

'Mummy!' they shout as they run in and hug her. They're so bloody happy she's here. As if this decision wasn't hard enough.

'Are you coming home again?' asks Arthur.

'That's what we're talking about,' says Sally.

I suppose she had to say that. I can't hold it against her.

'So you are?' asks Carrie.

'Well… it depends if Daddy lets me.'

The anger I've been repressing rises like a cartoon thermometer. That was out of line. You don't involve the kids. The amount of times I could have taken her down. Slagged her off. But I didn't. And now she's putting the blame on me – the responsibility for breaking up our family.

I turn to Sally. She flinches a bit when she sees my expression.

'Daddy needs to think about things. Mummy's just leaving.'

'I can stay around for a bit.'

'She's *leaving*.'

Sally takes the more-than-hint, says goodbye and goes. I tell her we'll talk tomorrow; that I'll make a decision.

I'll try to bury my anger, my resentment about her abandoning us and think about this clearly and collectedly.

The kids start crying the moment she's gone.

Sunday

As much as I want to give Arthur and Carrie to someone for the day to clear my head, I've promised them a Christmas tree, so we head to the 'Pop-Up Forest' by the main road. 'Forest' definitely doesn't feel like an appropriate description. 'Copse' would be overegging it. The place is like a graveyard for trees – a few semi-naked specimens in a car park; the rejects from the more organised families, huddling together for warmth.

As we wander around, even the kids' enthusiasm seems to be waning.

'Daddy, why do the trees look like this?' asks Carrie.

I try to think of how to answer as a random stray dog walks by and relieves himself next to one of the mangy firs. It feels like he's found his spiritual home. Or at least his spiritual home's bathroom.

I wander over to the guy in charge. 'Is this all you've got?'

'The restock's meant to be coming today, but it's not here.'

'What about later?'

'Dunno. Stock's low this year. Don't know if it'll be coming at all. I can do you a deal for cash if you want.'

To take what's there in front of you, imperfect and flawed – or wait for something better… something that may never come. Sally would know what to do. And she wants to come home.

I turn to the kids. 'Maybe we'll just come back another day…'

'No!' says Arthur. '*You promised us a tree!*'

I try to reason with them, but eventually give in. Because I'm a shitty excuse for a parent. I should know better. I should be someone who leads the way, who makes the right decision. But I just want to make them happy. To be their friend.

I carry the tree home over my shoulder. By the time we get there, my whole body's aching. You'd think it would've been lighter without all those needles weighing it down.

I set up the foliage-less wonder in the living room. It's lost even more on the way home. But the kids seem happy.

They decorate the tree while I go and pace round the bedroom. I try to convince myself that if Sally and I won't be happy together, it won't be good for the kids. But I'm not buying it. If I tell her not to come back, it's because I don't want her to.

And I don't think I do. She's hurt me. I can't trust her anymore. And I'm in love with someone else. But the kids… the bloody kids.

I go through to the main room and look at the tree, its bare branches decorated with baubles. It looks horrible. Like big-night-out makeup on a corpse.

And that's when I realise I can't do it. I can't look at this thing for the next few weeks, standing there reminding me of the fact that I just settled. I should have never listened to the kids. I love them. But they make terrible fucking decisions.

I sit them down.

'You know Mummy said she might be coming back?'

They nod enthusiastically, their eyes full of hope and promise. Promise that things might go back to normal again.

'She's not.'

I can see the heartbreak on their little faces.

'You'll still see Mummy. All the time. A lot more than you have recently. So now it's going to be like you have two families… which is twice as good.'

Tears start streaming down Carrie's four-year-old face. Arthur's trying to be the big man about it, biting at his lip to stop it from trembling, but he's barely holding it together. Teetering on the brink of crying. Just like me.

'I want things to be normal again, like it was before,' says Carrie.

'I do too. But they can't be. Things are just different now. But

I love you and Mummy loves you and we're going to love you both forever.'

Arthur finally breaks and starts balling his eyes out, I hug them both until they run out of tears. And eventually they do. But I know the pain will be with them for the rest of their lives.

After a few minutes of holding them in silence, I realise it's up to me to get things moving again. I'm their parent, not their friend. I need to lead the way. To inspire them to action.

'OK – let's get our coats on,' I tell them. 'We're going to go out and find a better tree.'

Evening

After the kids have gone to bed, I need a bit of time to get my head together before I call Sally, so I try to distract myself coming up with ideas for the custard campaign.

Predictably, this involves me sitting with a notepad and a pen contemplating how I'm destroying my kids' lives. But, the lush tree in our living room gives me hope. That maybe one day things will be better.

I realise I'm not going to be able to sleep tonight unless I make the call, so I pick up the phone.

Sally picks up on the second ring. There's no small talk, no hello, just, 'So what do you think?'

I pause for a bit. I was hoping for some chat about Christmas tree shopping to warm myself up.

'I'm sorry, Sally.'

'You're saying no?'

'I'm saying no.'

'Fuck you, Tom. Fuck you. This is our family we're talking about. You're breaking up our family.'

It's everything that's been going over in my head reflected back at me from the outside. The exact words that should destroy me. But they don't. Hearing her say them makes me realise something: it's not my fault. It's hers. And for the first time since she left, I realise that. And I let loose.

'OK, Sally. You need to stop talking for a second. I've done nothing but try to keep this family together for years. I've put up with your bullshit. With you walking out without even explaining why, and leaving me to do *everything*. But I'm fed up of it. I never tried to take the kids from you. But you wanted to take them from me.'

'Don't think you've won this, Tom.'

'I don't, Sally. In this situation, no one's bloody won.'

Sally is still speaking, but in my head the conversation is over. As I say goodbye and hang up the phone, I hear her saying, 'I'm going to fight you for custody!' and it doesn't even faze me. She doesn't have a leg to stand on. We'll sort something out. When we're both calm, we'll sort something out.

The words 'fight for custody' echo round my head though. And a few seconds later I know why. Custody. Custardy. Oh my God. Sally, I could kiss you. Well, if you weren't both not here and inhumanly angry with me right now. Fight for custardy.

The ad comes into my head fully formed. There's a mother and father arguing – things aren't going well. But they're trying to have a Sunday lunch together, trying to make things work. Then it gets to pudding time and Mum wants to give them cream. But Dad wants custard. And he's got to fight for it. He's got to *fight for custardy*. It's funny. I think it's funny. Maybe it should be the other way round, with the mum winning. I literally have no idea what's sexist anymore. But it's good. They said they wanted to appeal to a non-traditional market. This could be just the job. And in the end of course, the kids choose custard over cream – a victory. And when it happens, I won't have a single one of them turning Chinese.

Monday

I bounce into the office at 9:00 am. No one else is there yet, except Vin. He's in Amanda's office with a pad and paper looking despondent. I wave him a hello and he gives me an awkward smile and looks back down at his work. He's ostriching me. He's totally ostriching me. But I know that move. I invented that move. I bound into his glass-partitioned bunker without even knocking.

Vin looks up, uncomfortable, 'Look, I'm really sorry about the other night.'

'Doesn't matter,' I reply, 'I've got an idea.'

'For custard?'

'For custard.'

I explain the ad, and he loves it. We set to work on getting the pitch together, and by the time the rest of the office gets in, it's already half done. We work really well together. He's a good guy. With good ideas. Definitely my second favourite person in the office I've got off with.

I barely notice the rest of the department rolling in. JC looks over our shoulders at one point, making noises like he approves, but I manage to ignore it, like the persistent thoughts of Amanda hammering at the door of my consciousness, and dig back into the work.

It's not until we emerge from the office at lunchtime, that I realise Amanda's not there. I ask around. Most of them saw me leaving with her on Friday, so there's no chance of keeping that on the down low anymore. No one knows anything. Until finally I talk to Doug.

'She phoned in sick.'

'Oh. Right. Do you know what's wrong with her?'

'Don't ask me,' he shrugs. 'Like I'd be the first one she'd apprise

245

of that information,' he says, heavy with irony. 'She probably caught it from you anyway.'

The embarrassment I'd normally feel is tempered by a warm glow at what happened. We kissed. Sure, my wife fucked it up, but she's out of the picture now. We kissed.

I think about calling, but I want to talk to her face to face. It can wait till tomorrow. Vin calls me back into the office. We're going to try the pitch out on JC.

Tuesday

Still no Amanda. I texted her but she didn't get back to me. Maybe she's really sick.

It's probably nothing. Thirty-six hours – you don't need a doctor's note for that. And no-one's mentioned norovirus, so it might actually be legit.

At lunchtime, Vin and JC come back from the pitch meeting, emanating success. The client loved it. And that's not just according to JC. Vin seems to think so too, so that might actually be legit as well.

If things continue to move like this (and Amanda's not dead), life might actually work out. It might actually work out.

Wednesday

JC pops a champagne cork and manages to knock over the company's 2008 award for Best Advert. The glass smashes to pieces on the stone hearth. There's a tense moment of silence before JC declares, 'Plenty more where that came from,' and the office cheers. We got the account. We bloody got the bloody account.

By three o'clock, the whole place is a drunken mess. We're not getting anything done for the rest of the day, but no one cares. We're going home for Christmas with jobs to come back to, so everyone's fucking ecstatic. I feel like a massive weight's been lifted off my shoulders. A Christmas tree with all the green on it level weight. At one point some of the creative department even lift me onto *their* shoulders. I'm a hero. A bona fide hero. I don't think I've ever been a hero before.

My eyes drift over to Amanda's office. Where the hell is she? I called her last night, but it just went to voicemail. I'm starting to worry she's seriously ill.

'Golden boy!' JC shouts, pointing at me. 'Into my office – now.'

I follow JC into his inner sanctum. I wait for him to take his seat first – I've learnt my lesson from the first time with the beanbag. He sits down behind the desk, and I plonk myself in the chair opposite.

'Got something for you,' he says. JC reaches into the desk drawer and his hand emerges holding a Christmas gift. He slides it across to me.

It's the decision. His 'creative' take on a job announcement. I almost want to shake it to see what's inside, but it can't not be good. I just saved the company, for God's sake. It's got to be positive. It's got to be.

Slowly I unwrap it, and inside… is a copy of *Adver-ties*… And a calculator. A basic 24-key non-scientific calculator. The kind I wouldn't even be able to use for home accounts. But it's what it represents that matters: an X in red pen. A no. The black bloody spot. I failed. I don't understand how, but I failed.

I feel the disappointment come over me in a wave. I already thought I'd won. But I hadn't. I guess they're right – it ain't over till it's over.

'Why are you looking like that?'

I look up at JC like *isn't it obvious*? 'Because I didn't get the job.'

'What?' he says confused. 'No – you *did*. Shit – I got the parcels the wrong way round, didn't I? I just assumed the calculator was the good one. I know how you guys love calculators.' He picks up his phone and dictates a voice memo. 'Note for *Tit-Bits* – always write things down, otherwise you might forget them.' He presses stop, than has another thought. 'Or use a voice note, like I'm doing now.'

I turn the calculator over in my hand, smiling. I got the job. I'm no longer on a trial period. I got the job.

'Well, I'm a creative now, so I guess I'll have to try and wean myself off them.'

'That you will.'

We shake hands and I head back towards the party.

'Oh, and Tom…'

I turn round hoping JC hasn't changed his mind. 'Yeah?'

'You need to leave the calculator. It's technically John's.'

Slightly Later

Back on the office floor everyone's congratulating me. Carol gives me a reassuring squeeze on the shoulder. She's so strong. Glad I didn't take her up on the whole hand job thing – she'd probably have taken my manhood clean off.

Even John comes over to congratulate me. Strangely, he doesn't look that resentful. Probably hasn't got his calculator yet.

I see Vin over the other side of the office and head over to say thanks.

He gives me one of his standard big handsome smiles. 'Good work. Heard you got the job. You must be pleased.'

248

I nod. 'I am.'

'Well, it's been nice working with you. You'll have to come over to New York sometime.'

'That'd be… great,' I say, trying not to sound like that would be my first time going to America and absolutely awesome. 'When are you going back?'

'Tonight.'

'By the way,' I ask, 'have you talked to Amanda? Is she all right?'

'Oh,' he says, suddenly awkward. 'Hasn't she told you?'

'Told me what?'

'Sorry – I thought she'd have mentioned it.' He's trying to avoid telling me something. What isn't he telling me?

'She handed in her notice today. She's coming to work with me in the States.'

* * *

I find a message from Amanda on my phone from a few hours earlier, just after the party started and we text back and forth, agreeing to meet up for a drink. I manage to get Marta to babysit (with strict instructions to keep the chain on the door), and head straight to the bar after work. I don't want to be leaving the kids with someone, but this is important.

We make small talk about the deal, about me getting the job, about what we're doing for Christmas, and by the time we get down to business we're both pretty drunk. Hell, I was pretty drunk when I got there from work.

'I'm sorry I didn't tell you,' Amanda offers, by way of an explanation. 'I just wanted to be on my own while I thought about it. If you were there, it might have influenced my decision…'

It's a horrible way to hear that someone cares.

'Sorry, but I can't stick around for a guy,' she says looking me in the eye, 'As much as I want to… I can't.' I can't imagine being someone she'd even *want* to stick around for. It makes me feel warm inside at the same time as completely empty. Bittersweet is the word, I guess. Sitting there, I want to kiss her, but I know it would just make it worse.

'You know it's over with Sally…'

'I didn't. But… it doesn't matter. It just reminded me I had to think about myself. I'm sorry, but I just can't put my life in someone else's hands. I hope you understand.'

I do. I wouldn't want her sacrificing herself for me. I just wish she didn't have to make that choice.

'I could always see if there was a job for you over there.' She regrets it as soon as she's said it. 'I'm sorry – I shouldn't have said that.'

'No, I…' I think about me being in New York. Starting a life there, with Amanda and the kids. But no; I can't take them halfway across the world. Doing the exact same thing Sally was trying to. 'It's a nice dream…'

She nods.

'When are you flying?'

'Friday. I was meant to be spending Christmas with my parents, but we'll just spend the whole time arguing. I want to make a new start. Vin said I can spend Christmas with him.'

'That'll be nice. He's very handsome. And a pretty good kisser.'

'So I heard…'

We part as friends. Agreeing not to call each other tomorrow. It's for the best. We'd just be prolonging the agony.

But agony is what it is.

Thursday

It's the penultimate day of work before the holidays. I still remember when my primary school teacher explained what 'penultimate' meant to us, and how super sophisticated it sounded. 'Penultimate means the last but one, and "ultimate" is the last one.' I guess that made last night my 'ultimate' evening with Amanda. You could have fucking fooled me.

After the kids are in bed, Sally rings to apologise. She's actually being nice. It makes me think things might work out. Not together, but apart. She's back with Austin, but taking things slower. Which means she won't be moving to Canada… yet. But still, when you're a dying man, a reprieve can feel like a pardon.

Sally says she'll agree to joint custody and I can have the kids for Christmas Day. Well, most of it; she'll pick them up at six, but it's something. Especially because she still might relocate moose-wards, so it might be the last one I have with them.

But it makes me feel more optimistic, like one day we might even be friends. I even summon up the guts to ask what I did to make her so angry with me.

She considers the question for a second. 'I think… I think I was just angry that I didn't love you any more.'

* * *

We chat for another hour. Feeling out our new relationship – trying to work out how we relate to each other now. After a while I start to relax.

Enough to tell her about the new job.

'I knew you had it in you,' she says.

'Thanks,' I say. 'It's a bit of a pay cut, but—'

And then suddenly everything changes.

251

'What do you mean?' The intimacy between us is gone, she's back to being serious.

'Just that it's a bit less money.'

'How are you going to afford the flat? I've got to get a new place now Austin's going back – I can't keep paying half the rent.'

'I…' I'd just assumed we'd split it until the divorce came though. That I'd have time to think about a way to get promoted – to earn some more money. But I don't. I don't have any time at all.

Fuck. I've got to turn down the job.

Friday – Last Day of Work Before the Holidays

I'm back to where I was three months ago. No wife, no girlfriend and stuck in a shitty accounting job I hate. Life's like that. Constantly dangling hope in front of you like a carrot, but then taking it away. Or in my case you get the carrot, and it turns out to have insufficient calorific value to feed your family. It makes me realise what a waste of time the last few months have been. All this trying, striving. Maybe it's better not to try at all.

But I have the kids. And they have their mother. That's the most important thing now. Because I'm a dad. And maybe that's enough.

I arrange a meeting with JC for late afternoon. I want to bask in the glory of having succeeded for a few hours before I throw it all back in his face.

'So, Tombo. What can I do you for? Our latest junior creative in this flourishing departmento.'

'I can't do it.'

He pauses for a second, confused. 'You've got to believe in yourself, Tombo. You saved the company. And sure, most of your other ideas were bad, but you only need a few good ones.'

252

'It's not that,' I say, kind of smarting from the 'most of your other ideas were bad' comment. 'I can't afford to take the pay cut. Sorry. I thought I could, but things have changed at home.'

He nods seriously. 'Sorry to hear that, Tombo.' Then he thinks for a second, and looks like he's about to utter a profound revelation.

'Because you diddled Amanda?'

'No... I'm getting divorced.'

'Because you diddled Amanda?'

'No,' I say, 'I've been getting divorced for a while.'

'Oh, right,' he says, contemplating what this means. 'But you did diddle her?'

'I don't want to talk about it.'

'OK, OK. Just – I always wondered what it'd be like. Very sexy lady. Never made a move myself – relief now, as otherwise I'd be getting MeToo-ed left, right and centre, but still...' He suddenly has a lucid moment of awareness of the culture he's actually living in. 'Hey – do you think *Tit-Bits* might not go down well as a title?'

'I don't think it would be racist-washing-powder bad, but... you might be better going with something else.'

'Hmm,' he says, trying to open himself up to the blindingly obvious. 'Anyway, you heard Amanda's leaving?'

'Yeah.' *Thanks for reminding me.*

'Well, the upside is there's an opening for a new non-junior creative. After Custardgate, I'm sure the others would understand if I... offered it to you.'

'What? I—' Suddenly the door of possibility reopens in front of me. And on the other side, a future that could actually work...

'I guess that means we can give John the trainee job too,' JC continues. 'So... he'd be under you.'

I think for a second. 'Could I fire him?'

'No.' Oh well. Worth asking.

253

I almost can't believe it, but why the hell not? I'm a fully grown man. A parent. I'm used to responsibility, to doing a non-trainee bloody job. But none of this matters; it doesn't deal with the issue. I almost can't bear to ask, but I have to.

'How much does it pay?'

JC writes an amount on a piece of paper and hands it to me face down. What is it with salaries and people writing them down? They'd never do that with days of paid holiday. *Oo, twenty-two! And you may have noticed I also drew a cheeky little sketch of a parasol...*

I turn it over, hesitantly, knowing my next few years are in this figure.

And it's proper money. Proper mid-level, in-house accountant money. I don't have to move. I don't have to turn it down.

'Interested?'

I nod, grinning like a schoolboy.

Evening

By the evening, my grin's faded into a sort of mild depression about Amanda.

I feel so ungrateful. I've got exactly what I wanted. A dream bloody job. More than a dream job. I've got my kids. I'm keeping my flat. I'm sorting my life out. But I'm so down. Ridiculously down. Maybe I'm just not cut out to be happy. I've also got my parents staying. That might be part of it.

Claire texts me later. She apologises for not being in touch, but it turns out she and Martin are trying again this Christmas. Guess I won't have her turn up instead of takeaway any more. Kind of makes me wished I'd put some normal-sized condoms in Martin's stupid XL box. Cut off the blood supply next time he tries to have sex. Probably just make him even more arrogant though. 'I've outgrown extra large!'

But hey, only two days till Christmas.

Sunday – Christmas Eve

It's nice leaving London every once in a while. Feeling the bustle gradually fade away behind you as you get past the M25 and the motorway clears up.

Of course, it's nicer when you're the one driving. I'm currently sitting in the rear seat of my parents' car next to my kids, transported back to every holiday of my childhood, trying to remind myself I'm a 39-year-old man who's actually doing all right for himself. I try to convince myself I'm in an executive transport, being driven by a chauffeur, but it doesn't really work. Most chauffeurs don't own a turquoise Skoda and have their wife next to them complaining about feeling travel sick, and handing out refreshments.

Mum offers some Nescafe from a thermos, but I politely decline. Insisting on decent coffee is the only snobbery available to my generation. Sure, these pensioners can afford a decent house, but they wouldn't know a well-pulled espresso if it bit them on the overgenerous mortgage provider.

I kill about half an hour with the kids playing animal-vegetable-mineral. Carrie insists on coming up with her own ones, which definitely makes the game more challenging.

'Animal... OK – does it live in England?'

'Yes.'

'How many legs does it have?'

'Not sure.'

'Is it a mammal?'

255

'What's a mammul?'

'Is it furry?'

'No.'

'Is it small?

'No, it's really big.'

'Does it live on a farm?'

'No.'

'So it's a really big animal that lives in England, but not on a farm…. No… OK, I give up.'

'It's a dinosaur.' For fuck's sake. Lives in England?!?

I guess I didn't specify a time period.

Arthur continues with this farce, while I look out of the window. I like seeing the amazing houses you sometimes get by the motorway. You start fantasizing about living there, until you realise – shit – it's next to a motorway. Living there would be awful. I guess that's like other people's lives. They always look amazing from the outside. But from their point of view, they're probably as shit as everyone else's. Maybe that's why we all feel so bad about ourselves. No one's posting a picture of themselves in the back of their parents' car on Instagram.

'Mint?' says Mum, offering a Trebor.

'Yes, it's a mint!' says Carrie in reply to what she assumes is her granny's guess in her latest parody of Twenty Questions.

'You said it was an orange vegetable,' complains Arthur.

'Yes, but I changed my mind,' explains Carrie.

I sigh, accepting the Extra Strong Mint. Geez, that name isn't a joke. This must be how Carrie feels about her toothpaste. Maybe if you have enough of them they destroy enough taste buds to make thermos Nescafe drinkable.

We get to Aunt Eva's around four. I get a warm feeling inside as we roll onto the driveway. Aunt Eva greets us at the door with a big smile and a glass in hand. Marcus and Julian are already there and Uncle Jim has whipped up an eggnog which is so alcoholic, it could probably take out any Salmonella that was in your body *beforehand*. Within two minutes I'm sitting on a sofa, with a cup full of boozy custard (my Spirit Drink), and Carrie and Arthur are playing with Susie (Marcus' sister)'s kids. It's like we've been transported to another dimension. A dimension where everything's all right.

I used to love coming here for Christmas as a kid. The whole place is just so *festive*. There are decorations everywhere, rather than the lone plastic tree my parents had at their house. There's a proper fire, candles, Christmas music playing on the iPod… It feels like you're in a film or something: people seem to like each other, no one's wearing loungewear; it even *smells* nice. It's fucking weird.

I end up in a long conversation with Julian in front of the fire. He's a really successful theatre designer, and, now I'm a 'creative', he considers me 'one of his kind.' He's telling me how he came up with the set for this new West End musical version of *Cinderella*, told from the Ugly Sisters' point of view. She ends up forcing the glass slipper onto her foot – it shatters and cuts an artery in her foot and she dies in a pool of her own blood, realising that the true love of her life was her sister, not some ridiculous prince.

'That sounds really depressing.'

'It totally is,' says Julian, his teeth almost escaping from his smile. 'But it's also positive – it's about the importance of family'. Could have fooled me.

'What happens to Cinderella?'

'Well,' he continues, excitedly, 'the slipper was her only hope of snaring the prince, so… she grabs a piece of the glass and slits her wrists!'

'I think the kids did that version as their nativity last year.'

Julian plays mock-hurt. 'There's no need to be sarky. It's totally brilliant,' he says. 'It's got that real fairytale magic, but without the ridiculous happy ending – best of both worlds.' I love his enthusiasm, but I don't know. When you see how crappy the actual world is, maybe a happy ending isn't so bad.

After the kids have gone to bed, I wrap the remaining few presents and do the Christmas Eve parental business before ending up in a game of Balderdash. We sit down, all eight of us at the table.

'Well, at least it's not Scrabble,' Mum jokes, trying to be nice.

'Lucky for Tom,' laughs Dad, like he's made some conceptual jump that wasn't implied in the original comment. Laugh all you want, big man. Little do you know, the official Scrabble dictionary is currently waiting for you under the Christmas tree.

The game is actually hilarious within about five minutes. Susie tries to bluff us by claiming that the acronym F.R.E.D stands for the 'Federation of Reptiles, Extinct and Dormant.' Everyone's in stitches, like she thinks reptiles have formed a fucking Star Trek mission, boldly going where no extinct reptile has gone before. The whole thing is just amazingly fun. And, as I think about these people around me, the kids asleep upstairs, I realise that maybe what Julian was saying is right. This is what's really important – family. Sure, they're pains in the arse most of the time, but once in a while things fall into place, and you realise why you go through it all. And I'm sure that has nothing to do with me winning a board game for once.

Dad is in a foul mood afterwards because only one person went for his fake definition of 'taradiddle'. I'm surprised he didn't know the actual meaning from his archaic reference books. It's not long before Mum and Dad go to bed, followed by Eva and Jim, and I slump in a sort of warm post-eggnog victory stupor by the remnants of the fire.

Marcus comes through from the kitchen with a hot chocolate and sits with me for a while before bed. He's happy. Married life seems to be suiting him. We chat for a while – about Sally, about the kids, about his hangover after the wedding… eventually things turn to less pleasant territory.

'What happened to that girl you came with? Amanda, wasn't it?'

'It didn't work out.'

'Sorry to hear that. Work get in the way?'

'A bit. More the Atlantic. She got a job in the States.'

Marcus nods, understanding. He could never have been a straight guy – far too much emotional intelligence. 'Well… that's a shame. She seemed great.'

'She was.'

Julian comes down the stairs wearing a rather flamboyant dressing gown that is far too thin to provide any actual warmth. He kisses Marcus on the head.

'You coming to bed or what? Your family are lovely and all, but I didn't marry them,' he says. 'I doubt Tom's going to come upstairs and give me a cuddle.'

'Sorry, no. There's actually a guy from work I've kind of been having a thing with.'

Marcus smiles, and takes his husband's hand. 'See you in the morning.'

They go upstairs. And I sit there till the fire goes out.

Monday – Christmas Day

The kids are up at six, so I am too. We open the stocking presents and no one seems suspicious that Santa seems to have become less generous and creative since Mummy moved out, so that's a result.

We have a big breakfast of bacon and eggs, and Coco Pops on

259

their own that I brought from home. Auntie Eva doesn't have Coco Pops. Like I said – classy. By the time we open the presents, the kids have already had a second breakfast of panettone and eaten an entire pack of chocolate coins, so are running around hyper, playing with various plastic *PAW Patrol* monstrosities and battery-powered animals. It's not long before Arthur is also attacking everyone with a semi-automatic Nerf rifle which, come the apocalypse, may actually be powerful enough to hunt our country's wildlife. The weak, actually existing kind. I'm aware that Carrie's imaginary dinosaurs might require something a bit more powerful.

We sit round the tree with glasses of champagne and smoked salmon blinis while the kids hand out gifts in the elf costumes I bought them. They look awesome.

My present haul is pathetic. Two packs of socks from my parents: one of sensible black ones, and the other, novelty. Dad points towards the pair printed with the words 'Taxi Driver' and mouths 'for work' at me, without a trace of irony. I thank him, then break into a grin as he opens his Scrabble dictionary, trying not to look like his world is falling apart. Others gifts received include various jams and chutneys (one's from Fortnum and Mason – thank you, Auntie Eva) and a Toblerone. Julian and Marcus are next to me, and all their presents look awesome – each one thoughtfully chosen and luxurious; special little accessories from posh London shops mixed with high-cost technology items. Jesus. Not a Toblerone in sight. Well, until my kids bring Marcus over a triangular-shaped parcel from my mother. In your face, Marcus – that ain't from bloody Liberty.

Sally used to buy me great presents. She was the one person who actually knew what I wanted and got me something good. It makes me sad. That I've got no one in my life that knows who I am any more.

I'm thinking about Sally when Carrie comes over with tears

rolling off her face, leaving dark green patches on the felt of her costume. She's too distraught to tell me what's happened.

'Is it about Mummy?'

Carrie nods.

'You'll see her later. She's going to pick you up at six and then you'll have a second Christmas with her and Austin. It'll be great.'

'I don't want Austin to be there. I don't know Austin. I want it to just be you and me and Arthur and Mummy. I want things to be normal again. I want her to be here.'

'Me too, love; me too.'

It's just before noon when the doorbell rings.

I hardly even notice it. Carrie's calmed down again and I'm in the middle of breaking up an argument about whether Chase from *PAW Patrol* could beat Kylo Ren in a fight. I try to stay neutral, but I'm pretty convinced Kylo Ren would have it. I don't say that, obviously. Besides, KR might have a dog allergy. It would explain why he wears that face mask.

'It's for you,' says Marcus, appearing behind me and the kids. I'm pretty deep into trying to form an argument about how cartoon dogs could hold their own against the Sith, so it takes me a few seconds to register.

I walk toward the door, away from the revellers. It hasn't even struck me that Sally might be early. But who the fuck else goes round to someone's house on Christmas Day?

'What the—'

Standing there, about 2,000 miles from where she's meant to be, is Amanda.

'Hope it's OK to come over. I was at my parents' house for a few days, so I thought I'd pop by… as I was in the area,' she says, trying to act like it's no big deal. 'I brought you your present.'

She hands over a little parcel, but I'm not paying any attention, I can't take my eyes off her face. 'I thought you were in New York.'

261

'I got offered another job. Here. They don't trust JC any more, so they want me to take over as Creative Director.'

'That's… that's amazing.'

'It is, isn't it?' She smiles.

I notice my mum poking her head into the hall and I suddenly feel the need for some privacy. 'Give me a sec.' I grab my coat, and head out into the front garden with Amanda.

It's not snowing, but it's one of those magical winter days where it might as well be. There's frost on the ground, and a crisp chill in the air that almost makes it all right that you're in an environment that can barely sustain human life.

'How did you know where I was?'

'Julian Facebook-friended me after the wedding. I sent him a message. He's pretty active on Instagram too. Well done winning Balderdash last night.'

I shake my head, laughing. Fucking Julian. Although, I have to admit he's quite seriously in my good books at this moment.

I suddenly realise I'm standing here surrounded by the beautiful English countryside with this woman. Who I love. Like I said, I'm not going to tell her. That can wait. And she's also my boss. That's going to take a bit of getting used to, but right now it's barely registering. All I'm thinking about is how she's the most beautiful woman I've ever seen in my life. And I want to kiss her.

A day kiss. A far sight from a drunken snog at an office party. Luckily, I've already had a couple of glasses of champagne. Thank God for Christmas.

'At the risk of getting fired, I think I'm going to have to kiss you.'

She mulls it over for a second before answering. 'I'll overlook it. We're not in the office right now.'

Our lips meet, a little oasis of warmth amidst the cold of the day, touching gently at first, softly adhering to one another as they part. And everything just feels so… right.

She looks up into my eyes, 'Can you… hang out for a bit?'

I want to. I really want to. I want to invite her in and spend Christmas with her and my kids and eat turkey and get drunk and sit on the sofa watching shitty television, but then I remember Carrie. Crying her eyes out earlier. I don't want to force Amanda onto them. I don't want her to be another Austin.

'I think I have to spend the day with Arthur and Carrie… I don't want things to be weird for them.'

Amanda nods, understanding but disappointed.

'It's probably better if we take it slow around them,' I explain.

'OK – well… I'll be here for a few days if you want to see me.'

'If I want to see you?' I can't help laughing. It's all I bloody want. 'Sally's picking them up at six. Could you come over then… ? I can't promise I won't destroy you mercilessly at Cranium.'

She smiles. 'Yeah. That sounds good.'

I stand outside, and watch her walk back to her car. I've got so much inside me I want to say to her. But there's time. Hopefully there's plenty of time.

We wave at each other as she drives away, and I head back into the house. With a present that might actually be all right.

As I go back inside to what might be the last Christmas day I ever spend with my kids, it somehow feels like my life's started again. And sure, I don't know where this relationship will go. But it's a start.

And when you started with an ending, maybe that's enough.

If you enjoyed reading this and want to hear about future books
by Spencer Brown, sign up for the mailing list at:
www.spencerbrown.net

Or join the Marotte mailing list for updates
on all our authors at:
www.marottebooks.com

Marotte

Serious about Funny

Acknowledgments

Massive thanks to my wife for her support, encouragement, and just being generally amazing. Thanks to my agent, Richard Scrivener, for all the work he put into the book, and for being 'on it' to a very unusual degree – very glad to have you! – and Victoria at VLA for the initial introduction. Thanks to Sarah, my incredible editor for her great work and taking out most of the more egregious jokes. Thanks to the incredibly talented Liam Relph for designing my ideal cover. Thanks to Jimmy Ruzicka and Annabel Knight for their early reads, and buddy for trying to get through it even though he doesn't read fiction. Thanks to Penny Bryant for her eagle-eyed proof reading (with apologies for ignoring her correct suggestions of using 'and I' and 'racewalking', and for my wilfully flitting between the American and English spellings of 'ass'.). And finally, thanks to my parents for whatever horrible act they committed to create me, their support, and for being nothing like the parents in this book!

About the Author

Spencer Brown began performing comedy with the Cambridge Footlights alongside John Oliver and Matthew Holness, before becoming an internationally acclaimed stand up. He has performed everywhere from London's *The Comedy Store* to Mumbai and the USA and his TV credits include *Nathan Barley*, *Edinburgh Comedy*, *Last Comic Standing*, and his own special on Swedish television, as well as the lead role in the 2019 horror comedy movie *Shed of the Dead*. As a TV presenter, he has fronted *ITV*'s *Lip Service* (alongside Holly Willoughby) and *Five*'s *The Sexy Ads Show*. He is also the writer-director of the multi-award-winning short film *The Boy with a Camera for a Face*. *The Rebuilding of Tom Cooper* is his first novel.